Deadly Errand

Deadly Errand

Christine Green

Walker and Company
New York

First published in the United States of America in 1992
by Walker Publishing Company, Inc.

Published simultaneously in Canada by Thomas Allen & Son
Canada, Limited, Markham, Ontario

Library of Congress Cataloging-in-Publication Data
Green, Christine
Deadly Errand / Christine Green.
p. cm.
ISBN 0-8027-3219-4
I. Title.
PR6057.R338D4 1992
823'.914--dc20   92-9232
                                                      CIP

Printed in the United States of America
2 4 6 8 10 9 7 5 3

For Katherine Clare
for her patient reading

Prologue

The hand in mine had grown progressively colder. It was three a.m. and raining. I felt inside the bedclothes and touched the patient's feet, but death had crept there first; they would never be warm again. The only sounds in the room were the sonorous ticks of an alarm clock and the wispy breaths of the old lady. Breaths that paused in erratic punctuation and I knew that by daylight the pauses would have become a full stop.

I gently unwound the hand from its feeble grip, walked to the window and pulled back the curtains. I hoped to be cheered up by the view – I wasn't. Outside, the bare branches of trees thrust against the glass like demented bats. Yet the sound didn't penetrate the room. Only inside the room seemed to exist. I closed the curtains, sighing. It was as though the two of us were waiting in a slow-motion world, but only I prayed for a fast-forward.

The clock seemed to tick louder and faster when Miss Florence Boughton finally reached her full stop. I straightened her legs, combed the thin silvery hairs, placed a pillow under the chin and, leaving Florence's face uncovered, walked quickly out of the bedroom. I'd never felt brave enough to be alone with a body with its face covered. There always remained the slight feeling that the corpse might suddenly sit up. Uncovered, I could pretend to myself that Florence still lived.

Downstairs, I passed the grandfather clock in the hall. There were traces of dust on the clock face and I paused beside it for a moment to tap the glass, willing the hands to come to life. There was no response.

In the kitchen I switched on all the lights, huddled over a one-bar electric fire and watched the rain spatter against the kitchen window. I wanted to close my eyes but couldn't. There's no need to stay awake now, I told myself, but sleep was chased

7

away by the night sounds: a trickle of water along a pipe, a creaking floorboard, the hum of the refrigerator, even the sound of my own breathing.

At seven a.m. the rain stopped and the house became silent again. Relieved, I rang the GP and the undertaker and then made tea and toast to celebrate the arrival of morning. The combination of daylight, food and caffeine made the world seem a marginally better place. In fact, I began to feel quite cheerful, an hysterical cheerfulness that needed fuelling with company. I resisted an urge to check on Florence, who lay, stiffening and untroubled, upstairs. She had been a one-nighter, just another patient. But I still hoped Florence had believed that the hand that held hers belonged to someone special, someone she knew.

Chapter One

As I walked towards the side entrance of Humberstones Funeral Directors I was aware that Hubert Humberstone watched my arrival from behind the slatted blinds. He wasn't exactly watching me, he was merely waiting for a glimpse of my shoes. Duty shoes – black and low-heeled – would be a disappointment to him, not only for sight but for sound. Shoes that padded rather than clicked on the bare floorboards were no fun at all to Hubert.

'Good morning, Miss Kinsella,' he called as he crept up the stairs behind me. I half turned and his eyes registered, in an instant, the shoes. The expression could only be described as his fondle-foot look.

'Good morning, Mr Humberstone. I didn't hear you,' I lied. I always heard him.

'Good night, was it?' he asked, moving closer.

'Yes, thank you. The patient died this morning.'

'One of ours?' Hubert asked hopefully.

'Pritchards, I'm afraid. Family tradition.'

Hubert shrugged and wiped his hands across the stray hairs on his head. 'Never mind,' he said. 'I've got some good news. We've got a client coming today.'

The 'we' irritated me but I managed to force a smile, even though as he sidled closer a smell of bacon wafted from his black suit.

'You'd better come in,' I said, opening the office door so that he could go through first. 'Sit down, Mr Humberstone. I'll make some coffee.'

Reluctantly he sat in the jumble-sale chair in front of my desk. It was more a deep pit than a chair and I could tell he felt at a severe disadvantage. As I filled the kettle I flicked on the light to cheer up the drab room. The light worked but the gloom didn't

9

lift. The bulb, covered by an off-white paper shade with green leaves, cast its light in the middle of the small room, leaving the corners in shadow.

'This room gives me the creeps,' I said, more to myself than Hubert. 'I must buy a lamp.'

'Be able to afford it now,' said Hubert. 'Now that you've got a client.'

Relieved that he'd dropped the 'we' I asked if he wanted sugar.

Hubert nodded, still looking ill at ease in the chair with its saggy bottom nearly touching the ground. He stretched out his long legs and pulled nervously at the sleeves of his jacket, which were too short to accommodate his gangly frame. His skin was also at full stretch and his brown eyes sat below a high forehead like raisins set in dough. Poor Hubert wasn't handsome, but I had become fond of him, in the same way I had been fond of some psychiatric patients. I found his oddness strangely reassuring, his dour moments quite cheering.

'How's business?' I asked, handing him a mug of coffee.

'Not bad,' he said. 'Good month to look forward to. The old always snuff it in droves in the cold weather.'

'Do you have to be quite so blunt?'

'It's my life, my bread and butter,' Hubert replied in a hurt voice.

I nodded and drank my coffee. Hubert may be slightly weird, I thought, but he is my landlord and eventually I'll get used to working above a continual conveyor-belt of corpses.

'Tell me about the new client, Mr Humberstone.' I always called him Mister but in my thoughts he remained for ever Hubert.

'Nice woman,' he said slowly. 'Expensive shoes, comes from Short Brampton. I buried her mother— '

'What does she want me to do exactly?' I interrupted, trying to chivvy him along.

'It's a murder case,' he announced.

'Medical murder or common or garden murder?'

'Murder. Proper murder. A stabbing.'

'Your burial?'

Hubert nodded. 'It's on Friday. The police have been hanging on to the body for three months but now the inquest is over, they've released it.'

'I've never dealt with murder. Did you recommend me?'

Hubert looked embarrassed. 'You can do it,' he said. 'The dead girl was a nurse. Right up your street.'

I laughed. 'The last case "right up my street" was that woman who wanted me to investigate the reasons for her husband's loss of sex drive after his prostatectomy.'

'He was eighty.'

'That's the point,' I said. 'Then there was the woman with the breast lump who wanted to file a complaint against her GP for examining both breasts.'

Hubert smiled, opening up his crow's-feet so that his eyes practically disappeared. 'This is a paying one, though. Plenty of money in the family. The publicity will do you a treat. You could even have a gold-plated plaque outside with "Medical and Nursing Investigations" engraved in big letters and Kate Kinsella SRN,RMN underneath it.'

'I don't want publicity,' I said. 'I want to get this agency a steady supply of solid cases. Not just cranks trying to get back at the medical profession for imagined misdeeds. A plaque outside would only attract passing nutters and I'd be swamped. Word of mouth and my card spread around the local solicitors is quite enough.'

Hubert looked a little crushed but was obviously going to persevere. 'I could let you see the body.'

'You're disgusting,' I said, feeling my stomach tense like a boxer's biceps. Bodies you'd been with as they died, people you'd known, were quite different from the corpse of a stranger, especially one kept in a fridge for three months. Be charitable, though, I told myself. To Hubert, dead bodies were as normal as clapped-out cars are to a used-car dealer. 'I might not be able to handle this one. I'll have to think about it.'

'Don't think too long,' said Hubert, checking his watch. 'She's coming at two – thought two might be a good time. You can have a proper kip.'

'Thanks. I don't want to keep you any longer, Mr Humberstone. I'm sure you've a funeral to attend or a bit of embalming to do.'

Hubert, thick-skinned but not stupid, raised himself from the chair with as much difficulty as, if not more than, Lazarus and walked to the door. 'Sweet dreams then, Miss Kinsella, and think of the spondulicks.'

I raised an eyebrow.

'Money, dough, bread, spondulicks,' he said. 'This could be the making of you. I'll give you any help you need. And remember, wear the right shoes and you can conquer the world.'

'I'll remember that. What's her name by the way?'

'It's Mrs Marburg. I told her you'd be sure to find the murderer.'

'Don't expect any commission,' I murmured under my breath.

'Pardon?'

'Thanks for the commission.'

Hubert smiled. 'My pleasure.'

I locked the door when I'd heard him reach the ground floor. I trusted him to a certain extent, but I did know that occasionally when I left the office, he touched the shoes in my cupboard. It was a violation of sorts, but it didn't worry me as long as he didn't touch the shoes with me in them. Hubert wasn't yet in his dotage, though his exact age was hard to guess, he being the type who passes from youth to middle age with a mere hairy diminishment.

Although I worked from and occasionally slept at Humberstones I did try very hard to keep separate from the undertaking part of the building. The full-time receptionist, Daphne Gittens, a cheerful pleasant woman, tried to encourage me downstairs but I resisted. Hubert relied mostly on casual staff and my chief fear was that he would try to involve me in the laying out of the bodies. Also, Humberstones consisted of two houses knocked into one and Hubert lived above the 'shop'. I hadn't yet been invited to Hubert's flat. And if I was invited, I knew I would refuse.

I was at the foot end of my wash, standing on one leg with my size six in the sink, when I realised I didn't even know how to begin a murder investigation. And if I couldn't start, how could I ever finish?

I'd come to Longborough to start a new life. I'd got bored with nursing, although I didn't want to give it up entirely, and I'd been given some money. A few months after Dave, my detective inspector live-in lover had been killed, not in the course of duty, a friend of his brought round a cheque. Dave's friends and colleagues had had a whip-round because not being married I didn't qualify for a pension. I'd eventually accepted the cheque feeling like a widow but minus the orphans. And then I hadn't known what to do with the money so I stuck it in a building society and waited for inspiration to strike. That took some time, until a chance remark overheard in a bus queue gave me the idea of setting up my own investigation agency.

'Any fool can be a private detective these days. You don't need any qualifications, all you need is a room and the bottle to go for it.'

Dave hadn't been that bright, I told myself, and he had a habit of blundering into situations, saying the wrong thing at the wrong time, even being in the wrong place . . . Surely, I thought, I could do as well, if not better. Naïvely, I had expected to function as a cross between Mata Hari and a young version of Miss Marple. Now, faced with my first interesting case my 'bottle' was fast emptying.

'Oh, sod it,' I said aloud, consoling myself that it was only tiredness that was making me so jittery.

Extricating my foot from the sink, I dried it quickly, took the phone off the hook, and went through to the 'bedroom'. A windowless box, it contains a sofa-bed in permanent readiness, a folding chair, an alarm clock and a small cupboard. This room also needed a lamp, but I didn't care, it was just a place to sleep in and the darker the better.

The alarm clock buzzed at one and although I switched it off, it was only a reflex action, and it was one thirty when I finally woke; heavy-eyed and irritable that I felt worse than before I'd slept. But after two mugs of strong coffee and a face salvage job, I looked, and felt, quite decent, quite optimistic even.

Mrs Nina Marburg, punctual to the minute, arrived closely followed by Hubert who announced her as though to a packed ballroom, and then hovered as if expecting to be asked in. I tossed my head at him, and with a disappointed sag of his shoulders he left, to do whatever undertakers do to dead bodies. One day I'll ask him.

'Please sit down, Mrs Marburg.'

She gazed at my faded floral in a mixture of amusement and disbelief.

'It won't bite. Really it's quite comfortable.'

'If you say so.'

I knew then that she wasn't sure I could do the job.

Nina Marburg eyed me with slight suspicion from the depths of the chair. She had the look of an anorexic pixie – tiny oval face, beginning to wrinkle at the moving parts. 'You're younger than I thought,' she said.

'I'm twenty-nine.' And I would have liked to stay twenty-nine but thirty loomed next month. My offer of coffee and chocolate biscuits she declined.

'You can never be too thin,' she said, glancing at my size fourteen pityingly.

'How may I help?' I asked, breaking my chocolate biscuit delicately into pieces and trying to eat it very slowly. It was my breakfast after all.

'My niece Jacky Byfield – I expect you read about it in the papers. She was murdered, stabbed, in the grounds of St Dymphna's three months ago. Just twenty-three, a lovely girl, very religious, really dedicated to nursing. Everyone liked her.'

Well, almost everyone, I thought uncharitably. But I nodded, to encourage her to go on.

Mrs Marburg's eyes, the colour of dish-water, began to overflow and she rummaged in her handbag for a hankie. She eventually found an embroidered job, and with it she dabbed her eyes with careful deliberation.

'Do you have a photo?' I asked.

Producing a passport-sized one from her purse she handed it to me silently.

Jacky had an oval face, quite pretty, but spoiled by heavy eyebrows. She was smiling – a cold, cheerless smile.

'The police seem to think she was the victim of a random killer, a psychopath, or that she disturbed a peeping Tom. We don't.'

'We?'

'My sister Clare and I. She's been a broken woman since – since it happened. Jacky was her only daughter, you see. They were very, very close. Anyway, the police seem to have given up: they've reduced the number of men investigating and more or less told us that unless he strikes again, they have nothing to go on.'

'What makes you think I can find out more than the police? Indeed, is there anything to be found out? Random killers have, of course, no connection with their victim.'

'I know that. You don't have to patronise me.'

14

'Sorry. I didn't mean to. I was thinking aloud.'

Her answering look would have shrivelled leather. She was much sharper than she appeared. More goblin than pixie.

'Tell me why you don't think a stranger killed her,' I asked in a suitably chastened voice.

Nina Marburg uncrossed her ankles and lined up her feet as if lining up an argument, or a lie, or both. She wore navy high-heeled shoes, narrow-fitting with buttons down the front. Very expensive. No wonder Hubert was impressed.

'Jacky had been having nasty phone calls for two months before she died, always at night, always when she was at home. She worked permanent nights, you see. Sometimes three, sometimes four a week.'

'Phone calls?'

'No. Night duties of course. Usually it was about two calls a week.'

'Was the caller male or female?'

'Jacky wasn't sure, she said the words were all muffled. Does it make a difference?'

'It could,' I said. 'Although some anonymous callers are women, most murderers are men.'

'Of course.'

'What exactly did this person say?'

For a moment Nina fiddled with her hankie, pulling it and twisting it. 'I don't know the exact words. Called her a bitch and a whore, that sort of thing.'

'That seems quite mild. What about threats?'

'It didn't seem mild to Jacky, I can assure you. It really upset her.'

'The police know about these calls?'

'Oh, yes. They seem to think it was mere coincidence.'

'Well of course it could be.'

'I expected you to be on our side.'

'I am, Mrs Marburg, but I really don't want to take your money under false pretences.'

She raised one of her eyebrows, which in that position I could see was only a pretend one, expertly pencilled.

'You see, if there isn't a chance of finding the murderer you would be paying me for simply going over the same ground as the police.'

15

'Men,' she said, 'have no real intuition. I'm sure you could find out more.'

Her voice, high-pitched and wheedling, sounded petulant, like a child's wanting sweets.

'Mrs Marburg, the phone calls in themselves, are flimsy evidence of premeditated murder. Have you any other reason for thinking Jacky knew her murderer? A jealous boyfriend, that sort of thing.'

She stared at me for a few seconds. 'I can see you don't want to take this case. Is it beyond you?'

'Not at all,' I answered, trying to sound confident. 'I just want as much information as possible, so that I can get a result.'

She was silent for a moment, then answered thoughtfully, 'She did take out life insurance the week before she died – that's all.'

'I'll do my very best, Mrs Marburg, but don't expect too much. I have to be honest and tell you this is my first murder case. I usually deal with medical frauds and mishaps.'

'That doesn't matter,' she said. 'Perhaps you'll find out a doctor's involved.'

She wasn't smiling then and she didn't smile as she left.

Chapter Two

I began the next day searching through my filing cabinet for old local newspapers. As my files were empty I'd filled them with newspaper articles reporting crimes, as a slightly eccentric way of convincing myself that I ran a proper working business. Feeling optimistic that I'd find something on the murder I cleared the whole lot out, and began to sift through them. There was only one report, saying that a youth was 'helping with enquiries'; the stop-press noted he had been released. Not much help, without a name. Then I typed out with my usual two-finger slowness the information I had acquired. It didn't amount to much, so I typed MOTIVE? in the middle of the page. Then I paused, for a long time.

It was almost a relief when Hubert knocked at the door. I knew it was him, because he always crept up the stairs so stealthily. And I rarely had any other callers.

'How's the detecting going?' he asked.

I gave him a withering glance, which he ignored.

'You looking for the murder report?'

I nodded.

'Don't worry – I've got a stack of back numbers downstairs. I keep them for obituaries.'

He returned in a few minutes with several papers. 'These are the main reports,' he said, advancing towards my desk.

'Thanks.'

Hubert stood his ground and I felt a little sorry for him; he was obviously eager for an update.

'Aren't you busy?' I asked.

'I've delegated.'

'I suppose you want to know all about it?'

He smiled eagerly, his false teeth gleaming heroically.

'There isn't much to tell really. Jacky's aunt and mother are convinced that she knew her killer. I get the impression that they think it's someone at the hospital. Their only reason for suspicion is a few weirdo phone calls and the fact that she took out life insurance a week before she died.'

'What about the police?' asked Hubert, giving the armchair a wary glance and then perching on the edge of my desk.

'The police don't seem worried about the calls. They probably eliminated them as just coincidental.'

'And you wouldn't?'

'I'm not sure,' I said. 'But I'd like to speak to the mother before the police become aware that I'm involved, and I'll have to wait until after the funeral – it just wouldn't be fair on the poor woman.'

Hubert repositioned himself on my desk and stared at my feet for several seconds. It was obviously inspirational, because he thought of something. 'Why don't you get a job at St Dymphna's? Then you could tap into all the gossip and rumours. All that chitchat in the early hours, all girls together stuff. You'd soon get a lead.'

'Why didn't I think of that? Great idea. Take a gold star and a form point. I'd give you a kiss, only you might expect me to make a habit of it.'

Hubert smiled sheepishly. 'I've never had a gold star before.'

'You were deprived.'

'I'll be off now then,' he said, still looking pleased. 'I've done my good deed for the day.'

I rang the local nursing agency straight away. The woman who ran it, Pauline Berkerly, was almost a friend. We'd trained in the same general hospital, at different times, but it still forges a bond, and she'd kept me supplied with part-time work ever since I'd arrived in Longborough. Pauline and her agency had been a good enough reason to come to Longborough in the first place. She was both discreet and kind and well known for her efficiency.

'Any night work at St Dymphna's?' I asked.

'Seven nights a week if you want it. But why on earth do you want to work there? No one actually chooses to work at Dymphna's.'

'Because of the murder?' I asked.

18

'Partly; also because it's geriatric, it's due for closure, and it's miles from anywhere.'

'Not your most favourite hospital then?'

'The proverbial thorn. Do you really want some work there, Kate? I've got some more easy private cases, just like Florence Boughton, coming up.'

Nursing the dying was Pauline's notion of 'easy'.

'I'm on an investigation,' I explained.

'Oh.' There was a long pause. 'Don't tell me anything about it,' she said. 'I'd rather be kept in the dark.'

'That's where I am at the moment – fumbling.'

'Well, Kate, keep your fumbling very low profile, won't you? The management there are a most peculiar crowd.'

'I'll be careful,' I promised.

Half an hour later Pauline rang back. 'You're in luck,' she said. 'They are desperate for staff tonight and tomorrow night. Go straight to Harper Ward, round the back of the main building. It's continuing care – is that okay?'

'Fine. Thanks,' I said, trying to hide the fact that I felt quite daunted at the thought of two twelve-hour shifts with the dying, the dependent, the demented. And the scene of a murder.

At lunch-time I decided to go out for a sandwich and a large doughnut, the latter being compensation for having to work the next two nights. I met Hubert lurking in the doorway; he'd probably been listening to my descent. He smiled, opened the side door and began to follow me out. I didn't say a word until we were walking up the High Street, side by side.

'Going my way?' I asked.

'Only to the Swan. You going to the Swan?'

'I hadn't planned to. I fancied a sandwich from the Bakery.'

'Oh,' he said, in obvious disappointment.

The Bakery, in the middle of the High Street, was always busy, but as we approached and I saw the queue stretching yards up the road, I realised my oral compensation couldn't wait that long. Besides, the Swan did wonderful chips.

The pub, although busy at the bar, was not unduly packed. The usual groupings of estate agents and bank clerks stood around talking in loud voices about a variety of life's issues that went 'up'. Redundancies were up, blood cholesterols were up, stress levels were up, their mortgages were up. I could only guess at what didn't go up.

Hubert fought manfully through the upwardly mobiles to get our drinks and order my pizza and chips. He came back with a pint of beer.

'You eating?' I asked.

'My weight's gone up,' he said morosely, staring at the head on his beer as though prolonging the moment of pleasure to come.

There seemed nothing more to say and Hubert didn't speak again until his glass was nearly empty. Then, in a quite unnecessary whisper, he said, 'I've got a bit of gossip you might be interested in.'

'Really?'

'Really.'

'Well, don't keep me in suspense. Tell all.'

'It's about – you know who.'

'Jacky?'

'Yes.'

'Well, I'm listening,' I said.

Hubert leaned forward then, as if his words might escape into the surrounding beer fumes if he didn't keep them confined. 'A neighbour of hers, lives at number eight, says that Jacky often came home in the early hours with different men. And . . .' He paused as my meal arrived.

'And?'

'And they often went inside.'

'Knocking shop, you mean?'

'Well. Not sure about that; she did live at home,' he said uncertainly.

'Perhaps they were just having a prayer meeting.'

Hubert was not amused.

'Do the police know about these men?' I asked, offering him a chip from my plate.

'They're bad for you.'

'The police?'

'The chips. You'll get fat.'

'Good.'

Hubert, a little affronted by my lack of concern for my figure, fell silent, sulky even. Then, perhaps fearing I'd get temperamental too, said, 'She did tell the police, but she says she doesn't think they believed her.'

'Why on earth not?'

'She's blind; well, half-blind and nearly eighty.'

'You're having me on.'

'I'm not.' Hubert sounded affronted. 'Another drink?'

I nodded.

When he returned he looked happier. I think he'd spotted the girl at the bar wearing red stilettos, his favourite colour.

'Anyway this neighbour,' he continued, 'her name's Ada Hellidon, says that although her sight's poor she can tell the difference between black men, white men, tall or short.'

'Is she quite sane?'

'As you or me.'

'I'll go and see her on my way home tomorrow. Thanks.'

Hubert smiled serenely and we spent another half an hour listening to snippets of 'up' conversation wafting towards us. Hubert managed to down three pints, which surprised me, and his eyes began to water slightly as if the beer had seeped up through his body and was overflowing. He insisted on walking back to the office with me and his eyes watered even more in the chill wind. I left him at the parking bay at the back of Humberstones.

'I'm going home for a nap,' I said. 'I'm working at St Dymphna's tonight. Thanks again for the suggestion.'

'You be careful.'

It was only as I drove away that I remembered guiltily that I hadn't even bought him a pint.

Driving away from Longborough towards Farley Wood and home I thought how much Longborough reminded me of a blown rose, all tight in the middle but bedraggled at the edges. Inner Longborough retained its old-world charm, with its wide main street and small shops, and market square and church steeple, but from the fifties onwards the outskirts had sprouted estates – 'like bleedin' warts' was one description I'd overheard in the pub.

As I drove on into the countryside it still felt a novelty after living in north London for most of my life. When I'd first arrived I'd felt very insecure driving through empty country lanes. It felt really odd not to be in second gear, with traffic front and back. Now I was used to it, I felt quite resentful of other cars. But today there were no other cars and although it was grey and overcast I still found the countryside held a mysterious fascination. Perhaps it was the lack of people, villages with their populations cocooned indoors, or in some far-distant office. Even the village church, which stood on high ground and overlooked my cottage, took on a sinister heaviness on bleak, cloudy days, although it was the graveyard surrounding it that troubled me most. My life seemed to be dominated by corpses but the only one that intrigued me was Jacky. Could it be true about the succession of men to the house? What about Jacky's mother? What on earth was she doing at the time?

The cottage, as I pretentiously called it, was a terraced house in a row of five. Two up, two down, and a conservatory which one day I would use. The front room smelt musty and unlived-in, but I felt glad to be home and I'd only just settled down on the sofa, covered myself with a duvet, and thought how decadent an afternoon nap seemed, when the door bell rang. Being vain about everything but my weight, I glanced at myself in the hall mirror as I passed – what a sight! My red hair stood in henna'd spikes, like the burning bush finally burnt, and my mascaraless eyes were a lost feature in an oval of face.

The woman at the door tried to hide her surprise that I'd been lying down. 'So sorry to disturb you, dear,' she said.

I ran a quick inventory – no clipboard, didn't look like a messenger from Jehovah, certainly not double-glazing or time-share. Far too cosy and sensible to be a salesperson.

'I'm on night duty tonight,' I explained.

'I'll not keep you long, dear. Just two things really, Neighbourhood Watch and the WI.'

'Come in then, Mrs . . . ?'

'Mrs Morcott – Pamela.'

'Kate Kinsella, Miss.'

I made tea and Mrs Morcott sat neatly in my armchair and expounded the virtues of Neighbourhood Watch. 'Everyone has to be so careful these days, don't they, dear?'

I nodded and smiled.

'What with psychopaths everywhere and burglaries every five minutes.'

'Surely not round here,' I said.

'Oh, yes, dear. There was a murder locally about three months ago. The police haven't caught the killer, so he's still at large. Scary, isn't it? A young nurse. Struck down in the hospital grounds. Raped as well!'

'Really. And the police don't have any clues?'

'None at all, it seems. But please don't worry. Our Neighbourhood Watch scheme means we can all sleep more easily in our beds.'

'That's great,' I agreed.

And Mrs Morcott then tried less successfully to interest me in the Women's Institute. 'Honestly, dear, we do have such a lovely time. We have speakers and quizzes and competitions. It's not all cooking and jumbles.'

'I really don't have the time, Mrs Morcott, but I am interested in Neighbourhood Watch.'

'Good. Good. I'll add your name to the list. Think about the WI, won't you? That poor murdered girl's mother is a member. She hasn't come, of course, since it happened, but we're hoping to encourage her back to the fold.'

Suddenly, Farley's Wood's WI seemed a lot more interesting. 'I'll think about it,' I promised. 'Thanks for calling.'

I tried again to sleep but couldn't. Thoughts of Jacky Byfield prevented that. A religious nurse, her mother a member of the WI, seemed an unlikely amateur prostitute. She also seemed an unlikely victim for crank phone calls. The fact remained, though, someone had hated her enough to kill her. Or had she seen something that night that meant she had to die? And was it true she'd been raped? The newspapers said nothing about rape. The endless possibilities circled in my mind until I decided it was time for 'breakfast', because food is the best way I know of passing time without having to think too much.

At seven thirty I drove the six miles to St Dymphna's in pouring rain and loud Mozart. Outside the hospital two huge ornamental streetlamps cast a watery glow around the entrance. Iron gates with stone pillars led to the drive, which was flanked on either side by mature pines and oak trees. The building at the end of the long drive seemed more country manor than NHS. A single chandelier shone feebly from what could have been reception. A sign saying 'to Wards Grant, Melba, Truman and Harper' directed me through two stone arches to wooden sheds which looked exactly like stabling blocks. The sign on one said 'Porter's

Lodge' and on the other 'Catering'. Both were in darkness. I parked the car as I came to another smaller, narrower arch. A lone bike stood propped against a wall. I walked through the archway and on to a covered walkway – all black wood with posts every few yards. The walkway led to another long wooden shed. It reminded me of all those old prisoner-of-war films, although I suppose the walkways were an added refinement.

The kitchen window of Harper sported a yellowing net curtain, ill-hung, but at least the lights on inside made it seem more welcoming. One half of the ward was in complete darkness. As I opened the wooden door it was the quiet I noticed. No hustle and bustle of visitors leaving, no nurses walking to and fro. To my left in a row of about eight beds lay what looked like the victims of some gruesome catastrophe. Most looked comatosed, rather than asleep, their bodies in foetal positions or awkwardly propped up on pillows. The ward curtains were open, each bed facing dark, rain-lashed windows. The weather, though, had ceased long ago to be a matter of concern for the ladies of Harper Ward. The nursing office separated the two halves of the ward and as I walked in I noticed that the right-hand-side patients seemed a bit fitter. Four old ladies slumped in straight-backed chairs with wooden arms. Others gazed at me anxiously from their beds.

I was the first of the night staff to arrive. A young staff nurse sat at the desk writing the report. She looked up and with obvious effort smiled.

'Agency?'

I nodded and smiled in return.

'Take a seat. We're a bit behind as usual. Typical day in this madhouse.'

She sounded very depressed. I was beginning to feel depressed too. At five past eight I was still the only night nurse.

'I'll give you the report now,' she said. 'Someone's bound to turn up soon.'

She didn't sound convinced. The report contained such gems as 'didn't eat her supper' or 'bowels well opened' and even 'still stiff as a board'. At least the technicalities weren't going to be a problem. Halfway through the report an auxiliary nurse turned up – small, cheerful and bubbly.

'Hi. Sorry I'm late. Stupid kid of mine cut his knee open just as I was leaving. You agency?'

'Berkerly,' I said, smiling. I felt more cheerful now.

'Don't worry about anything. I've been on the last three nights. Routine's always the same.'

We listened to the rest of the report and I tried to catch on to a few names but they all seemed to blur in a time-warp of similar ones – Ivy, Nellie, Hilda, Edith, Grace, Minnie, Dollie.

When the staff nurse had gone, along with another nurse who had appeared from a sitting-room at the end of the ward, my companion turned to me and introduced herself. 'I'm Linda Brington. I'll show you round first and then we'll do the night drinks. That okay?'

'Fine. I'm Kate Kinsella.'

Linda bustled out quickly. 'This is what I call the "baby's end",' she said as we walked past the sleeping patients. 'There's the sluice, bathroom, loo, and staff loo. Clinical room's at the end of the ward, next to the sitting room.'

I followed her pointing finger.

'Never forget to close the smallest windows will you? Some buggers will manage to get in anywhere.'

As we walked back we closed the curtains until we reached the door. Linda dropped the door catch and then shot the bolt. 'We keep it closed until the morning. Never open it unless you're sure it's someone you know.'

'We're not likely to have someone try to get in, are we?'

'Have done in the past but I'll tell you about that later. Could you start doing the drinks for the patients sitting out?' Linda moved off quickly down the ward. She was obviously going to organise me completely.

As I approached the three patients grouped around a table, a tiny gnome-like old lady wearing a cotton mob-cap peered at me intently.

'Hello, Mrs Bluefrock. Are you back then?'

'I'm back. Would you like a drink?'

'What's she say?' she asked no one in particular.

'Would you like a drink?' I repeated, mouthing the words carefully.

Before she could answer another patient sat up in bed shouting, 'Pleasa, pleasa. pleasa.'

This seemed to strike a cord with more patients and one screamed out, 'I'm pissing myself!'

25

'I want the commode,' another wailed.

It was Linda who restored peace; walking into the ward she quickly summed up the situation. 'Gladys, stop whingeing. Eva, you'll have to wait. Ivy, tea?' Her familiar voice had a calming effect and the ward soon became quiet again.

'Don't worry, Kate, they always play up new nurses; they get insecure.'

When eventually the drinks had been given out at one end of the ward we moved down to the other. Little of my previous nursing experience could have prepared me for the sheer frailty of these old ladies. The contorted bodies, the skin so delicate and easily bruised, the eyes which stared ahead without seeing. We worked together steadily, moving from bed to bed, washing, powdering, putting on clean nighties, giving tablets, saying 'Goodnight, God bless.'

'Kiss me, Mother,' said one. 'I haven't been a naughty girl, have I?'

'You've been very good,' I said kissing her cool cheek.

By eleven the ward was quiet, the night light glowed and Linda walked into the office with a tray of tea. I felt exhausted, my back ached from lifting and rolling and heaving but Linda still seemed fresh and alert.

'Not a bad "change",' she said. 'Sometimes every bed is wet.'

As we drank the tea I asked how long she'd worked at St Dymphna's.

'Too bloody long.' She laughed. 'Mind you, it's better than staying in every night.'

Before I had time to ask why, the phone rang – it was night sister.

'I'll be there in fifteen minutes. Everything all right?'

'Fine, thank you. No problems.'

There was no response, just the sound of the phone being slammed down.

'She's an old crow,' said Linda. 'She resents coming up here. Has to take a taxi and bring a porter with her. It's ever since the murder of course. She'll stay about three minutes, that's all.'

'It's a strange set-up, isn't it? Why on earth aren't the night sisters on site?' I asked.

'Cutbacks. We're closing down. There's only one problem.'

'What's that?'

'No one wants the patients. The private nursing homes don't want them, the General doesn't have room. I think the managers are hoping the patients will just die off before the new financial year.'

'Why don't the nursing homes want them?'

'Too much like hard work I suppose.'

'What about the staff, will they be redeployed?'

'Some will. Most of us are looking for new jobs now. Ever since the murder we've all been a bit nervy, it gets really creepy here at times.'

'Murder,' I said in mock surprise. 'What happened?'

Linda didn't get a chance to reply as a loud rapping on the door disturbed us. I'd neither heard footsteps nor a taxi draw up. I guessed it was night sister, but that didn't stop my bottom from lifting from the seat in surprise. Linda, though, was on her feet first.

'Who is it?' she called.

'Night sister.'

Linda unlocked and unbolted the door.

'I can't be long. Taxi's waiting.'

She looked me up and down as I came out of the office. I did the same to her. In late middle age she looked as if life had treated her unfairly. Lines of anguish lay across her face like the National Grid. Pale blue eyes, with creased lids, flickered nervously in a face that had probably once been pretty. Her floppy white cap looked as tired as her face.

'Berkerly Agency?' she asked.

I nodded.

'Don't forget to get your time-sheets signed.'

'I won't,' I said, smiling, trying to be pleasant.

'Come on, let's get this round done.'

She was so fast I could barely keep up.

'Ward's tidy,' she said, as she walked out of the door Linda held open in readiness for her.

I laughed when she'd gone. 'Is she usually like that?'

'Like a bat out of hell – always,' said Linda. 'Mind you, she's had a hard life. Her only son died in a motor-bike accident and her husband's an alcoholic.'

For a while then we fell silent. Linda took out a magazine and I read a newspaper. Occasionally the central heating thumped, the strip lighting buzzed and a patient mumbled incoherently in her sleep. But it was the sounds outside I heard more acutely, an owl hooting, the wind in the trees, the rain against the windows, a far-distant car. It was a little later that I heard footsteps. I looked up startled.

'It's okay. It's only the security man,' said Linda, looking at her watch. 'He always does one round at midnight, then about two, then about five.'

'Was he here the night of the murder?'

'Huh!' said Linda. 'He was supposed to be. We had to find Jacky. He was nowhere to be found.'

'Who's we?'

'Me and the staff nurse from Melba Ward. Jacky had gone across to get some more incontinence pads about midnight and she didn't return.'

'Did you know her well?'

'I'd worked with her quite a bit. Too religious for me; she was a bit goody-goody. Didn't drink or smoke or swear. Still, she didn't deserve to get murdered.'

'I don't suppose anyone does.'

Linda looked at me sharply. 'Don't you believe it,' she said. 'Some people ask for it.'

Chapter Three

'Who do you know who's asking to be murdered?' Linda hadn't volunteered any names, so I decided to take the bull by the horns.

'That boring fart who sits at home in front of the telly. He's a prime example. That's why I work nights; I'd be divorced by now or he'd be dead if I didn't.'

'How would you murder him, if you had the chance.'

She paused, her eyes bright with interest, then she smiled. 'We'd be in bed,' she said. 'He'd be fast asleep as usual and then – I'd sit on his head and suffocate him – he's only a little bloke.'

My expression must have amused her because she began to laugh so raucously that I joined in.

'Oh, God,' she said between laughs, 'you've got a morbid sense of humour.'

When we'd finally regained control she asked, 'Are you married?'

'No one would have me,' I said. 'Well, one or two would have. Wimpy ones. I fancy the rugged, intrepid kind. You know the type – they paddle a raft up the Orinoco.'

Linda didn't, she looked puzzled. 'Haven't you ever lived with a man?'

'I did once, for three years. Dave – he died.'

'An illness?'

'No, accident.'

Somehow I couldn't tell her my one time live-in lover had been felled by a stray brick as he passed a building site. He'd been drunk at the time. Died instantly. Not exactly a hero's death, especially for a police inspector. I hadn't been heartbroken; shocked – yes. Live-in he may have been, but he spent most of his time in the pub or working. Even so, since Dave, there had been no one else.

I suppose he was intrepid in his own way. And he did die near the canal in Camden Town. That was his Orinoco.

Linda must have felt awkward at my silence because she got up abruptly. 'I'll do a round.'

I followed her out and we walked past the beds, checking no one had died surreptitiously. One or two lay mouths open, breaths hardly perceptible. They looked not just dead, but long dead.

Back in the office we ate toast and drank tea and amused ourselves planning how we would spend a quarter of a million pools win. It was a sobering thought that somehow we managed neither an evening out nor a new outfit on our winnings.

'That's another dream shattered,' announced Linda. 'Just as well I don't know how to fill out the coupon.'

At one a.m. our cheerfulness began to wane and Linda suggested we start our breaks. I chose second break, from three to five.

'We don't get paid for our two-hour break,' she explained as she collected her cloak from a hook on the office door. 'You can do whatever you like. Give me a shout if you need a hand and bang on the door at three. If I do go off to sleep I die!'

'Should I expect anyone while you're gone?'

'God no!' Linda burst out. 'You might hear the security man as he thumps by. You'll soon recognise the sound of his boots. Just occasionally he calls in for a cup of tea, but he always taps on the kitchen window and calls out. More often than not he— ' She broke off as she picked up the tea-tray. Following her out to the kitchen I waited for her to continue, but she didn't.

'The police don't call in then?' I asked.

'They did just after the murder, for weeks! Mind you I think they came more for a chat and a cuppa than anything else. At the beginning CID men came and questioned us, trying to find out if we had alibis. Well, of course, those on duty did – each other. And those off duty had husbands or boyfriends to vouch for them.'

'Surely they didn't suspect the staff?' I said, trying to inject a tone of mild incredulity into my voice.

Linda shrugged and began to rinse the mugs. 'I think it was just routine. They have to investigate all possibilities, don't they? Anyway the Detective Inspector seemed to think it was strange she wasn't raped. He thought a psychopath would only have sex on his mind.'

I wiped the mugs with a paper towel and said nothing.

'And,' Linda continued, 'I told him rape was violence, not sex, and he mumbled something about "Bloody feminists" and left me alone after that.'

As we walked down the ward doing checks and turns I said, 'Do *you* think it was peculiar she wasn't raped?'

She gave me a slightly startled look as if I'd said something outrageous. 'No. Why should I?'

'No reason. I just wondered.'

I must have looked mystified because she started talking quickly, as if to justify her reaction.

'Jacky was a bit of a weirdo really – any man who decided to rape her wouldn't have found it easy. She knew every martial art going – karate, kung fu, judo. She was only small but she was tough. Strange, really, she didn't put up more of a fight, but then she was stabbed in the back. I suppose she didn't have a chance.'

'You were going to tell me about someone getting in here at night,' I said. We were standing at the day room door.

'Was I?' She looked blank. 'Oh, I remember. Someone once forgot to bolt the door at the bottom end of the ward. A drunk came staggering in with a bag of chips in his hand and started offering them round.'

'You got rid of him then?'

'Yes. No problem. You're not nervous at the thought of being on your own, are you?'

'No, of course not.' But I was. Every noise, mumble and cough seemed magnified once I sat alone in the office.

One of the patients shouted, 'Bill, Bill, where are you?' When I explained Bill was fast asleep, she said, 'Lazy sod. You go and wake him up.'

I checked her medical notes – Bill had been dead twenty years.

A clanging cot-side sent me rushing to the other side of the ward where Edith had managed to trap her leg between the bars. When I had pushed her leg back and given her a drink and covered her up she shouted indignantly. 'I know what you're up to, you – you – prostitute.'

After that the ward became quiet again, and between rounds I tried to read the patients' notes. But concentration only came in short rallies and I kept thinking about the night Jacky was killed.

31

That night, in the dark, she must have felt safe to have walked through the grounds alone. She could defend herself. Who did she have to fear? Or was there someone afraid of her, someone who had to silence her to save themselves?

Linda didn't need waking.

'I only dozed. The rain against the windows down there sounds like drumbeats,' she said as she brushed her hair. 'Were they all right?'

'Fine,' I assured her. I made her a mug of tea and then went down to the day room. Vinyl-covered chairs lined two walls; in one corner sat a television set as blank and sinister as a glass eye. In the other corner was a bird cage, covered with a tablecloth. There were no lamps or tables. It smelt of urine. I sat myself between the two chairs Linda had covered with a clean sheet and watched the curtains flutter at the French window and listened to the rain and murmurings from the ward. Dozing was easy, sleep was impossible. The bird in the cage began to thrash about as though making suicide attempts by throwing itself at the bars. I took the tablecloth off and wished the budgie well. He or she seemed to understand, because all it did then was try to knock its companion toy budgie from their shared perch.

The two hours between six and eight seemed the shortest of the night because we were so busy. And I hardly noticed how tired I was until I drove away from the hospital. My concentration was definitely impaired and my eyes seemed to stare fixedly ahead in a sort of robotic trance. I had planned to go home but at the T-junction home was a right turn, the office left. There was no contest, I turned left. It was then I remembered that I was supposed to be seeing Mrs Ada Hellidon.

Via tortuous country lanes I managed to find Short Brampton. The village interior looked quaint, with stone cottages crushed together incestuously. So close were they, it was hard to imagine any knocking-shop activities going on there. There was no shop of any kind. Short Brampton was far too posh for shops.

Ada Hellidon's cottage was easily distinguishable, as it was the only one in need of renovation. The front door, which led directly on to the road, was covered in mud and dust and the paint had peeled back, like some nasty skin disease. I knocked hard on the door.

'Who is it?' screeched the reply, like a parrot on heat, and even when I answered, the screech became louder, more insistent. 'Who is it?'

Hubert had obviously forgotten to say that not only was she half-blind but deaf as well. As Kate Kinsella meant nothing to her I shouted through the letter-box, 'Mr Humberstone said I'd call.' But the front door still didn't open, and eventually I called, 'It's the district nurse.'

She opened the door then. A tiny old lady with skin the colour of a nicotined finger and hair of a pale purple hue. 'About time,' she said. 'You're new. The doctor's been promising me you'd call for weeks. It's my leg ulcer, you know. Come on in then.'

I followed her in, her legs moving more briskly than mine, and with no trace of swelling or varicose veins.

The cottage smelt vaguely of paraffin and stew. Old stew.

'Just you look at this,' she said aggressively, as if she expected me to argue. Already she'd peeled off her stocking, thrust her ankle on a footstool and was pointing to a small Elastoplast on her leg.

'I'll take it off, shall I?'

It was a stupid question and her answering look confirmed it. 'Where's your bag?' she demanded.

'I'll have a look first,' I said as I peered under the edge of the plaster.

'Mind what you're doing,' she warned, but I'd already done it and the plaster was off.

All that lurked underneath was the healed scar of a previous ulcer. Healed long ago. Ada Hellidon's thin upper lip curled slightly and she sucked in her equally thin lower lip until it disappeared. Her expression didn't look embarrassed. She just looked perplexed. I felt the same way. For a private detective I was doing quite well as a district nurse.

'Is it all right?' she asked. 'Not gone gangrenous, has it? I can't see very well.'

I assured her it wasn't gangrenous, that I'd bathe it and that it would be better left exposed.

She misunderstood or pretended to. 'A bath,' she said. 'I haven't had a bath for two years. I need someone to get me out. You'll bath me. I'm lucky I'm on Economy 7, there's plenty of hot water.'

She made Economy 7 sound like a conferred honour. I agreed to the bath as there wasn't much else I could do.

33

Mrs Hellidon began to chat as I helped her undress.

'I've lived round here all my life, you know. I know everyone.' She paused and grimaced. 'Well, I used to know all the villagers. People my age are dead now. Lucky buggers. Mostly young people in the village now. Mind you, they get bumped off by lunatics. Not surprising really. Young girls having sex all the time. Wouldn't have been allowed in my day. It went on. We knew that. But we did it on the quiet. Down by the river in the dark, that's where it went on.' She smiled then, a smile of remembered pleasure.

'Didn't that girl who was murdered live round here?' I mouthed carefully.

She noticed. 'I'm not deaf,' she said. 'That Jacky Byfield, you mean. Used to live at the end cottage. She was a right one, I can tell you. Churchgoer as well. Men in and out all the time. Only recent, though – a few months before she got killed. Before that, she had a proper boyfriend. Ever so smart he was. Had lovely short hair, nice suits, sort of posh.'

'I thought you couldn't see well.'

'Nothing wrong with my sight, only close up. I can't see your face properly but I can see longways. I'm only long-sighted and I'm not daft. Dr Hiding says I've got a very sharp brain for my age. I gave a good description to the police. I watch from the window, you see. Sit in my chair most days, just watching. I'm the only one left in the village during the day, in this bit anyway. I belong to Neighbourhood Watch. I am the bloody neighbourhood.' She chuckled delightedly.

Once she was in the bath I didn't have the heart to hurry her along.

'Did this girl Jacky live alone?' I asked as I soaped her back.

'You give my back a good scrub, there's a dear. I haven't managed to get at it for such a long time.'

I didn't repeat my question, partly because Ada seemed to be enjoying herself so much, but mostly because I was too tired to think straight. I knew the answer anyway.

'That girl's mother,' she said, raising one foot, looking at it carefully and then returning it to the water. 'That Jacky's mother – has a man!' Ada made it sound like a terminal illness.

'Oh dear,' I replied.

'Funny family altogether,' she continued. 'The husband left years ago—'

'Not dead then?'

'Dead? I suppose he could be. He just left, disappeared years ago when Jacky was about three. I saw him leave, walked right past my front door. Had two suitcases with him and a couple of suits slung over his arm. Never saw him again in the village.'

The bath over, I'd managed to help with drying and powdering to Ada's complete satisfaction. Getting dressed was almost finished, when she said, 'Oh, it's been lovely, dear. Thanks ever so much. You will stay for tea.'

I stayed: the whole situation was so ludicrous I had to do the whole bit. We had chocolate biscuits with the tea.

'You'll come again, won't you, dear?' It was a plea rather than a question.

'Of course,' I replied. 'Next month.'

Ada frowned. 'Two weeks,' she said.

'Three.'

She nodded. 'Done.'

As I left she handed me a jar of jam. 'Plum,' she said. 'My best.'

'I think I ought to explain,' I began. But she didn't let me continue.

'Don't you worry, dear. You'll get the hang of things. It's always hard for new young nurses – I'll put in a good word for you with Dr Hiding.'

I basked for a moment at the idea of being thought young. Then I remembered how bad her sight was. She noticed my car, though.

'You ought to get a new car,' she said, 'like all the other district nurses.'

Driving away I realised that now I'd have to pay Dr Hiding a visit. And I'd have a lot of explaining to do.

Chapter Four

In the afternoon Hubert knocked on my office door. I was just getting dressed.

'You'll have to wait,' I called. He waited.

'You look terrible,' he said as I opened the door.

'Thanks.'

He stood there looking vaguely keen and expectant.

'Come in,' I said grudgingly. I still felt hung over from sleep.

Hubert sat himself on the corner of my desk. 'It's the funeral on Friday,' he said. 'Jacky's – at the Church of the Second Coming – interment. You ought to go, meet the suspects.'

'And interview them as we stand by the grave, you mean. Or spot the one who looks like the devil incarnate.'

A crestfallen look crossed his face as if he had lost one of his customers to the Co-op. I ignored his expression, but put plenty of sugar in his coffee.

'Do you know Dr Hiding?' I asked, handing him the coffee.

'Is he a suspect?' Hubert's voice sounded suspiciously joyful.

'Don't think so. What makes you say that?'

'No reason. The police surgeon is one of the GPs at the practice. There's three of them – Hiding, Benfleet and Kingsthorpe. Benfleet is the police surgeon. He's got bunions, used to wear winkle-pickers in the sixties.' Hubert's eyes glazed over dreamily. Surely he wasn't turned on by the thought of bunions? I hoped it was the winkle-pickers.

'You should have been a chiropodist. Feet are definitely your forte.'

'Wanted to be,' muttered Hubert, staring into his coffee. 'But it didn't run in our family. My father thought it was very odd I should want to fiddle with feet.'

'Dead bodies being more normal?'

'Nothing more normal than death,' he said.

He was right of course, but feet were normal too. Unless of course you were Hubert, then feet seemed to have quite mystical qualities. Capable of really stirring the imagination.

'What's the Hiding practice like? I need to register in the area.'

'I suppose you think there's a choice. This isn't London, you know. There's only one surgery in town. You're on a Hiding to nothing.'

'You're sharp this afternoon.'

He grinned without showing his teeth.

'Do I need an appointment?'

'For what?'

'The doctor.'

Hubert looked amused as if I'd asked a silly question. 'No. You just go along. I've only been once or twice, I'm not ill often. I've heard about Hiding, though.'

'And?'

'You'll find out.' His smile fixed. I think he was trying to be enigmatic. He just looked ridiculous.

When he'd drunk the coffee I elbowed him to the door. It seemed he wasn't quite ready to leave because before I'd managed to open it, he turned back and spoke in his confidential tone. 'I've heard a whisper.'

'Yes?'

'It's about Jacky.'

'Is it a secret?'

'What's that supposed to mean?'

'Nothing, sorry. You were saying.'

Hubert leaned forwards and bent his head towards mine. 'I've heard, from a reliable source, that' – he paused, as if embarrassed – 'that Jacky was a – virgin.'

Even saying the word made Hubert's face mottle puce. I realised then why he'd never married. Why he preferred feet and shoes. The vocabulary of footwear could never embarrass him.

'How reliable?' I asked.

'If you must know, Dr Benfleet's post-mortem assistant told me, in confidence of course. Jacky was virgin intacto.' He whispered the word virgin.

'Virgo intacta,' I corrected, trying at the same time not to sound patronising. 'It seems funny, given that in the pub you told me Jacky was practically a prostitute.'

'I did not.'

'You did. A succession of men going in and out – those were your words or at least the gist of them.'

'That's what the neighbour said.'

'I know. I saw her this morning. Gave her a bath.'

Hubert was shocked. 'You did what! That's a funny carry-on for a private detective. Are you sure you know what you're doing?'

'No I don't, but I'm trying.'

I felt suddenly depressed, but Hubert didn't. He looked expectant, even excited.

'There's something else,' he said. 'Jacky didn't die from the stab wound. She had something wrong with her heart valves, really rare; she would have died young anyway.'

That did surprise me. I supposed a combination of shock and haemorrhage must have triggered a cardiac arrest. No wonder the body had only just been released. Did that make the crime manslaughter or attempted murder, I wondered?

'For a private detective you should know better.' Hubert left then, looking really pleased with himself.

I think he meant Ada's bath, but I'm not sure.

Shortly afterwards I phoned the surgery. I didn't believe that you could turn up without an appointment. A receptionist who had obviously taken a course in telephone smile-talk answered.

'Good afternoon. Longborough Health Centre. May I help?'

'I hope so. I'd like to see Dr Hiding. I'm not registered yet.'

I waited, expecting the smiley voice to change, for her to say, "What's wrong with you?" and then, "Come in a fortnight." Instead she spoke with cheerful heartiness, 'Certainly, my dear, any time this afternoon, until six thirty.'

'Today?' I queried, just to be sure.

'Yes indeed. Dr Hiding would be pleased to see you then.'

Longborough Health Centre lay tucked away on the outskirts of town in the middle of a thirties-style council estate. It would have been out of place in any small town. Externally it was a riot of domes and turrets and haphazardly arranged windows, many no bigger than portholes. In fact, some were portholes. Inside, it looked as if the ceiling were missing. Bare piping hung in the roof space as though part of the decor. In the middle of the upper reaches was a platform, obviously some sort of room. A spiral staircase led upwards. Perhaps eccentric architects came cheaper or maybe the threesome had run out of money. Anyway it didn't look finished, and it was as dark as a cave, enlivened only by the green of numerous potted plants that gave the impression it was a cave somewhere in the jungle. I was impressed with the musak though. Mantovani, I guessed.

Only two people waited in the open-plan reception area and I continued to be impressed when I was summoned after five minutes.

Dr Hiding sat at his desk but stood up as I entered the room. He was good-looking in a scholarly way. Heavy-rimmed glasses and a grey cardy made him appear older and no doubt wiser than he really was. He shook me firmly by the hand which, strangely, made me feel like some rare exotic species.

'Welcome, Mrs . . . ?' he queried. 'How may I help?'

'It's Kate Kinsella – Miss. It's nothing really,' I began apologetically, as though something less than major injuries needed an apology. 'I've got some low back pain and I haven't registered yet.' The backache wasn't exactly a lie. I always have a slight backache, most nurses do. He'd been writing my name but stood up abruptly, walked to my side of the desk and I thought he was about to feel my back. Instead he held my hand and stroked it slowly and rhythmically. I was at the same time mesmerised and disconcerted and I must have shown it.

'Just relax, Miss Kinsella. Here we treat our patients holistically. The whole person, not just bits and pieces.'

'Oh, good,' I murmured. 'That's nice.' I could feel my IQ slipping away from me like water from a colander. I almost forgot why I was really there. It didn't seem the right moment to mention Mrs Hellidon.

He continued to tower over me, stroking my hand. Eventually he said, 'Right, my dear, take your clothes off and pop on the couch.' The 'my dear' irritated me and his keenness to get me undressed worried me; it seemed in advance of either my condition or our relationship. I followed his eyes to the curtain and he resumed his position at the desk. I didn't have much choice. It was strip or be unholistic.

Lying on the couch in my bra and knickers I resolved always to

39

wear decent underwear in the future. The elastic on my knickers had begun to shed itself – little stringy bits kept appearing – and my bra, once white, was now a dull beige. He approached the couch with a firm tread and began to get physical with his stethoscope, patella hammer and his hands. He explored my spine inch by inch. Told me to sit up, sit down, stand up, bend over.

'Ah,' he said, as if he had discovered a new condition.

'What is it?'

'It's only muscular,' he said. 'A course of massage and exercises will sort you out. You can get dressed now. It would be a good idea not to wear high heels any more. With your weight, it's throwing your back out of shape.'

I got dressed feeling as if I'd emerged from a chrysalis as a fat hunchback.

He was filling out some notes when I returned. He nodded for me to sit down.

'Dr Hiding, I did have another reason for coming,' I said hurriedly.

'Oh?'

'Yes, I called on Mrs Hellidon in Short Brampton yesterday. I was in uniform and she thought I was a district nurse. She wanted me to look at her leg ulcer – long since healed – and I gave her a bath.'

'That was very public-spirited of you,' he said, with no trace of surprise. He seemed to think it was perfectly normal.

'There's more to it than that. You see, I called on her for some information.'

'What sort?' he asked, peering from beneath his glasses and smiling fixedly.

'I'm a private detective.'

'Really. You don't look the type.'

I supposed he meant fat hunchbacks don't look the type.

'It's interesting work, is it?'

'Very.' I didn't tell him my speciality. He could have something to hide. 'I'm investigating the murder of Jacky Byfield, the girl who was stabbed in the grounds of St Dymphna's.'

He nodded but didn't answer. I quickly tried to dredge up my IQ a few points. If I asked outright about Jacky he would give me a lecture on confidentiality and patients' rights. Probably those rights came holistically – even post mortem. I decided on a more general approach.

'Such a tragedy,' I continued. 'Such a fine girl, so religious, so virginal.'

'Indeed she was,' he murmured. 'Indeed she was.' He'd obviously known her quite well. Staring out of one of the porthole windows he said, 'She was such a healthy girl, physically and mentally. Well, now she's got her wish.'

'Her wish?' I echoed.

'Yes indeed. Eternal life. That's what we all strive for, isn't it? A pure life, albeit hard, in the here and now and then the joy of everlasting life. That was her heart's desire, of course.'

'Naturally,' I muttered.

He didn't seem to notice the sarcasm in my voice. For a while he seemed to forget I was still sitting there. Perhaps he was praying. I began to feel quite uneasy. Hubert's enigmatism hadn't been unfounded and somehow my back had stopped hurting altogether.

'One question,' he said, resuming eye contact. 'A personal one.' He paused awkwardly.

'Yes.'

'Your sex life.'

'Yes?'

'Is it fulfilling?'

Stupidly my mouth opened and then closed. I coughed to fill the gap. 'Quite normal, thank you,' I managed to stutter. Why should I admit to him that it was on hold at the moment?

'Coming to Jesus stops us needing, stops us having to satisfy the flesh. Sustains us. Am I making myself clear?'

'Perfectly, I'll bear it in mind.'

'The Church is like a lover, you know. When Jesus comes again all will be revealed, all will be eased. His love is more passionate than human love, more all-embracing.'

I nodded as the sermon ended.

'My massage sessions are every two weeks. Tuesday evenings from six to eight. There's no need to make an appointment.' My visit was over. I stood up. As I got to the door I realised he was behind me. He shook me vigorously by the hand as he gave me his benediction. 'Jesus saves, Miss Kinsella, Jesus saves.'

But he didn't save Jacky, I thought, while muttering 'Hallelujah' in response.

On the way out I registered with Dr Benfleet. His bunions would be preferable to Hiding's second coming. The receptionist didn't even blink.

Returning to the office I spotted my reflection in a shop window. I wasn't a hunchback at all. I bought two cream cakes to celebrate. One for me, one as a peace offering for Hubert. He wasn't fat anyway and if he didn't want it, I'd eat them both.

Back at Humberstones I braved the lower sanctum to find Hubert. I found him in the Chapel of Rest – he seemed to be admiring a tasteful selection of flowers ranged in front of an ornate cross. There were two coffins on display. I didn't want to know who was in them. I called from the door, 'You could have warned me.'

He swung round. 'You wouldn't have believed me.' His eyes moved to my feet and glinted. When he looked up my black patents seemed to be reflected in his eyes. 'Odd, isn't he,' he said. 'I go to Benfleet. Very good with feet, on account of his bunions, I suppose.'

I was about to tell him about the cream cakes when he said, 'You've had a phone call. From Jacky's aunt. She wants you to attend the funeral tea.'

'What joy.'

'Could be very useful – in between the ham sandwiches.'

I hoped so, I really did. If Jacky had been as irritating as Dr Hiding I wasn't surprised she'd been murdered. And I wouldn't have been surprised if Hiding was hiding something.

'I've bought us some cream cakes,' I told Hubert.

He looked inordinately pleased. As we left the chapel he said, 'That coffin on the right is Jacky's. She's been embalmed.'

I was sure he was joking but I couldn't eat my cream cake. Hubert ate them both.

Chapter Five

My companion of the night, Olwen Jones, looked as old as some of the patients.

'It's me first night on, Staff,' she announced. 'Been off sick with my back for six months. Still, I'll do my best.'

Olwen, although plump, assumed a stooped position, as though she were permanently ready for action. This was very misleading, and halfway through the evening's work I suggested we stop for ten minutes. Olwen looked ready to drop. A cigarette seemed to revive her and she peered at me through thick bi-focals.

'I needed a break, Staff. I forgot how tiring it is. My doctor didn't want me to come back to work at all, said I should go on long-term sick. But I retire in six months and I wanted to see it out. I've been at St Dymphna's for forty years.' She puffed reflectively on her cigarette. 'Forty years,' she repeated. 'The changes I've seen you wouldn't believe. Forty years.'

Mutterings and groanings from the ward cut short our break.

'Come on, Olwen,' I encouraged. 'We'll soon be finished.'

Although our patients could no longer tell the time they did seem to sense we were late. Dolly, who wore the mob-cap, reproached me. 'You should know better, Mrs Bluefrock. Coming here late, expect you've been with that man again. You should get a proper job instead of taking up space in my house.'

I agreed that I should.

'And you,' she said, peering at Olwen, 'you're fatter than ever. I've never seen an arse like it.'

Olwen laughed. 'You're on form, Dolly. 'I've missed you.'

Once Dolly was settled and had been given her usual tot of brandy she cheered up. 'You get to bed now, girls, thank you and God bless.'

The best part of night duty is connected with lights. The

switching off of the main lights at night and the switching on again in the morning. Standing by the light switches I checked all was quiet both ends of the ward.

'Good night everyone,' I called. There was no reply. They were all cocooned in their duvets, warm and untroubled. By morning the plastic mattress covers and the plastic covers of their duvets would have cooked them as though in a sandwich toaster. For now, though, there was peace.

'I'm knackered,' said Olwen, sitting down heavily on one of the office chairs and beginning to forage in her shopping bag. Triumphantly she produced a packet of chocolate biscuits. I made tea and soon Olwen's pale face looked less anxious.

'Didn't think I'd cope at first. I'm past it now, I know that. But I've enjoyed working here. Mind you, there's not much excitement here these days. In the old days there was always something going on.'

'Well, I call a murder exciting enough, but I suppose you don't know much about it, being off sick at the time.'

Olwen smiled wryly and shrugged. 'Don't you believe it. I probably know more about the murder than anyone— ' She broke off. 'Apart from the murderer of course.'

'You knew Jacky well?' I asked.

Olwen paused for a while as if not quite sure. Murder, like suicide, seems to make people doubt their memories of that person. As if all their ideas and thoughts and feelings had been scrambled in a computer and the dead person has become a stranger. A mystery. A jigsaw puzzle personality that takes a long time to reconstruct. For close relatives and friends all that takes a very long time. Guilt clouds the memory too. Eventually Olwen said, 'She'd only worked here three years but I worked with her quite a bit.'

'And did you like her?'

Olwen looked past me and shifted her bottom in the chair. 'She was okay.'

Condemnation indeed.

As if sensing I was about to ask more questions she stood up suddenly. 'I'll just check the patients, Staff.'

When Olwen came back from her tour of the ward it was obvious she wanted to change the subject. She sat with crossed arms and frowned. 'It's funny,' she said reflectively, 'being away for six months has made me see everything differently. I never felt old before and now I realise I'm nearly ready to be a patient myself. I've got no kids, my husband's been dead these three years. You worry all your life about paying the mortgage and then once it's paid you have to sell it to be able to afford private care. Well, I'm getting out.'

'Retiring, you mean?'

'I'm off to Spain, I've decided. I'll sell the house before the DSS can force me to sell. Once the money's gone that's it. I'd rather be old and poor in Spain in the sun than crouched over a gas fire in England.'

'Perhaps you'll find a man out there,' I suggested.

Olwen laughed, her good humour returning. 'Pigs might fly. Anyway only a younger man would do, a toy-boy. The old boys I meet look all right on the outside, then when you get to know them better they tell you about their haemorrhoids, their constipation and, worst of all, boast about how they used to perform. No, I don't need a man. I just want to be warm, near the sea, go to the occasional tea-dance and relax with nothing and no one to worry about.'

'You could get bored.'

'Boredom is a wet Sunday in England, watching *Songs of Praise* on the box and wondering how many more miserable Sundays you can live through.'

I nodded. I hate Sundays. The longest, loneliest day of the week.

Our mood had begun to go downhill fast. But food came to the rescue. Olwen had brought baked potatoes, sausages and bacon that only needed reheating. The food lifted our mood and Olwen began to reminisce about the old days: the hard work, the fun, the parties, the affairs.

'Surely the affairs still go on?' I protested.

'Hardly at all,' said Olwen, 'unless of course if you counted Jacky and Dr Robert Duston.'

I was intrigued. Perhaps here was a motive – jealousy, thwarted sexual desire. Dr Duston desperately trying to lure Jacky to his bed and then in a frenzy of rejection killing her. One stab in the back, though, hardly constituted a frenzied attack. It seemed almost half-hearted, but perhaps the killer had been disturbed mid-attack or perhaps in the dark it had been a ghastly mistake.

'They were having an affair?' I asked, wondering if an unconsummated relationship could ever be called an affair.

'Suppose so,' said Olwen. 'In a casual sort of way. No one ever saw them out together but she did visit him in his room.'

'Here?'

'Yes. In the main building.'

'When she was on duty, you mean?'

Olwen took off her glasses and rubbed her eyes, then she stared at me as if trying to focus her eyes and her thoughts together. Her face looked naked without her glasses. 'Oh, yes. "I'll just pop over and see Robert" she'd say, bold as brass.'

'Does he still work here?'

Olwen nodded. 'He's a registrar, shares his time between here and the General. Not bad looking, about thirty, single.

The phone interrupted us. It was one of the night sisters checking that all the patients were likely to last the night. If a patient died and the houseman or registrar were busy then they had to come. I reassured her that everything was in order, including the patients.

Olwen wasn't pleased. 'We're just a backwater now. They'd just like to forget about us altogether. Did anyone come last night?'

I nodded. 'I thought a night sister always came.'

'Not if they can help it, especially if an RGN is on and she seems to know what she's doing.'

The phone rang again almost immediately. 'It's Mick O'Dowd, security. All right if I come over to see Olwen?'

She looked pleased. 'I'll put the kettle on,' she said.

By the time the tea had brewed Mick O'Dowd had arrived. 'Hello, Ollie, old love, nice to see you back,' he said, giving her a hug. 'And who's your good-looking friend?' he asked, his eyes flicking over me without a trace of sexual interest.

Mick O'Dowd, I'd decided, liked women. Probably not a womaniser but a man who felt happiest in the company of women. Well, he'd chosen the right job. Olwen plied him with thick buttered toast and well-sugared tea and I had the feeling it was going to be a long visit. An informative visit, too, I hoped.

As they chatted I wondered if he had known Jacky well enough for tea and toast. His greased black hair and gold chain worn outside his uniform shirt certainly didn't suggest her type. But perhaps he'd been as friendly with Jacky as he obviously was with Olwen.

'How long did the police keep you?' Olwen was saying.

'Bloody hours. Why they should suspect me I don't know, I wouldn't have— ' He stopped as if realising I was there.

'I'll go over to another ward or sit in the day room if you'd like to talk privately.'

'Don't be daft,' said Olwen quickly, 'you're one of us now.'

Somehow that sounded vaguely ominous and I shivered slightly. Olwen noticed. 'Borrow a cardigan from the cupboard, Staff, your arms are all goose-pimples.'

As I left the office I heard Olwen say, 'They're not still asking you questions?'

In reply Mick's voice seemed tinged with bravado, 'Only once a week now. "Anything to tell us, Mick? Want to get it off your chest?" I just keep my mouth shut.'

Looking through the linen cupboard, I noticed we needed more sheets. It was the excuse I needed to visit Melba Ward and perhaps have a word with Mick on his own. He could walk with me through the grounds.

When I returned to the office Mick was saying, 'In her own way she fascinated me.'

Olwen muttered, 'Yeah, like a snake.'

'Who's like a snake?' I asked with a smile, trying to sound casual.

Olwen was quicker than Mick, 'Oh, just one of the night sisters.'

She was lying, I was quite sure of that.

For a while then they talked in riddles of people I'd never met and places I'd never seen.

Eventually Mick stood up. 'I've got to go, girls. Do my duty.'

'Will you walk me over to Melba?' I asked. 'We need some more sheets.'

'I'll go,' said Olwen.

'No, I'll go. I need some fresh air.'

Olwen shrugged. 'I'll ring to let them know you're coming.'

Outside the air did seem fresh but as we started walking I soon began to feel cold.

'You should have worn a coat,' said Mick as he placed one arm round me and crushed me to him.

For a moment I held my breath and tensed. I swear I could feel the adrenalin pumping. My nursing tutor used to say "Adrenalin,

47

girls, is for fear and flight." Or was it fight and flee? I couldn't remember.

'You scared?' asked Mick as he slackened his pace.

'Should I be?' I tried to walk faster, hoping soon to see the lights of Melba Ward instead of just bushes and trees.

'It was just here,' said Mick slowly, as he stopped and looked around.

'What was?' I asked stupidly, realising as soon as I spoke what he meant.

Mick released me. 'Just here. I found the body just here.' He stared at the ground and I joined him, just staring at a patch of bare earth as if Jacky were still lying there; as if somehow we could conjure her back.

'I thought . . . ' I began. 'I thought Linda Brington and Claudette found her.'

'Well, that's what the police think,' said Mick, giving me a sideways glance that dared me to answer. 'Here we all stick together.'

I pulled the cardigan tight around me and walked on quickly. Mick O'Dowd followed behind, his footsteps a dull thud on the hard ground. I looked over my shoulder, once, nervously. Did Jacky do the same thing that night? Was the same person following her? Perhaps she breathed a sigh of relief when she realised it was only Mick O'Dowd. Did she ignore him, turn away, walk on? What would I have done?

The outside light of Melba Ward shone reassuringly in the gloom. Mick walked by my side now, and when we reached the door he said, 'Bye, Staff, nice to meet you. See you again. Take care.' He sounded so ordinary, so easy, so good-natured. Do murderers urge their victims to take care, I wondered?

A young staff nurse greeted me at the door. She seemed pleased to see a new face. 'Hi – I'm Claudette. Kettle's on – office is straight in front.'

She disappeared into the kitchen and I walked into the office. This room was larger and more square than Harper's, the windows were higher and the vivid blue curtains with appliqué moon and stars gave it a more cheerful look. Otherwise, the equipment was the same, even to the position of the desk which faced the wall.

At the desk sat a slim, middle-aged woman. She half turned and raised a hand in welcome. Her hair and make-up were not

48

quite defined enough to make her face come alive. As if discretion was her byword. Her uniform dress, although crisp and fresh, was a dull yellow. And in the harsh strip lighting rogue grey hairs glinted in her short brown hair, alien, not only in colour but in their frizzled texture. I wondered why she didn't pluck them out. Her eyes, a greenish-blue, were bright and with their thick lashes her most attractive feature. Like me, she wore no rings and I noticed her fingernails had been neatly and completely bitten away. I guessed she was divorced.

'Hello,' she said. 'You must be Kate from the agency. I'm Margaret Tonbridge. Take a seat. Tea will take a while.' I saw then that she was working on some embroidery. She continued to work, the needle moving in and out, in and out. Monotonously. In silence. At last she put down her work. 'There. That's finished. Do you sew?'

I shook my head.

'Very soothing, embroidery. I could teach you the basics.'

'I haven't got the patience,' I explained. 'Not with things.'

She ignored that. 'You'd acquire it with practice,' she said. 'I'm patient – any sort of handicraft teaches patience.'

I smiled. 'I'm sure you're right,' I said. But I didn't agree. I thought sewing was a masochistic occupation, fraught with dangerous things like hooks and needles and scissors and sore fingers and irritation. I looked towards the door, finding the silence worrying. Where the hell was the tea?

'The tea won't be too long now. Claudette's a bit obsessional. She has her routine – wash hands, rinse mugs, scald with boiling water, dry with paper towels, then wash, rinse and scald teaspoons, wipe tray, wash taps, wipe taps, lay tray, make tea. It takes a long time.'

At that moment Claudette appeared with the tray. There were biscuits, and I wondered if she used tongs to put them on the plate. As she put down the tray I noticed the raw, steak-red hands, the scraped-back hair, fine and dry as though washed as often as the hands. I supposed she was in her early twenties. I'd seen Macbeth once. She reminded me of his lady.

'Has Margaret been telling you how long I take to do things? It's very irritating I know, but it's just the way I am.' She seemed proud of the fact.

'Have you had any treatment for your condition?' I asked.

Her eyes widened in surprise; obviously no one had been quite so blunt before. 'No, of course not. It's not a condition anyway, it's – it's – '

'A nuisance,' Margaret provided helpfully.

For a while a frosty silence descended: Claudette poured the tea and I tried to think of something useful to say. Useful to me.

'I talked to Mick on the way over,' I said, 'about the murder. Scared me rigid.'

Claudette spoke first, her hands moving to her hair and patting her head as though fixing her words into place. 'Scares us all,' she said. 'I shall be glad when they catch him. Sometimes at night, in the quiet, I imagine him creeping about outside.'

'Were you both on duty the night of the murder?'

Claudette glanced at Margaret as if seeking confirmation. Margaret nodded, looking up for a second from the needle she was threading, and then resuming her in-out motion.

'Did you hear anything that night?' I asked.

'Not a thing,' said Claudette. 'You heard a car, though, didn't you?'

Margaret answered thoughtfully, pausing mid-stitch. 'Yes. It was about twenty past twelve. I'd done a round at midnight and then I checked all the plugs were out. I looked at the clock in the day room.'

'And I was in the kitchen tidying up,' murmured Claudette.

'Mick tells me you and Linda Brington found the body?'

Claudette stared at her water-worn hands. 'Yes,' she said.

I waited for her to continue but she didn't. 'How awful,' I said. 'What on earth did you think?'

'Think?' she echoed. 'I didn't think. I just looked at her, lying there on the ground like a rag doll. I couldn't believe it.'

'I would have run off screaming,' I said. 'What about you, Margaret?'

She looked at me blankly. Claudette, too, looked blank.

'We just stood there, it seemed like a long time. She was face down with the incontinence pads still in her hand.' Claudette's voice had dropped to a whisper.

'Were you scared?' I asked.

'I was shocked.'

'Didn't it occur to you he might still be around, lurking in the bushes?'

'No, that didn't occur to me.'

I wondered why. 'Did you touch the body?' I asked.

It was one question too many. A look of suspicion passed between them. I was sounding like a policeman.

'I'm sorry,' I smiled. 'I read too many murder stories, a morbid hobby.'

'You should take up sewing, it's more constructive,' Margaret said.

'I'd better be off, Olwen will think I've— ' I stopped myself just in time.

'I'll come halfway with you,' said Margaret. She picked up one of the cloaks from a hook on the back of the door. 'Here, wear this one,' she said. 'I'll wear Claudette's cloak.'

'I'll be fine on my own,' I protested.

'That's what Jacky thought,' she said grimly.

Chapter Six

I gave the office a miss for the day. Hubert seemed a bit peeved when I phoned, but as there were no messages it seemed sensible to sleep in a proper bed for once. Not that I slept well. In my dreams Claudette had grown fangs and was chasing me. Her outspread cloak, billowing like huge black wings, threatened to engulf me. She gained on me, moving closer and closer until the cloak was over my head and I could see the lining was not black but red. And the red was blood. Blood that dripped over my hair, my forehead, my face. Trickling in slow motion over my body like treacle from a spoon.

When I woke to find myself merely steaming under the duvet, I felt quite cheerful, even though I had the funeral to attend. And nothing suitably funereal to wear. I prefer loose, colourful clothes. Clothes that I can sag into and not worry about the odd bulge. In the end I decided to wear the only straight skirt I own, a dark mauve, and a black silk shirt of Dave's. Seemed appropriate really – a dead man's shirt. I rang Pauline Berkerly to arrange more work at St Dymphna's. All she could offer me was a single night on Melba Ward and a night nursing a tetraplegic. I turned down the tetraplegic.

Pauline did promise, though, to check on the names of any agency staff working around the time of the murder. Perhaps they wouldn't be so cagey. Who was I kidding? The staff at St Dymph's weren't cagey, they were just lying. But why? Who were they trying to protect and would they protect a murderer? What troubled me most of all, though, was Jacky's unpopularity. Once I found the reason for that, there could be a motive. Motive plus circumstances equals murder, I told myself – twice – but it didn't help.

I sat at the kitchen table so that I wouldn't crease my newly ironed clothes, watching the clock and wishing the funeral time would arrive. Was Jacky wearing a cloak that night, I wondered, and was the wound very bloody? Stab wounds can be very deceptive. A minor-looking slit with hardly any outward bleeding can be internally devastating. The fact that Jacky had dodgy heart valves seemed academic. The murderer couldn't have known that, no one had, but he or she did know where to thrust the knife with deadly accuracy.

The Church of the Second Coming, opposite a derelict shoe factory, stood squat and ugly against a dark sky. The tin roof, a shade of cabbage green, boasted a wooden cross with the message 'Jesus Saves' and a poster on the door promised 'He will return'. I sat in my car watching people arrive.

The mourners met each other outside in groups of twos and threes – nodding, patting arms, occasionally hugging each other. Funerals seem to bring out the need for physical reassurance, as if by touching each other people are saying, 'I'm not dead, see, touch me, I'm still here.' I'm not an expert on funerals, though; I've only been to two – Dave's and my father's. And then of course I didn't take much notice of the other mourners or the place. I do remember the weather, though – both in May, both sunny days, with the flowers wilting in the heat.

The hearse arrived, followed by the chief mourners. I managed to glimpse Nina Marburg's side view and the woman I presumed to be her sister didn't turn her face. A tall, youngish-looking man walked between them. The coffin had already been carried in. Hubert, I was surprised to see, acted as front pall-bearer. Humberstones must have been short of staff as Hubert usually delegated such jobs. His expression remained as blank as the wooden coffin he helped to carry.

I waited a few minutes to make sure I saw as many faces as possible and then I planned to slip in at the back of the church. I'd just decided I'd better make a move when a group of four youths approached the church, stood outside jostling each other, began laughing, pushed each other around in a good-natured fashion and then walked in. But after a few yards they stopped, the tallest one throwing an empty beer can over a hedge and then shouting to the others, 'Carm on!'

They turned back then and, keeping well together, walked through the church door.

I'd crossed the road when the Range Rover drew up and parked on the double yellows and I couldn't avoid falling into step with Dr Hiding.

'Ah, Miss Kinsella, we meet again.'

His tone suggested he knew I'd registered with Dr Benfleet. I smiled.

'A sad occasion,' he said, taking me firmly by the arm and guiding me into the church. 'But we must remember that Jacky is, at last, happy in heaven.'

He made it sound as if someone had done some difficult conveyancing and Jacky had finally settled down in a mansion by the Thames.

The interior of the church glowed with the light of imitation candles ranged along the window-sills. And at regular intervals between each bulbous candle sat jam jars of dried leaves and flowers that cast spidery shadows against the windows. The seating was wooden and separate and the coffin had been placed on a trestle table behind the lectern. There didn't seem to be an altar and generally it all seemed very sparse. The congregation too was sparse. I counted about thirty, mostly old ladies.

Dr Hiding sat beside me and gave me a nudge. 'The hymns,' he whispered, handing me a two-page leaflet. Their pastor, I noted from the heading, was Edward Cable.

'Brothers and sisters,' he began. 'Brothers and sisters,' he repeated more loudly, more warmly, 'we are gathered here today not just to mourn the passing of our sister Jacky Byfield but to celebrate her return to the loving arms of Jesus.'

He paused and someone shouted 'Praise be' and 'Jesus saves'.

'Let us join in our special hymn for the dead, "Safe in Our Saviour's Arms".'

It was an almost jolly hymn, sung to the tune of 'When the Saints Go Marching In'.

After that, Edward Cable welcomed those who had never been to the church before. 'I welcome you,' he boomed, 'all the brothers and sisters welcome you, but, most of all' – he paused and in the silence there was a ripple of anticipation, like a football match just before a goal is scored – 'Our Lord welcomes you.'

'Hallelujah' and 'Praise be' and 'Amen' circulated around the congregation.

'Let us pray.'

I lowered my head but didn't close my eyes. I was too busy looking at the backs of heads. All the women, except me, wore a hat. Very dull hats too, berets and scarfs and felts. The four boys weren't praying either, but whispering amongst themselves. They gave the impression of tight, teenage restraint, about to be unleashed at any moment. I noticed the seemingly young shoulders of a man in the second row. His dark grey suit and short haircut spelt the 'smart, quite posh' description of Jacky's boyfriend, ex-boyfriend. I looked round for Ada Hellidon but couldn't see her. One elderly lady sat head forward in a wheelchair on the end of my row in the corner. She seemed to have been parked there alone.

The pastor continued with his rambling prayer which by now had turned into a sermon. He was getting quite emotional about forgiveness.

'Forgive them, Lord. O, Lord Jesus, sweet Jesus. When our time comes, O Lord, let us come with hearts unsullied by thoughts of vengeance. Let us look to your return to save us – we the chosen ones. We will forgive all those who trespass against us. Our sister Jacky would be the first to forgive her enemies – today and for ever, she is with you in paradise.'

'Praise the Lord.' 'Amen.'

'Amen. And, as we follow the coffin let us sing "Come Back to the Fold of Jesus".'

Slowly we followed the coffin to the cemetery outside. Why, I thought, did the pastor refer to 'them' and her 'enemies'? Why should Jacky have enemies in the plural?

The graveyard contained about six fairly recent stone crosses. Artificial roses and daffodils graced one or two graves. In the others, the vases were gloomily empty. There was nothing to suggest age or permanence. Once we were all assembled Pastor Edward Cable didn't waste the drama of the moment. This burial contained no 'dust to dust' eulogy but a loud 'Into thy hands, O Lord,' then a pause.

'Amen.'

'Hallelujah.'

After that, one or two voices rose up in spontaneous prayer, most of it unintelligible.

No one had cried until this point but as the coffin was lowered I noticed Nina Marburg stumble at the graveside. The woman in black next to her moved forward and held out her hand. They were obviously family, both sharing the same slight body, the small face. But my client was years older than her sister. And her sister, Jacky's mother, was extremely pretty. They each threw a red rose on the coffin and then hugged each other. The other mourners were silent. Tears filled my eyes, remembering. Hubert must have seen, because he smiled at me, a reassuring sort of smile. It seemed strange to think that he was the one person in Longborough whom I could call a real friend.

Post-funeral depression had set in and I wanted to rush away from the church but Dr Hiding blocked my exit to offer me a lift. I pointed across the road to my car. He looked so disgusted when I refused, it did at least make me smile. As I walked to the car I noticed the back view of a tall, thin woman pushing the old lady in the wheelchair. She looked vaguely familiar. Stopping a few yards on, she rearranged the grey felt hat that had flopped over her charge's eyes and bent over to say something. There seemed to be no response.

It was cold and I shivered. I wanted to go home but the funeral tea had to be endured and I was after all on an investigation. I couldn't afford to get morose and disinterested. I had to meet people, be inquisitive, ask pertinent questions. My mind, though, remained calm and blank. If religion was the opium of the people I could understand why. It had stultified me.

Even Leonard Cohen failed to cheer me and it rained in irritating stops and starts. Dr Hiding's Range Rover followed me all the way to Short Brampton. I drove very slowly, giving him every opportunity to overtake. He didn't even attempt it. He had taken hostages, though, for I caught a glimpse of the boys in the back seat. Had they been bribed, I wondered, or was Dr Hiding's chilling presence enough to coerce them to the funeral tea?

The house was indeed only four doors up from Ada Hellidon but what a difference four doors can make. This was the end house in the cul-de-sac, stone-built, detached and impressive. A house with interesting outbuildings and plants that crept up walls. The sort of house that proclaims 'No Hawkers or Circulars'. A house where, no doubt, preserves were made and eggs pickled.

The well-ruched cream curtains hadn't yet been pulled and inside I could see people moving around. I hoped there would be sherry or better still scotch. I needed a drink. It seemed doubtful though, amongst such company. I suspected the boys had brought their own.

Clare Byfield met me at the door and seemed as pleased to see me as if I'd been an old friend. 'I don't expect we'll get much chance to talk about your progress but I'm glad you're here.'

I wondered what progress she thought I'd made but I murmured my condolences.

'At least I've had a few weeks for the initial shock to wear off and of course Alan has been such a comfort to me. Poor Nina, though, has had to weather everything alone. But we're trying to be strong; Jacky would have liked us to be strong.'

I nodded. 'Perhaps we could meet soon,' I suggested, 'on our own?'

'Yes, yes of course. I'm used to being questioned. The police didn't leave us alone at first. But of course now they seem satisfied it was a stranger . . . ' She paused and stared into space for a moment. I wondered if she thought her sister was wasting her money employing me.

'I really meant just a chat about Jacky, her likes and dislikes.'

She stopped staring then and her grey eyes focused on me. 'Oh, I see,' she murmured. 'I'm here most days. Alan is too. He works from home mainly.'

I was about to ask what he did exactly at home when he turned up, tall, dark and much younger than Clare.

'Darling,' he said. 'I wondered where you'd got to. Are you feeling okay?'

'Oh, yes, Alan. I was just coming to find you. This is Kate Kinsella – I told you about her. This is Alan Westone.'

He smiled at me then and at her, gratified. Then, holding out his hand, she took his hand in hers as though receiving a precious gift. Don't be cynical, I told myself. I wondered if Jacky had felt like me – invisible.

I wandered through into the lounge and although it was crowded I could smell alcohol. People grouped together in huddles, but the room still had a large and spacious feel. The walls were covered in a magnolia paper with a silver regency stripe. Two matching sofas in palest blue were arranged opposite each other in front of a gas fire with artificial logs. The older ladies had been ranged in threes on the sofas, as if the seating arrangements had been made in advance and now they were obliged not to move. Each of them sat silently concentrating on holding glasses of sherry in one hand and a plate of nibbles in the other. Younger guests left their groups occasionally to make little sorties to mingle or collect food and drink, but after a short time they would return to the safety of their original group.

I decided to eat and drink before I spoke to anyone, and I made my way to a table in the corner that was covered with a white lace tablecloth and laden with the usual buffet fare: vol-au-vents and quiche and bridge rolls and salad. Not imaginative, but it was a funeral tea. Near the food stood a drinks cabinet, dark oak with lighting behind the bottles so that the drinks seemed to glow invitingly. I helped myself to a sherry when I saw other people doing the same.

After two sherries and several vol-au-vents I began to circulate. I wanted to talk to the boys and Jacky's ex.

The boys stood in a huddle, drinks and cigarettes in hand, occasionally laughing in loud nervous bursts. As I approached they eyed me suspiciously.

'Excuse me,' I said. 'I'm a reporter with the *Longborough Echo* and I wondered if you'd contribute a few words about Jacky.'

There was a long silence as if they were trying to read each other's minds or work out who should be spokesman. Eventually the tallest one spoke. He gave the impression of being Corporal, partly because of his sharp crew cut but also because the others seemed to look towards him for a response.

'Yeah, okay,' he said. 'What about her?'

'Well, how did you first meet? How well did you know her?'

He laughed loudly, his friends joining in. They stopped when he stopped. And the low chatter in the room stopped too. People paused mid vol-au-vent to stare at us. Glaring at them he said in an aggressive whisper, 'I didn't bleedin' fancy her, you know. We didn't hardly know her at all – did we?'

His eyes caught his mates for confirmation. They nodded.

'It wasn't like that. She was okay but not tasty. If you know what I mean.'

The others sniggered.

'We're homeless, you see, bin chucked out. We get let back in by our mums, though – don't we?'

Again the others nodded in unison.

'Jacky used to let us stay the odd night. Gave us breakfast in the morning too. Dead religious she was. Used to try and get us to church. She was on to a loser there – wouldn't get us going to church – you know what I mean.'

'But you came to the funeral – why?'

'Bloke from the Volunteer Bureau said if we didn't he wouldn't get anyone else to put us up. We 'ad to come. See, we get chucked out quite often.'

'All of you?' I asked in amazement.

'Yeah. He's me brother, see,' he said, indicating with his thumb the boy beside him. 'He's Damian, I'm Duncan – Dixon. That's Steve and Jace.'

Steve and Jace smiled at being mentioned.

'We going in the papers then?' asked Damian.

I nodded.

'You ain't taking notes, are you?'

'I remember everything.'

'Get 'er,' murmured one.

Duncan swigged at a can of lager and offered cigarettes around. They were becoming bored with me, their eyes roaming over the guests in a bid to find something or someone of interest. Finding none, their attention reverted to me.

'So the Volunteer Bureau sent you to Jacky whenever your parents threw you out?'

'Yeah. That's it,' said Duncan, blowing smoke directly into my face.

'And you get thrown out regularly. What for?'

'Nothing really. Drinking, being late – all the usual.'

'Do you still come to the house now?'

He grinned, the others looked from one to the other, waiting for Duncan's wisdom. 'Nah. Jacky's mum won't have us. Says we're dirty pigs. We are, though, ain't we?'

They all laughed then, on cue at Duncan's little joke.

These then were 'the men' Ada had seen entering the house. What a disappointment. But I persevered. 'Did the police tell you about Jacky's death?' I asked the group, trying not to look at Duncan.

59

But he answered just the same. 'Well, they didn't exactly talk to us,' he said, smirking. 'They questioned us. Wanted to know where we were that night.'

'And?'

'Well, we all had alibis, didn't we? We were all together at a mate's house until about two in the morning. Then his mum came home – she'd had a row with her boyfriend and we got chucked out.'

'Occupational hazard,' I murmured.

'What?'

'Nothing. Thanks for your help.'

I moved away from the boys and went over to the 'bar' for another sherry. Duncan had glowered at me as I left; perhaps he'd been expecting payment. Theirs seemed a solid enough alibi and no doubt they had been interviewed separately. Without Duncan beside them, the others would have been reduced to telling the truth.

I spent the next few minutes looking for the 'posh' young man. I found him, ill at ease, talking to an elderly lady who kept snatching nervously at her own knee – probably her rug was missing. He agreed to talk to me in the utility room which was the only place I could think of. His name was Kevin Stirling, and his body was of normal size but his face and head seemed small in comparison. The thin nose and brown eyes that darted nervously away when I looked at him made me think of ferrets. I told him I'd met Jacky at the hospital.

'I met Jacky at the church,' he explained. 'It was the love of Jesus we had in common at first. But then I became much more fond of dear Jacky, just as a wonderful friend, you understand. She was my ideal soulmate, my alter ego if you like.'

'I see.'

Kevin continued, there was no stopping him. 'We used to walk home after church at first; occasionally she'd come to my house but more often I'd come here. I was always welcome.'

'Of course,' I murmured.

'I can't believe she's dead, you know. We had such wonderful times together. We loved the same music, enjoyed long walks, the countryside, even the same TV programmes – nothing violent of course – nature documentaries, that sort of thing.'

'So what went wrong?'

'Wrong?' he echoed.

'Well, you were no longer going out with her.'

'That's true but things were getting – very intense, shall we say.'

Yes, let's say that, I thought, but I didn't let him off so easily. 'You mean you wanted to get her into bed and she didn't?'

His eyes flickered at the question as if his brain had to do a double-take. 'I can assure you,' he said irritably, 'my intentions towards Jacky were marriage and one day children. Our break-up had nothing to do with carnal desire.'

I was losing him, I could tell. His eyes concentrated first on the washing machine and then on the door. 'I'm sorry, Mr Stirling,' I said softly. 'I just wondered why such a compatible couple should, well – separate.'

Kevin sighed. 'Oh, if you must know, we had a row. No, it wasn't a row – it was just an argument about her voluntary work. She never really had enough time for me. We met at church of course, but apart from that she was always so busy. It got worse and worse and in the end I gave her an ultimatum – voluntary work or me. She chose the former.'

'I see.'

'Do you?' he said dully. 'If she had lived, no doubt we would have got together again some time. I just wanted to be with her all the time. Jesus came first of course – with us both. But . . . I still miss her.'

I nodded and patted his arm. He looked about ready to cry. 'Do you know anyone who may have wanted Jacky dead?' I asked.

'No – no one. She didn't have any enemies. Why should she have any enemies?' Kevin's voice had risen in agitation.

'What about the anonymous calls?'

'Those!' His thin lips curled in contempt. 'The police asked me about those. It wouldn't surprise me if those homeless yobs weren't responsible.'

'Why?'

'I don't know. But they're useless individuals, work-shy louts. That's all they are.'

'Jacky didn't seem to think so – she helped them.'

'True,' he murmured. 'I think she was misguided, naïve.'

'The night of the murder?'

Kevin's eyes glittered angrily. 'Yes?'

'Where were you?'

'I was at home, of course, with my parents. The police have established my innocence completely. I wouldn't have harmed Jacky, would I?'

'No, of course you wouldn't. Thank you for talking to me.'

He smiled in relief. The utility room had become claustrophobic for us both.

I went back to the lounge with Kevin following miserably behind. He resumed his seat next to the old lady who had by now fallen asleep. Kevin was no murderer, I felt sure. His blandness hid no passion, no real anger, just a peevish sort of jealousy. His greatest arousal probably came from singing hymns. I was about to cross Kevin Stirling off my ever-dwindling list of suspects when I remembered that a single stab wound in the back was a passionless type of murder.

I drank another sherry and watched Kevin. He was watching me, his ferrety eyes trained on my bosom. He'd crossed his legs to expose white short socks and black hairs. He wore black slip-on shoes with thick soles. Would Hubert think that significant, I wondered?

Helping myself to yet another sherry I realised I wouldn't be driving myself home tonight. Before calling for a mini-cab and saying my goodbyes I would call on Ada Hellidon. The fresh air would do me good and I could take her a vol-au-vent and a couple of bridge rolls.

Her house was in darkness save for the front room light. I knocked and knocked but there was no answer or sound of movement. I shivered.

'It's the district nurse,' I shouted in desperation. Then I peered through the letter-box. I smelt the paraffin first. Then my eyes caught a glimpse of a black shape on the floor. Ada lay there. Dressed in black, ready for the funeral.

Chapter Seven

A neighbour with a key let me in. Ada lay tidily, on her side with her legs drawn up, at the bottom of the stairs. Her hair seemed to glow in the dinginess of the hall like a purple halo and as I switched on the light the pink lampshade cast the scene with an almost surreal warmth.

She looked not dead but sleeping. There were no signs of violence and her hair curved into the nape of her neck in tight, unspoiled, newly permed curls. She wore a black coat and a grey skirt which had managed not to expose her knees and on her feet were red slippers. Not fluffy ones but the type with leather uppers and fur-lined. But still slippers.

I told the neighbour who stood open-mouthed with shock that she should ring the police from her house. There was no need to call an ambulance yet.

Kneeling beside Ada I felt for both radial and jugular pulses. There were none. Her skin was cool but had not quite the icy coldness of the many hours dead. There was no sign of rigor mortis and I thought death had probably occurred within an hour or so. Judging by her closed eyes and peaceful expression, death seemed to have called too suddenly to cause either pain or fear. Had she fallen downstairs, I wondered, or had she had a massive heart attack or stroke halfway down the stairs?

I stepped over her body and walked upstairs to check the carpeting. The orange and brown stair carpet was secured firmly on each stair by stair-rods. At the top there was a fitted carpet leading to the bedrooms and the bathroom. There were no badly worn areas, no fraying edges, no loose or rucked patches. Nothing there to have made her fall.

Within minutes the police had arrived. A uniformed Inspector, accompanied by a sergeant, gazed for a moment at the body with barely disguised disappointment.

'Looks like an accident,' said the Inspector miserably. 'Did you find the body?'

I nodded.

'Name?'

I gave my name.

'Not yours. The victim's.'

He ignored me then to make a cursory inspection of the stairs until interrupted by the police surgeon, Dr Benfleet.

'Hello, Gerry. Accident?' he asked the Inspector.

His answer was given with a toss of the head stairwards and a mumbled, 'The usual.'

Benfleet bent down to examine the body. But he couldn't bend far because his belly got in the way. He sank on to his knees, and began straightening the body. I stood pressed against the hall wall trying to be inconspicuous. Looking up suddenly he asked, 'WPC?'

'Nurse.'

'Good. Help me roll down her stockings.'

We turned her gently on her back and removed her stockings and then, starting at the head, he began his examination. There was slight but recent bruising on the left temple. Making a few notes he began to scrutinise Ada's body for signs of injury. I kept quiet.

Eventually he stood up, stretched himself, smoothed his silver hair into place, patted me on the arm and, looking at the Inspector, said, 'Dead about an hour and a half, natural causes by the look of it, probably shock due to fractured pelvis. There's some bruising, most of it new.'

The Inspector gazed for a moment at the staircase. 'Stairs aren't that steep surely, not to fracture a pelvis?'

'Osteoporosis. Weak bones, old boy. Very common in elderly ladies. Even spontaneous factures are quite usual.'

I could keep quiet no longer. 'Could she have been pushed?' I asked.

Dr Benfleet gave a low chuckle. 'Ah! that old chestnut. Yes indeed, my dear, she could well have been pushed. But try proving it. It's very hard to distinguish between bruises; one tiny shove, that's all it would need. Not a good method of murder.'

I raised an eyebrow in surprise.

'Can't be sure they'll die, can you? They might manage a few dying incriminations.'

My question had managed to irritate the Inspector.

'What exactly are you doing here?' he asked.

'I knew Ada. I nursed her once. I found the body and wouldn't like to think she had been murdered.'

'This isn't New York,' he said. 'Harmless old girls don't get murdered in Short Brampton. She fell down the stairs. There are more deaths through accidents in the home than anywhere else.'

'Nurses get murdered,' I said, but he ignored me.

'Leave your name and address with my sergeant; we'll be in touch if there is anything we need to know.'

I was dismissed, although Dr Benfleet gave me a wink as I left.

As I walked towards Clare's house I noticed both Clare and Nina waiting for me on the front door step. At least I thought they were waiting for me but instead they were saying goodbye to the funeral guests. The arrival of the police had perhaps made some of them leave early just so they could hang about outside watching. Dr Hiding was just leaving.

'Miss Kinsella, there you are. I was concerned. I thought for a moment you had decided to drive home. And I did notice you drinking rather large amounts of sherry. I'll give you a lift.' With his hand on my arm in a vice-like grip I didn't have much choice. And anyway I felt too depressed to argue.

On the way back to Longborough Dr Hiding drove my car with one hand on the steering wheel, the other on my thigh. The hand didn't move so I tried to forget it was there. Every so often he turned slightly towards me, smiling. I tried to keep the conversation on the subject of Ada's death, telling him how I'd found the body. That, surely, would dampen his ardour.

'Had the CID arrived?' he asked.

'Uniformed, an inspector and a sergeant.'

'Inspector Dallington?'

'Yes. He seemed to think Ada's death was an accident.'

'The CID will be called in if there's any doubt at the post-mortem. They are an ungodly bunch but they get results.'

I wasn't convinced. 'They haven't made much progress with Jacky's death so far.'

'And you have?'

'Well, no . . . but it is very complicated.'

He laughed. 'Prayer, my dear, is the answer, and of course finding the protector.'

'Protector?'

'Yes. Someone, somewhere, knows or guesses who the murderer is. Invariably they get conscience-stricken and begin to ask questions. God works in unusual ways.'

'Amen to that.'

The thought struck me that if that was the case, someone I'd already met could be in danger. Or poor Ada had started asking questions and had been given the ultimate answer.

When we arrived in Farley Wood it also struck me Dr Hiding would now be without transport.

'Where do you live exactly?' I asked.

'Within walking distance, on the old Longborough Road. From here I'll be home in about fifteen minutes. I'll pick my car up tomorrow.'

'It's very kind of you to drive me home. Thank you.'

I tried to sound polite but firm. But that didn't stop him making a sudden lunge and trying to kiss me and grab my breasts simultaneously.

'Dr Hiding! Pull yourself together,' I managed to say as I prised his lips from mine. 'Jesus won't want you for a rainbow.'

His face puckered but it brought him to his senses. 'A minor aberration, Miss Kinsella, I do assure you. I find you so desirable. We could walk with God together, we could marry. Celibacy is such a hard road and I get so lonely.'

As he spoke I could smell the whisky on his breath and behind his glasses his eyes lurked, pink and watery, like lychees floating in syrup. 'Dr Hiding,' I said, 'you have been drinking. In the morning you'll be sober and you'll remember this conversation with embarrassment. I shall do my best to forget the whole incident. Good night.'

He got out of the car then, wordlessly, and began to walk away with bowed head. I watched as he walked past the church, lifting his head towards the spire, a dark shape against a darkening sky. But now he walked more upright, his shoulders squared once more in righteousness. God must have spoken to him forgivingly, and I couldn't help wondering if he needed

66

forgiveness on other occasions, and for more serious 'aberrations'.

The phone was ringing as I opened the front door. It was Hubert.

'I've heard the police are swarming over Short Brampton. What's happened? Are you all right?'

'I'm fine. Swarming is a slight exaggeration, though, for a duo of police. And how did you find out so quickly?'

Hubert chuckled. 'A friend of a friend rang.'

'Not touting, I hope,' I said. 'You'd not be disappointed, though. There's been a fatality – Ada Hellidon is dead.'

There was silence for a moment. 'God rest her soul,' he said. 'Do you think it was an accident?'

'Seems most likely, but I suppose we won't really know until the PM.'

'You just take care of yourself. You could be next in line.'

Somehow that thought had never crossed my mind. 'I'll see you later,' I told Hubert.

'Good,' he said. 'I think you could do with a bit of help.'

'I'm sure I can manage perfectly well on my own, Mr Humberstone.'

'I didn't mean that sort of help,' he replied. 'I meant some treatment to help you relax and release your deductive powers.'

'Sounds wonderful – but what do you have in mind?'

'Reflexology.'

I felt the laughter grip my chest and I had to cough to ward it off. 'It sounds very appropriate,' I said between coughs. 'Are you any good?'

'Good! I'm a star pupil.'

Thoughts of Hubert massaging feet amused me for a few seconds until I realised it was *my* feet he had designs on. Not only, it seemed, could my life be in danger, my feet were also at risk. And I wasn't sure which worried me most.

The following morning, on Saturday, I went back to see Clare Byfield in Short Brampton. Dr Hiding's Range Rover was no longer there, but the neighbours seemed to be out in force, making the most of bright but wintry sunshine by sweeping their front paths or cleaning their cars.

I managed to talk to Ada's right-side neighbour, a short woman with tiny hands and feet which ballooned into a large round shape as though her extremities had pumped up her body. She wore a bright blue padded jacket which added to her girth but her unlined face and curly brown hair made her age difficult to guess.

'I'm a newcomer here,' she explained cheerfully. 'I've only lived in this village for ten years.'

Freda Banks rested the broom she was using against her chest, and as she breathed, the broom handle rose and fell between the cleavage of her breasts like some mesmeric extra limb. I tried not to look at it.

'I work full-time so I didn't know Mrs Hellidon all that well. Nice lady, but a bit of a gossip. Noticed if people didn't take their milk in straight away, that sort of thing. And she seemed to have a down on the Byfields.'

'In what way?' I asked.

By now, I'd taken out my reporter's notepad and my pencil and was attempting to write down every word. Mrs Banks, trying to be helpful, spoke very slowly as if I were either deaf or daft, or both.

'Now then,' she began, 'Mrs Hellidon told everyone she met about the "goings-on" as she called them. Am I speaking slowly enough for you?'

'Yes. Yes, thank you. Please go on.'

'Well, to be honest, I think poor Mrs Hellidon was a bit jealous.'

'Jealous of what?' I asked, my pencil poised.

'Money, visitors, that sort of thing. She was very lonely, I'm sure. So she just watched the comings and goings from her front window.' Mrs Banks placed both hands over the broom handle and stared into space for a moment.

'Whose money?' I asked. 'Clare Byfield's or her boyfriend's?'

A frown crossed Freda's forehead. 'Oh, no, dear. You don't seem to understand. It was Jacky's money she seemed to mind. In fact it worried her. But, as I told her, nurses earn a lot more these days and Jacky didn't waste her money. She didn't drink or smoke. She did go on holidays but not to anywhere all that exotic, although Mrs Hellidon seemed to think a trip to Blackpool quite something.'

'I see,' I murmured, but I didn't. I was confused. 'What really puzzles me,' I said, 'is if Mrs Hellidon was a gossip and not friendly towards the family, why on earth was she invited to the funeral?'

Freda's eyes widened in surprise. 'Oh – but she wasn't invited. She told me. She wouldn't have gone to the funeral anyway, she was strait-laced C of E. And Clare Byfield couldn't stand her. Whatever made you think she'd been invited?'

'No reason,' I lied, remembering Ada's body, all in black. Had she only pretended that she'd been invited? Was that why she still wore her slippers?

I thanked Freda Banks and left her sweeping the front path, her body swaying and wobbling to the steady rhythm of the brushstrokes.

The front door of the Byfield house opened before I'd even knocked.

'Do come in,' Clare said, smiling. 'I saw you come up the drive. I'm just so glad we've got the chance to have a quiet chat. Alan has gone out for a while. Come through to the kitchen. It's my favourite room. Do you have a favourite room?'

She didn't seem to expect an answer, so I stayed silent.

The kitchen did have charm, with a pine dresser, onions hanging in strings, decorative plates on the wall and a refectory-size pine table. Dried flowers in a basket on the dresser, a large bowl of oranges on the table, plus the smell of freshly ground coffee gave the room a feeling of warmth and plenty. Its only disappointment was the absence of any signs of baking.

Clare mentioned Ada first. 'Poor Mrs Hellidon. That came as quite a shock. She always seemed reasonably fit. I didn't like her much but I certainly didn't wish her any harm. Do they think she had a stroke or something?'

'A fall, it seems. One thing puzzles me about her death, though.'

'What's that?'

'She was all ready for the funeral and yet one of her neighbours said she hadn't been invited.'

Clare glanced away. 'Would you like some coffee?' she asked, her eyes fixing on the filter machine as though willing it to spring to life. I accepted. The coffee-making seemed a clumsy affair, Clare's nervousness apparent in every gesture she made. Cups clattered loudly into saucers, cream trickled down the side of the jug and dripped on to the tray.

'Oh, dear,' said Clare. 'I find it so hard to concentrate these days. Look at the mess I've made.'

'Please sit down, Mrs Byfield,' I said. 'I really don't want to keep you too long.'

The implied threat seemed to work. She sat, expectant, still nervous.

'Is it true Mrs Hellidon wasn't invited to the funeral?' I asked.

'Quite true. I really detested that woman. She was an interfering, gossipy old harridan. Not the sort of person I wanted at my daughter's funeral.'

'Could anyone else have invited her?'

Clare sniffed delicately. 'No one! My sister certainly wouldn't have. She disliked her, too.'

'Fine. That's all I wanted to establish,' I said, trying to sound encouragingly satisfied. 'Now, though, I'd like to ask you a few personal questions about Jacky. Do you feel up to coping with that at the moment?'

'Oh, yes. I'd like to get everything sorted out, once and for all. What do you want to know about my daughter?'

'I'd like to know exactly how much money Jacky had in her bank account. I have reason to believe she was quite well off.'

For a moment there was silence, a silence in which Clare stared at me in pained disbelief. Then she laughed, without humour. 'Don't be so ridiculous,' she said. 'All Jacky ever had was her salary. Admittedly she had a very careful attitude towards money, but she certainly wasn't well off and it's ludicrous to suggest she was.'

'You'd have no objection, then, to my seeing her bank statements.'

'No, of course not. Although there are no recent ones. I had a massive sort-out some weeks ago.'

'Is her bank account closed?'

'Not yet. I have to wait for the Letters of Administration, so my solicitor tells me. Everything takes so long in a case like this, doesn't it? I'm going to see my solicitor, Mr Harlstone, today; perhaps you'd like to come with me?'

'On Saturday?' I queried.

She nodded. 'Longborough is quite progressive in some ways,

you know. Harlstones keeps open on Saturday morning because the estate agents are open.'

Clare Byfield then gave me a quick head to foot glance, as if to check my presentability for the local solicitor, and managed to make me feel about as welcome as a parasitic worm. It seemed to me Jacky had probably felt that way too.

She left a note for Alan with love and kisses almost jumping off the page, and I drove into Longborough and parked outside the discreet offices of Harlstone, Harlstone and Firs.

Inside, the receptionist, a middle-aged lady, sat stiffly at a desk and enquired equally stiffly, 'Are you expected?'

Clare nodded.

'Mr Harlstone senior or junior?'

'Senior,' replied Clare, forcing a smile.

After about ten minutes Mr Harlstone senior came out to greet us as if his receptionist had summoned him by thought alone.

'Dear lady,' he said, advancing on Clare and shaking her hand. He was tall but with a slight stoop and thin floppy white hair and glasses on a piece of elastic dangling on his chest.

'Dear lady,' he said again.

Clare introduced me briefly and he smiled and guided us through to his office.

'Do sit down, ladies,' he said, indicating what could only be described as a bench to sit on, just like one of those brown forms I remembered from school PE.

We sat awkwardly close to each other, upright and alert, whilst Mr Harlstone moved great piles of pale blue and dusty beige folders to either side of his large desk so that he could see us properly. He sat down on a high winged leather chair and fixed his glasses on the end of his nose.

'Now, then,' he said. 'What can I do for you?'

I realised then that he didn't have a clue as to who we were or why we'd come.

Clare explained our mission and after a lot of searching and opening and closing of folders he mumbled, 'Ah, yes – young Jacky. I do have the Letters of Administration. She didn't make a will, unfortunately. Everyone should make a will. I tried hard, I can assure you, to persuade her to make a will but she remained very stubbornly opposed.'

'Surely,' I said, 'she didn't have that much of an estate to worry about.'

Mr Harlstone stared at me sternly for a few seconds. 'Her current bank account was in a fairly healthy state, about four thousand pounds and of course there was her insurance policy and . . . ' He paused, his eyes flickering over us as though he was uncomfortable or had something uncomfortable to tell us. 'And . . . ' he continued, 'and she did intimate to me that she had a large sum in a London bank – quite a large sum.'

'How much?' asked Clare sharply.

'I did say she only intimated, she wasn't exactly direct but I got the impression she had a deposit bank account under a false name – for about twenty-five thousand pounds. That was, of course, when I suggested she made a will . . . '

'Impossible!' said Clare angrily. 'How on earth did she get that sort of money?'

Mr Harlstone shrugged. 'It may not be true,' he said.

Clare had edged forward on the bench and was rubbing her knees in anxious thought.

'Have the police found out where the money is?' I asked.

'Ah . . . well . . . unfortunately I forgot at the time. My son was away ill and I was very busy and you know how it is . . . Anno domini and all that . . . '

'So they don't know?'

'Sadly not,' said Mr Harlstone, shaking his head.

'Will I get the money?' asked Clare, rapidly getting over her shock.

'If there are no other claimants. For the current account that is. As for the other account . . . '

'What do you mean – other claimants – I'm her mother.'

'Her father still lives, though, and he is entitled to a half-share.'

Clare's mouth opened silently and then closed again. Her face had paled and she swept her hands nervously through her hair.

'About the account in the false name?' I asked. 'How do we find out about that?'

'Now that could be difficult,' answered Mr Harlstone. 'If not impossible, unless you have the pass book. Without that, there is no way of knowing what name she used. The money could just sit there . . . if it really exists.'

It existed, I felt sure. But where the hell was the pass book?

Chapter Eight

'You've had two phone calls this morning,' said Hubert as I arrived at Humberstones. His tone was accusatory. He stood by the office door gazing in.

'You can come in,' I said. 'I'm going to open a bottle of whisky.'

I thought he looked disapproving but he walked in and sat down eagerly in the armchair. He even managed a smile. 'You cracked it yet?' he asked as I opened the bottle.

'Here's your whisky and don't upset me.'

For a moment he swirled his drink and stared into its depths. 'Are you going to tell me or shall I go?' he said, without even tasting my whisky. Hubert either knew something I didn't or thought he did. His tone was so crisply defiant that I decided that, along with the reflexology course, he was probably taking assertiveness training. I drank half my whisky.

'Not much to report really, Mr Humberstone – except that it seems Jacky may have mysteriously amassed twenty-five thousand pounds. And no one seems to know where it came from, least of all her mother.'

Silence from Hubert. Not a flicker of surprise crossed his face.

'You knew, didn't you?'

'Guessed. Don't forget I knew Ada Hellidon. She was a shrewd old girl,' Hubert said, as he raised his glass and drank his whisky in one brave gulp.

'How did Jacky make that sort of money? That's what I keep asking myself. And where did she keep her pass book? No doubt the police and her mother have searched the house from top to bottom and if it wasn't in the house— '

'Maybe,' interrupted Hubert, 'Maybe.'

'You're not being very encouraging. I was hoping the money angle might lead somewhere.'

'I've heard a rumour,' said Hubert. 'About a suspect.'

'Murder suspect?'

'Yes. The police are going to make an arrest soon. They seem to think a peeping Tom called Kennie Litchborough killed Jacky.'

'Have they any evidence?'

'I've only heard they're expecting him to confess. It seems he's admitted to hanging round the hospital hoping to catch a glimpse of nurse's uniforms and that's all.'

Suddenly I felt a glimmer of optimism. Perhaps the police had got the wrong angle – not a suspect, more an observant informer. Someone who had perhaps seen or heard more than he realised.

'Do you know where he lives?'

Hubert smiled and I noticed that his skin had improved, and he definitely looked happier and healthier. 'He lives in one of the houses at the back of the hospital, 2 Leys Court, with his mother. She used to be a prostitute.'

'I didn't realise there were houses at the back of the hospital.'

'Small estate, used to house some of the staff when the hospital was big and thriving.'

I poured us both another whisky. 'Mr Humberstone,' I said, 'you are not only a fund of knowledge, you're also quite a fascinating person. My ambition in life is to marry you off.'

'Too late,' he said.

I raised an eyebrow and was about to go into my 'it's never too late' routine when Hubert said, 'I'm already married. I've been married for twenty years. Mind you, we only lived together for a year. Then she found out. She accused me of love at first foot, said I was perverted and she'd make sure I'd suffer financially for the rest of my life.'

'And you have?'

'Oh, yes. But there's never been anyone else for either of us. I don't mind keeping her. I see her once a week, we have a drink and a chat, I slip her some money and then I look forward to seeing her again the next week.'

The whisky made everything particularly poignant and I had to force myself not to think of Hubert and his doomed love, in case my judgment became clouded and in my imagination Hubert became Heathcliffe and hearses became horses.

'Are you all right?' asked Hubert.

'Fine, fine. Just drank the whisky too fast. I'll be off to see Kennie Litch . . . '

'Litchborough.'

'That's him.'

'I'll call you a taxi,' said Hubert. 'And just you take care. He could be the murderer, you know. Not all perverts are harmless.'

'I'll bear that in mind. And, by the way, who phoned this morning?'

'Jacky's aunt and Kevin Stirling. He wants you to ring him back.'

Hubert rang for a taxi and I resolved to drink more slowly in the future.

On the way to Kennie's house I began to wonder why Kevin had phoned me. Not to confess, surely? Although he struck me as the type who would think it necessary to confess to the most trivial of sins, would he simply deny, even to himself, a serious crime, like murder?

The Litchborough home backed on to open fields but the front looked towards the hospital grounds. A woman in late middle age opened the door. She wore blood-red lipstick, blue eyeshadow and a gold chain around her ankle. I got the impression she was still gainfully employed.

'I'm from Action for Victims of Wrongful Arrest, that's AVWA for short. I'm from the Sexual Division,' I said, smiling sympathetically and flashing my UKCC card with self-attached passport-size photo.

'Come on in, dear,' she said unhesitatingly. 'We have been having a few problems lately. You sit down and I'll make us a nice cup of tea.'

The house smelt of stale cigarettes and disinfectant; a switched-on, but silent colour television sat in one corner, with a brown and white striped settee a mere four feet or so from the screen. I sat down on the settee next to a sleeping tan-coloured mongrel.

A sleeping male slumped in the only other chair. I presumed he was Kennie, knackered after a night's peeping Tommery.

'That's it, dear, you make friends with the dog,' said my hostess as she carried in the tea on a tin tray. 'He doesn't like many people, especially the police. Here's your tea and a biscuit to go with it.'

'You're Kennie's mum, I take it,' I said as I struggled to accept the tea and avoid the dog who was now awake and snuffling at me most suggestively.

'I'm his mum all right. He's been a trouble to me all his life, I can tell you. Ever since he was about four. At first I thought it was a joke, sort of childish nonsense but it didn't stop. Believe you me, I went everywhere with that boy. Most of the doctors we saw said he'd grow out of it, in time. That's a joke, he's twenty-six now. Not going to change now, is he? He's harmless, though, completely harmless.'

'What exactly does he do, Mrs Litchborough?' I asked in a whisper.

For a moment she stared at me. 'You call me Renée, dear, I'm not married. Isn't your hair a lovely colour, so curly as well. Mine's always been straight. Have to have it permed every few months. Now then, dear, you wanted to know about Kennie. Well, first off, he's not all that bright. I don't think he knows what he's doing. Exposes himself, see. To young girls mostly but especially in uniform, nurse's uniform, school uniform. He likes uniforms. And watching, of course. Seems to turn him on. I try to keep him in, but I have to work, don't I?'

I nodded. Kennie began to stir.

'He's a lazy git,' said his mother fondly. 'Has to take these pills to calm him, which is why he's always sleepy. Come on, Kennie, wake up. This lady here is going to help you get off.'

Kennie seemed to wake immediately, primed to be on the defensive. 'I didn't do nothing. I didn't do nothing. And I didn't see nothing.' Kennie's round childlike face screwed up in anguish and his voice grew higher and higher. His skin, the colour of semolina, showed two red blobs high on his cheeks – the jam in a plate of milk pudding.

'Calm down, Kennie, I only want to help you,' I explained. 'I'm sure you haven't done anything bad. I only want to find out if you saw anyone else doing bad things.'

There was silence for a moment while Kennie looked from me to his mother.

'You answer the lady's questions. She's trying to help you. She's not going to ask you to sign any confessions either. So just speak up and be sensible.'

'Have the police asked you to sign a statement?'

76

Kennie nodded. 'I can't read though, but I haven't told them that yet. But I can write my name.' He grinned slyly.

'Tell me about the hospital grounds, Kennie, and who you see there at night.'

He thought for a moment, looking worried. His mother lit a cigarette and blew smoke rings into the air. His eyes followed them.

'Kennie, try and remember – is there someone you like specially at the hospital? A nurse?'

Eventually he said, 'Yeah. I like the uniforms.'

I sighed inwardly, trying to be patient. 'Kennie,' I said, 'when you leave here to walk to the hospital – what do you do next?'

'I stand by the entrance behind the bushes and watch the nurses coming and going. Then I walk around a bit and wait.'

'For what?'

'For when they come out again.'

'You mean you wait there all night?'

'No. Not all night. I watch them. Sometimes the nurses go to other wards.'

'And did you see Jacky Byfield the night she died?'

Kennie's eyes flickered with fear and he looked towards his mother pleadingly. 'Mum,' he said, 'what do I say?'

'I've told you. Just tell the bleeding truth or I'll clip your ear. I told you he wasn't all there,' she said. 'He'd need to have his wits about him to get away with murder – wouldn't he?'

I nodded in agreement. 'Come on, Kennie,' I said. 'What did you see that night?'

He looked at the floor and began to mumble. 'I saw her leave the ward, she was carrying something. She was going to another ward. I followed her. I waited outside the ward and when she came out I followed her again.'

'Was she wearing a cloak?'

'No. Just her dress. She went into the main building. The next time I saw her she was lying on the ground. I ran away. I was scared. I didn't touch her or anything.'

'That's good, Kennie. You're being very helpful. There's only one thing I don't understand. Why didn't you wait for her to come out of the main building?'

He looked up, and seemed less worried now. 'I did wait for a

77

bit, but then I saw someone else going towards the porter's place. And I followed her.'

'Was the person you followed a nurse?'

'Yes.'

'Do you know her name?'

'No.'

'Would you know her again?'

'Not sure. I only saw her from the back. She was wearing a cloak.'

'What were they doing in the porter's lodge – could you see?'

'I looked, but the curtain was pulled.'

'What did you do then?'

'I'm not saying. I'm not saying any more. It's none of your business. I didn't hurt anyone.' Kennie's voice rose hysterically and he began to tremble. I could see beads of sweat appear on his forehead and his face paled alarmingly.

'Now then, Kennie, don't get in one of your states. You'll only start off an attack.' Renée walked over to him and patted him awkwardly on the shoulder. 'He's asthmatic, gets ever so bad when he's upset,' she said. 'Perhaps you should go now.'

'Just one more question, Kennie. Did you hear a car come into the hospital grounds that night?'

Kennie's breathing had already begun to rasp and he looked up at his mother pleadingly.

'You answer, there's a good boy. Then I'll get your inhaler,' said Renée, still patting his shoulder.

'I didn't hear no car,' he said slowly, looking not at me, but at his mother.

Renée rang for a taxi for me and Kennie was dispatched to his room after a quick burst of his inhaler.

'Sorry he wasn't more help,' said Renée. 'Will you talk to the police about him and tell them to leave him alone?'

'I'll do my best,' I promised. 'But I have to be careful. If they know I'm involved they might try even harder to prove Kennie's guilt. You'll just have to make sure Kennie doesn't confess. If they take him in for questioning again, try to have a solicitor present.' And a doctor, I could have added.

In the taxi I tried to work out exactly how helpful Kennie had been. Very, I decided. But even so, all I had really found out was that St Dymphna's at night was a lot more active than I had realised. Mick O'Dowd, it appeared, was having an affair, or at least, an assignation, and so of course was Jacky.

Back at the office I rang Kevin Stirling. He worked in a men's outfitters called Hobbs and Sons.

'I can't talk now,' he said. 'Will you meet me after work?'

I agreed to see him just after six outside the shop. I arrived early, just before closing time, and Longborough's High Street shops began exuding their last customers into the rain and darkness. They hurried home, heads down, seeming shrunken, as if by being less tall the rain wouldn't batter them so much.

I switched off the engine and let the rain cover the windscreen. I don't possess an umbrella and I didn't plan to leave the car. So I sat, watching the rain and Hobbs's front door and I thought about how a nurse could make twenty-five thousand pounds. There was blackmail, robbery, drugs. Drugs! Perhaps Jacky's doctor friend was supplying her with stuff and she was selling it on the black market. Then I remembered. It wasn't impossible to steal drugs from a hospital, just almost impossible. The regulations covering controlled and dangerous drugs are so strict, no one, not even a doctor, could manage to nick so much as an aspirin without someone finding out and reporting it. Smuggling from abroad was much more likely but from the little I knew about Jacky that seemed far fetched. But having several grand was far fetched too.

At about ten past six Kevin Stirling left the dreary-looking shop he worked in and stood for a moment scanning the street for my car. He carried a large black brolly. Kevin had probably been a boy scout. Eventually he saw me and with utmost caution he crossed the road. Somehow I didn't think he was Jacky's partner in crime.

'Filthy night,' I said as I opened the car door.

He sat down, bringing the cold and wet into my warm car. 'Thanks for coming,' he said. 'I wanted to speak to you desperately. Can we go somewhere to talk?'

'There's the pub or the Burger Palace,' I suggested.

He was silent for a moment as he brushed the hair back from his face. 'I don't drink,' he said.

'The Burger Palace then.'

'Okay.'

He sounded miserable and his thinly pointed nose glowed red and he began to rub his hands nervously. I drove in silence, waiting for him to speak. He didn't. Not until we were sitting down, between the plastic fronded plants and plastic-topped tables of the Palace did he talk.

'This coffee's strong,' he said.

'We haven't come here to discuss the merits of the coffee,' I said. 'You have got something you want to get off your chest.'

He frowned and looked between the plants as though about to impart national secrets.

'We are the only customers, Kevin.' I felt I could call him Kevin. It made me sound more of a friend.

'It's about Jacky,' he said. He paused, both hands round his plastic cup of coffee. 'I . . . I have something to confess. I did a terrible thing . . . I wanted to tell you at the funeral but it didn't seem the right place. I just can't live with it any longer. I'm not eating or sleeping. I can't work properly. Sometimes I dream Jacky is in heaven, she's happy and smiling and giving me the thumbs down sign.'

'How do you interpret that?'

'It means I'm going to hell.'

'I don't believe in hell. Only a sadist would invent hell. Hell is only a concept to keep us all in control.'

'I wish I could believe that,' he said. 'I just wish I hadn't done it.'

'Killed Jacky, you mean?'

'Oh, God, no! You don't think that surely. I couldn't. I couldn't kill anything.' His small eyes had widened and his upper lip quivered. 'Please don't say such things. Do I look like a murderer?'

'All murderers look different, Kevin. If it's not murder you want to confess to, what exactly do you want to tell me?'

'It was me who . . . I made those phone calls.'

'I see.'

'You don't sound very shocked,' he said, his voice edged with disappointment.

'I'm not. Why are you telling me? Why not the police?'

My reaction came as a surprise and for a moment he stared at me as though I'd cheated him of the satisfaction of his confession. 'I will tell the police but I wanted to tell you first. To explain.

I thought if you believed me and understood, perhaps the police would too.'

I sipped at my coffee, wishing I'd ordered a hamburger. 'Tell me about it, Kevin,' I said.

'I've got a very possessive nature. Jacky was only my second girlfriend. Everything was fine at first, just like I told you. Then I thought she was keeping things secret from me.'

'Another man, you mean?'

'Perhaps,' he said uncertainly. 'There was this doctor she talked about, said she hoped she could save him. Bring him to Jesus. But it wasn't just that. At times she seemed so secretive, all dreamy and preoccupied. Sometimes she would go off on her own and not tell me where she was going. When I asked her about it, she would just laugh at me and tell me not to be so stupid and jealous.'

'And did that make you angry?'

Kevin thought for a while. 'I didn't show I was angry. But I was inside.'

'And you never showed anger towards her?'

'How could I? I was terrified of losing her. I just kept seeing her and trying to find out what she was . . . '

'Trying to hide?' I said helpfully.

'Yes.'

'What did you hope the phone calls would achieve?'

Kevin lowered his eyes and then looked past me towards the window and the dark night outside. 'I thought she might turn to me for protection,' he murmured. 'Might see me as her knight in shining armour. It didn't work like that, though, did it? And then someone killed her.'

'I think I may have found a motive for her death, Kevin.'

He looked blank. 'Motive?' he said.

'Yes. Would it surprise you to know Jacky had money in the bank?'

'No, of course not,' he said sharply. 'She was always trying to save. There was her salary and even though she had a fairly new car she certainly didn't waste money.'

'So about how much would you expect her to have had in the bank?'

'Oh, I don't know. About two thousand pounds I suppose.'

I was managing to irritate Kevin; he had confessed and now he wanted to escape.

'Not a bad guess. She had four thousand pounds in her current account and about twenty-five thousand in a deposit account.'

Kevin's mouth fell open unattractively. 'You're joking. She couldn't have. It's not possible. I don't believe it.'

'It's true, Kevin. I'm sorry. Her mother will confirm it if you don't believe me. The money is in a false name and her pass book is missing.'

I bought Kevin another coffee and laced it well with sugar to relieve his stunned silence.

'She was hiding something, then. I wasn't just paranoid. But what?'

'I was hoping you might be able to tell me.' But even as I spoke I knew that was a forlorn hope.

Kevin's expression of bafflement gave me my answer. He finished his coffee slowly and finally said bitterly. 'You've managed to sully her memory for me. That was all I had and now you've spoilt even that.' He stood up. 'I'm going home now. Give me a few days and I'll go to the police.'

'I'll give you a lift.'

'Don't bother. I'd rather walk. It will give me a chance to think.'

I watched him go out into the rain, walking several yards before he remembered his brolly was still in my car. I ran after him and called him but he ignored me and walked on. Somehow his slumped shoulders reminded me of a child who had just seen his balloon burst by a nasty bully.

I drove home to the cottage, had a hot bath, ate a bowl of cornflakes and a bar of chocolate, and finished a murder mystery. Having failed to guess whodunnit, I went to bed convinced that I had as much chance of finding Jacky's killer as Hubert had of becoming a film star.

Chapter Nine

I started the next day with an apology. I'd forgotten to ring Jacky's Aunt Nina. She ignored my apology. 'I've just found out about the money,' she said. 'I can assure you I didn't give Jacky large sums of money.'

I didn't confess that thought hadn't crossed my mind.

'Mind you, I did give her presents of money for her birthdays, but never very large amounts. It's all very worrying, isn't it?'

I agreed that it was indeed.

'Have you made any progress with your investigation?' she asked.

'I'm moderately optimistic, all things being considered.'

She murmured, 'Good, good.'

I was about to breathe a sigh of relief that the phone call was nearly over when she said, 'I do hope you won't uncover anything . . . nasty. If you know what I mean.'

'Murder is a very nasty business, Mrs Marburg. The killer may well strike again. I'm sure you wouldn't want that.'

'No, no, of course not. You have to carry on, of course.'

Nina didn't sound really convinced but morally she probably felt she had no option. Perhaps deep down she had always suspected that Jacky had given someone a reason to kill her and that her niece wasn't quite the poor innocent her lifestyle suggested. Although I didn't yet know the killer, I promised myself I wouldn't give up until I did, even if Nina Marburg withdrew her financial interest. And I couldn't help suspecting that was why she had called me yesterday.

It was Sunday, grey and bleak outside, and by the time I'd skimmed the papers I felt restless and lonely. The day stretched ahead as bleakly as the weather. I checked in my freezer; I had two pork chops, a frozen chicken and an apple pie. On the vegetable front I had three carrots, four potatoes and ten Brussels sprouts. I also had a bottle of plonk. A feast enough to invite someone to lunch. But who? Names did not spring easily to mind. In the end I invited Hubert.

Hubert seemed surprised but keen. 'I don't get many Sunday dinners,' he said.

'Don't expect the works,' I said. 'It's only chops.'

I was dishing up as he arrived. 'Smells smashing,' he said, handing me a bottle of champagne. He wore an ensemble in beige, complete with beige cardy and matching tie. Somehow casual clothes made him seem more normal, and we talked for a while about the upturn in the death rate and how he wanted to improve his business. Somehow that seemed normal too. We were both in the death business.

We drank the champagne first, and after that we didn't care how cheap and nasty my wine tasted. But I did notice that I'd begun to get despondent halfway through the bottle.

'I'm not making much progress, you know,' I said. 'I've got suspects by the dozen, but a tenuous motive and no real clues.'

'There probably are clues,' said Hubert, wise with wine and food. 'You just haven't recognised them yet.'

'I'm beginning to think I wouldn't recognise a clue if it stood up and barked at me.'

Hubert laughed. 'Let's put down the sequence of events and a few prime suspects and see if we come up with a name.'

I agreed; it was one way to spend a Sunday afternoon.

I cleared the kitchen table and with pens and paper we poised ourselves to brainstorm. I drew a diagram with Jacky in the centre and the people she knew radiating from her.

'You haven't told me yet about Kennie Litchborough,' said Hubert as I sat staring at my diagram.

'He's simple-minded; he saw Jacky that night but I don't think he murdered her, although I think he may have seen who did. But being so simple it was hard to get much real information. I only managed to give him an asthma attack after finding out that one of the nurses met Mick O'Dowd, the security man, in the porter's lodge that night.'

'Have you spoken to him yet?' asked Hubert.

'Not really. The police seem very interested in him, but I suppose they would as he was on duty that night.'

'Who found the body?'

'That's a very good question. Kennie said he saw the body, but I don't know if he told the police that. Two nurses – Linda and Claudette – admitted to finding the body but Mick O'Dowd also told me he found the body. But he hasn't admitted that to the police. Quite honestly, I think they're all lying. All covering up for each other. And then of course there's the doctor – Robert Duston. They knew each other and it seems the night she was murdered she went to the main building to see him.'

'What does he say?'

'I haven't met him yet.'

'But have you met all the staff who were on duty that night?'

'Not all. Some were agency and I'm sure only the two wards were involved. I've still got one nurse to see who was on duty that night but it's difficult to pretend to be just another agency nurse.'

Hubert frowned. 'Do you think she was blackmailing one of the staff and they are banding together to protect each other?'

'Could be, but that's going to be very difficult to prove.'

'Yes,' Hubert agreed. 'But there's always a weak link in a chain and in my experience men are weaker than women, emotionally anyway. I think you should concentrate your efforts on the men. Eliminate the male suspects one by one and you'll find the answer.'

Hubert was cheering me. I smiled and offered him the last of the wine.

'I've eliminated the two Ks already.'

Hubert looked puzzled.

'Kevin Stirling, the ex-boyfriend, who admitted to me yesterday that he made the anonymous phone calls. And Kennie Litchborough. That just leaves the doctor, Mick O'Dowd and at a pinch Jacky's mother's boyfriend, Alan Westone.'

'Only three male suspects,' Hubert commented, writing down the names. 'You could be on to your next case in no time.'

'I hope you're right, Mr Humberstone. Could we have a rest from this now and you can tell me all about reflexology?'

Hubert beamed delightedly. 'This is one of the best Sundays I've ever had,' he said and launched into a less than brief history and description of the wonders of foot massage. I declined a demonstration. And while he chatted I remembered Ada

Hellidon's slippers and her being dressed in black ready for the funeral. Hubert had got to the area of the foot corresponding to the bowel and was telling me how massage there could cure constipation and haemorrhoids when a thought struck me. Of course Ada was ready for a funeral – but it wasn't Jacky's.

Before Hubert went home I asked him how I could find out whose funeral Ada had been planning to attend.

'Just leave it with me. I'll find out through the grapevine.'

'Should be the coffin line,' I said. But I could see by his expression my facetiousness hadn't amused him.

Shortly afterwards Hubert left and I decided to attend the evening service at the Church of the Second Coming. I didn't know who I wanted to see, or quite why I was going, but it would while away a Sunday evening and I might find out something useful.

Unlike the funeral, the congregation was large and fairly youthful. Although, saying that, I supposed the average age to be about forty. Sunday night was 'How I came to Jesus' night. Three saved souls were to tell us in some detail how they became born-again Christians. The first was a middle-aged man, unremarkable save for a twitching eye. I tried not to focus on the eye but his twitch was more interesting than his life story.

I did manage to look for Kevin but there was no sign. The old lady in the wheelchair was again parked in the corner – still alone. And apart from her and the pastor there was no one else I recognised.

The testimonies were interspersed with serious praying, which the pastor started dramatically, 'O Lord Jesus. Listen to the poor sinners. Hear them. Grant them not only peace and love but the gift. The gift of tongues. Your sign to us, the chosen ones, that our Lord and Master Jesus Christ lives within us and manifests Himself in many languages. I will walk among you now and place my hands on my flock. Let us beg Jesus for his rare and beautiful gift.'

From the faithful came passionate pleas: 'Oh, yes Lord.' 'Praise the Lord.' 'Me, Lord, me.' 'Hosanna.'

I tried to be as unobtrusive as possible. Hysteria rose in the air as palpable as smoke. Edward Cable moved between the rows of chairs and laid his hands on the heads of those who were kneeling. I only counted three not kneeling and I was one of them. The other two were elderly.

Then suddenly from the front came an orgasmic groan and a

woman stood up and began talking in esoteric gibberish. The man beside her clutched the chair in front and began to cry out loudly, 'Jesus . . . J . . . Jesus . . . Jesus . . . J . . . J . . . Jesus' – over and over again. I felt definitely uneasy. The end of the service couldn't come quick enough, I just wanted to go home.

The service lasted three hours. Thankfully I joined the queue to be met outside by Edward Cable.

'I'm so pleased you have come to our service. I believe you attended the funeral of our dear sister Jacky. A true child of Jesus.'

I nodded and smiled.

He held me firmly by the hand. 'We all miss her, you know. She was so much loved by the elderly ladies. Her weekly visits will be sorely missed.'

Then inspiration struck. 'Perhaps I could take over some of those visits,' I said. 'For a short time anyway.'

'Praise be. The Lord must have sent you. If you'll wait behind I'll give you a few names and addresses.'

I walked back into the church, sat at the front and waited. Edward Cable was a trusting soul. Trusting enough to allow a complete stranger to visit his aged flock. When he returned I asked if he would like references.

He seemed surprised. 'The Lord takes care of His people. The Lord has sent you to replace Jacky. To do Jacky's work. To give succour and comfort to the elderly.'

'Just temporarily,' I murmured. But he wasn't listening; he was busy writing down names and addresses. 'I'm not sure when I'll be able to start.'

'Start in the Lord's time, my dear. In the Lord's time.'

Clutching my list I left, vowing never to return. I saved reading the list until I got home. I drank hot cocoa laced with whisky and read the names as I lay in bed. There were five in all. Two in Farley Wood, two in Longborough, and one in Leys Court behind the hospital. It was that one that interested me. Tonbridge? For a moment I couldn't remember where I'd heard the name before. Tonbridge. Margaret Tonbridge from the hospital. A relative, I assumed, and living near Kennie. Perhaps my dallying with religion hadn't been a complete waste of time after all. I wanted to see Kennie again and now I could combine the visits. I almost looked forward to working at St Dymph's again; compared with the church, it seemed like a haven of sanity. Had Jacky been quite sane, though, I wondered? Stray boys, old ladies and nursing seemed masochistic to me. What was she trying to prove? Or what sin was she trying to absolve? And who found her out?

St Dymphna's as a haven of sanity seemed like a sick joke when I arrived on Monday night. Over the weekend the managers had decided to close two wards, Grant and Truman, and squash as many as possible into Melba and Harper. Several patients had chest infections, two were dying and two of the day staff were sick. Thankfully I was working with Linda Brington.

'I'll just get on with the routine things, Staff, you see to the two who are pegging out.'

That wasn't as easy as it sounded, for one of the dying was awake and frightened. 'Sally, Sally,' she called. 'I'm dying, I'm frightened. Where are you?'

'I'm here,' I said stroking her hand. 'I'm here all night.' I knew from the report that Sally was her daughter. Sally was dead. There was no one else. I stayed with her, gave her sips of warm tea and gradually she sank into a deep sleep. The sounds of her death rattle were lost in the general torment of the ward.

By eleven Linda and I were saying to each other, 'We're winning,' and thoughts of tea were just about the most important thing in our lives. Then I heard Linda shout from the top end of the ward. 'Oh Christ!'

I rushed up to the bedside. 'What's the matter?' I asked calmly, seeing neither blood nor fire.

'It's so bloody inconvenient,' Linda was saying. 'She was always a selfish old . . . '

My eyes followed hers. The patient was quite dead. Bolt upright, looking cheerfully triumphant, at least that's the way I saw her.

'Better now than later,' I said, trying to placate Linda. 'I'll make some tea then we'll call the doc and let the undertakers know. It won't take us a trice to lay her out.'

Linda smiled wryly. 'It's just so typical of her to die without giving us proper warning . . . ' She paused, 'I'm talking rubbish, I know. It's just that we'll probably be laying out three tonight. It's so depressing. And I bet we've only got two shrouds.'

We began to laugh as we drank our tea. A siege mentality or hysteria or both. I'd rung the night sister whose tone was

sharp, as though we were somehow to blame for the incon-
venience.

'Try to hang on to the rest,' she said brusquely. 'There's enough
dying down here without having to worry about you lot. Have you
rung the doctor yet?'

'He's being bleeped.'

'Good.'

The phone banged down. We giggled again, only to be startled
into silence by loud knocking on the door. It was Dr Robert
Duston, or so his badge told us. Tall, dark and stunningly
attractive, I looked at him in surprise and managed to stutter
that we had had an unexpected death. My virtual incoherence
sent Linda scurrying from the office in a fit of giggles.

'What's the matter with her?' Robert Duston asked.

'Just circumstances,' I replied, handing him the patient's notes.
Attractive he may have been but there was no warmth in his dark
eyes and I doubted he had a sense of humour.

'Before you see the patient, Doctor, would you mind if I ask
you a personal question?'

He scowled. 'What's on your mind?'

'It's a bit of a cheek, I know, but I was a one-time best friend
of Jacky Byfield. She wrote to me that you were friendly and yet
I was at the funeral and you weren't.'

'Are you trying to find out if we were having an affair? Because
if you are, the answer is, we were not. She was a pain in the neck.
A religious maniac, who plagued me for months. A nice enough
girl, I suppose, for someone who liked the pure and virginal. I
don't, Staff Nurse. Do I make myself clear?'

'Crystal.'

He walked past me into the ward. I followed on behind and
watched him treat the dead woman to a very cursory examination,
which didn't really surprise me. She looked very dead now that we
had laid her flat.

'Anything else?' he said.

'Two more, probably tonight.'

'I'll see them now. If they die after two, get the night sisters
up.'

When he'd gone Linda reappeared. 'Your face was a picture,'
she said. 'Your eyes came out on stalks. He may be handsome
but he's a surly sod. Jacky was the only one who liked him.'

'He didn't seem . . . ' I stopped. Linda would wonder why I had asked him about Jacky.

'No, he doesn't. Still, it's his business, isn't it?'

Together we approached the bed of the dead woman. 'Laying out' now consists of washing the corpse, putting in false teeth, combing the hair and putting on the stiff white shroud. Years ago it was much more complicated. The road to heaven has definitely become faster. The checking of the patient's belongings took the most time: two flannels – check; one lavender talc – check; two pounds fifty – check; three nighties – check. And so it went on. Until at last our one-time patient was labelled and all her treasures were safely in a black plastic bag. Packing belongings is a salutary lesson to the materialistic. You really can't take it with you.

Wrapped in a white sheet the corpse lay there bright in the ward's dim light. We paused for a moment.

'Do you know she didn't drink or smoke, was a housewife all her life and had been a childless widow for thirty years,' said Linda. 'Makes you think, doesn't it?'

The 'laying out' seemed to have made her introspective and that in nurses often led to philosophical discussions about the meaning of life and deaths as we'd known them. Not that I knew any nurses who were afraid of death. Just of protracted life. Still, we needed cheering up.

'Talking of drink,' I said, 'there's some sherry in the cupboard. Shall we have some before the undertakers come?'

Linda smiled half-heartedly and shrugged. 'Okay. I bet it's British and been there for yonks – better than nothing though.'

Pritchards, Funeral Directors, arrived during our second glass of sherry. The hospital, it seemed, had a standing order with them to remove bodies at night. I imagined Hubert being disappointed that he hadn't managed to acquire the commission.

'Hello, girls, you all right?' said the younger of the two men. 'Which way?'

I pointed to the bed.

'Do you want to pull the curtains round the other beds?' he asked.

Pulling the curtains around the beds is traditional practice in most hospitals. Since all the patients on general wards know when someone has died, I could never see the point. And, anyway, mortuary trolleys have such a distinctive trundling sound you'd have to be deaf not to notice. But our patients were deaf, and demented, and they would, in the main, fail to notice if a helicopter landed in the ward.

'No, just go ahead,' I said. 'They're all fast asleep.'

Linda and I watched from the office door. The men didn't need our help. She was small and frail. They lifted her gently on to the cold hardness of the trolley and placed the lid over her. Then they progressed noisily down the ward. As death trundled past us, the men smiled and spoke in unison.

'Cheerio. Have a good night.'

It was a relief that the body had gone. We finished our sherry and Linda asked if she could go to first break.

'Not that I'll be able to sleep. I'm a bit superstitious,' she explained. 'Whenever there's a death here, something else always seems to happen. Once I saw something in the day room. I wouldn't go in there for weeks afterwards.'

Linda hadn't struck me as the nervous type but I could see by the anxious look in her eyes she was perfectly serious. 'What did you see?' I asked.

'I think it was a patient. It was in the summer and it was hot so I'd opened the French windows and turned the chair to face them. I'd dozed off, and for some reason I opened my eyes and there in the doorway stood this old woman. Grey hair, Crimplene dress. I screamed and started to get up but she just disappeared. It scared me to bloody death. We never did find out who she was. But we'd had a death that night and, even now, I'm convinced it was her.'

'Why don't you bring a chair in the office? I'll stay in the ward and sit with the dying ones.'

'Are you sure?' Linda asked. But I could see relief in her face and the pained, scared expression disappear.

I helped Linda carry a chair into the office and I sat in the ward by the patient called Dottie, who every few moments mumbled 'Sally, Sally,' between dry, cracked lips. The water I gave her trickled unswallowed from her mouth and all I could do to soothe her was to hold her hand and stroke her forehead. My eyelids began to grow heavy and I had to fight the urge to lay my head beside Dottie's and sleep with her.

All I could hear in the ward were the sounds of breathing or snoring, so the sudden footfalls startled me. I went to the kitchen window but in the darkness I couldn't see a thing, just the path and the frame of the walkway.

There was silence outside for a while and I went to the door and pressed my ear to it. But there was no sound. Then I heard it again, a noise like the crunch of feet on hard gravel. And I realised it was not coming closer but receding, going round the side by the staff loo. I rushed to the loo, fearful the window was open. It was, but only just. I stood on the lavatory seat and without opening the window any more I peered out. At first I couldn't see or hear anything but then I caught a glimpse of feet. Feet in running shoes. Ankles in jeans. A man. He was lifting his feet softly like a cat. Coming closer.

Chapter Ten

Kennie stopped underneath the window. In that moment of recognition my foot slipped, plunging painfully into the lavatory bowl. Struggling to keep my balance my mind screamed 'Linda', but no sound came from my lips. And then for a moment as I fell sideways – oblivion. The great blackness coming down like the swift closing of an up-and-over garage door.

I knew I was on my side but I felt it necessary to try to work out my position in relation to the walls and the door and the ceiling. That seemed impossible. I was in positional limbo.

'Stay still,' Linda was saying. 'Did you faint?'

I murmured something about looking out of the window and Linda set about prodding me and asking if I could feel my legs. That seemed to jolt me awake.

'Feel them!' I said. 'The right one is killing me.'

'Try moving your toes,' suggested Linda. 'I'll be back.'

I became aware of the fact that my head was only a few inches from the wall and there was blood on the wall and I knew then, without a doubt, that was the reason my face felt sticky. I wondered in a vague way if I was bleeding badly but decided I wasn't. Linda came back with wet cloths, dry dressings and as I gazed up at her, a worried expression.

'Shall I call the doctor?' she said.

'Am I that bad?'

'It's only a tiny cut,' she said as she inspected my eyebrow.

'So my modelling days aren't over?'

'Very funny. Do you feel like getting up now?'

She helped me up. I'd sprained my ankle, and the mirror told me that I'd also have a black eye in the morning.

Linda shuffled me back to the office and went off to make tea. 'You'd better take off your wet tights and your shoe,' she said on her return. 'I'll stuff your shoe with paper and I'll rinse your tights. They'll be dry by the morning. Are you sure about the doctor?'

I hadn't noticed how wet I was but now I became aware of the cold I shivered and began to wriggle out of my soaked tights. 'I'll be fine. I heard someone prowling about. I had to see who it was.'

'You should have called me. Who was it – Kennie?'

I stared at her stupidly for a moment. 'You knew!'

'He's a harmless little prat. He just hangs around hoping to get a glimpse of the nurses. Some of the girls even give him cups of tea.'

'But why was he creeping round by the staff loo?'

Linda laughed. 'He was probably going to pee in the drain that's round the side.'

'You don't think he could have killed Jacky, then?'

'Good God, no! Have you seen the way he walks? Like a constipated camel. He couldn't possibly have crept up on Jacky. She was quite good at martial arts, you know. She wasn't hefty, but she was quick and she would have heard Kennie's feet a mile off.'

'So whoever killed her, she either didn't hear or she ignored because she knew who they were?'

'I suppose so,' said Linda grudgingly. 'But it's all over and done with now. After all,. the police seem to think a total stranger killed her.'

'But what if the killer is one of the staff? We're all in danger until he or she is caught – aren't we?'

Linda watched me warily like a dog surveying his own live-in cat. 'You didn't strike me as the worrying type, Kate. But you seem very interested in Jacky's death. Anyone would think she was a friend of yours.'

I feigned an attack of giddiness then and I felt quite proud of myself until I realised it was for real.

'Come on,' said Linda, 'you need a proper rest. I'll walk you down to the day room.'

I didn't argue but on our slow walk down the ward I did check the patients. 'What about the turns?' I said.

'I can manage the lighter ones on my own and get one of the other girls to help with the rest. With any luck our two sickies will last till morning.'

Gratefully I sank into one of the armchairs and Linda fetched me a pillow and a blanket. The budgie hadn't been covered and he chirped merrily for a while and the curtains fluttered noisily but neither kept me awake. I slept, hearing nothing, and without dreaming.

When I woke up the birds outside were singing but it was still dark. The clock on the wall showed five a.m. I stood up too quickly, forgetting about my ankle and my head. Both throbbed in unison as I limped into the ward. At the far end Linda was lifting a patient on to the commode.

'I can manage,' she insisted, but I helped her just the same. From then on the patients called incessantly and although I still limped, I coped reasonably well, if a lot more slowly than usual. But by the time the day staff appeared at seven thirty, my head and ankle were dancing a tango of pain and I gave a very brief report before departing thankfully for home.

Feeling a true martyr I decided to call in at Humberstones. My intuition told me Hubert might have some news. If he did, he refused to give it to me.

'God. What a sight. Have you been in an accident?' he asked, making me feel instantly worse.

I explained I'd slipped down a loo. He didn't believe me.

'I'll drive you home,' he said. 'You'll sleep better at home.'

I didn't argue, but I did try to get him to tell me what he'd found out. He wasn't to be persuaded.

'I'll tell you later,' he said. 'When you feel better. It's nothing that can't wait, my duck.'

'You've never called me that before, Mr Humberstone. You must be local born. A true country boy.'

He grinned and led me out to his car, loading me into the front seat as if I were one of his more cumbersome corpses. I was too tired and stiff to care. I dozed in the car and when we arrived Hubert insisted on helping me upstairs and on to the bed. I slept fully clothed until knocking at the door woke me.

Slowly I made my way downstairs. It was Mrs Morcott of the WI.

'Oh, my dear. I'm so sorry. I've disturbed you again and you've had an accident. You poor thing . . . '

'Come in, Mrs Morcott. You'll have to forgive me if I'm not very communicative.'

She bustled in, still apologising. 'Do tell me if there's anything I can do for you, anything at all. I've really only come to invite you to join us on one of our day trips – a mystery tour – could be really exciting.'

I declined, thanking her for thinking of me.

'Well, I won't keep you, dear,' she said. 'I saw you at the funeral and I told myself not to forget to invite you to a more jolly occasion.'

'I didn't see you, Mrs Morcott,' I said.

'No, dear. I did try to catch your eye but failed. I didn't go to the funeral tea so I didn't get a chance to say hello. Such an interesting service, terribly sad of course. I was talking to a little lady next to me in the church. She'd seen Jacky just two weeks before she died. "I mustn't forget to visit you next time," Jacky had said. "I'll just put you down in my diary." And the very day she was due to visit that lady – she was murdered.'

I nodded and murmured, 'Tragic.' It was all I could think of by way of polite response, because all that echoed in my mind was diary, diary, diary! Where the hell was it? What detective misses at least looking for one? Most people have a diary, even if they don't use it. Was her mother failing to tell me about it because it reflected badly on Jacky or was it in fact missing? Or more to the point had the police got there first? I would have to search Jacky's room for the diary and the pass book. Although I felt it very unlikely the pass book was there and if it wasn't there, where else would Jacky have put it or hidden it? With the pass book I could see if Jacky had paid in her monies on a regular basis, establish a pattern.

After Mrs Morcott had left, I drank tea, had a bath, camouflaged my face as best I could and decided I felt much better. I rang Clare Byfield and she seemed quite happy for me to see Jacky's room.

'It's as she left it,' she said wistfully. 'Just as she left it.'

Later in the day when I saw the room I could see that it was. Neat, clean and as bare as a nun's cell. The bed was covered with a fine patchwork quilt.

'Did Jacky make the quilt?' I asked Clare as we stood at the door looking in. 'It's lovely.'

'No, someone gave it to her. I can't remember who. It was some time ago.'

By the bed was a low mahogany table on which stood a lamp with a tasselled shade. On a lace mat lay an open Bible and by its side an alarm clock – the old-fashioned sort that goes tick-tock loudly. I was disconcerted to realise it had been rewound and still ticked and tocked. A large wardrobe, circa pre-World War One, dominated the room, the only other furniture being a chest of drawers and a wicker chair painted cream. Sitting there was an elderly teddy bear. His black eyes seemed to stare at us disapprovingly.

'I'll leave you to look round on your own.' Clare spoke as if I were a prospective buyer inspecting the house.

I closed the door when she had gone and as I did so noticed the picture on the wall behind it. 'The Light of the World'. I wondered why she'd put it where it was hardly visible from the bed. Somehow the picture completed the room. It was an old lady's room. Add a few sepia photos in ornate frames, some laxative tablets and a bottle of aspirins, and it would have been perfect.

The wardrobe contained a few classic skirts and blouses, mostly in shades of blue and beige, four summer dresses and five pairs of shoes – all polished to perfection. I half expected shoe-trees but there were none. The shoes rested on a pile of magazines, all *Ideal Home*. The bottom drawers of the chest of drawers contained neatly folded plain cotton underwear. A faint whiff of lavender escaped from the drawers and I shuddered. It reminded me of old ladies, death, in such a sweet smell. The top drawer yielded more of interest – a few letters, a row of pearls, a wrist-watch, a brush and comb set in mother-of-pearl, three or four antique-looking silver spoons – and a diary. There was no make-up, nothing young and frivolous about this room. It was neat and organised to the point of being secretive. And I knew without any doubt I would find nothing of any real value in the diary.

Downstairs I asked Clare if I could take the diary and the letters to my office.

'Yes, of course,' she said. 'The police have already seen them, so why not you.'

'Jacky's room is a bit sparse,' I said. 'Was her room always like that?'

Clare stared at me for a moment and then a soft smile lit her face. 'Oh, no,' she said. 'Once she had a lovely room, with posters and bright colours and loud music blaring out all over the house.

She went to pop-concerts and discos and had lots of fun.' The smile of happy reminiscence left her face abruptly, to be replaced by the tight controlled look of someone unable to face such bittersweet memories.

'When did all that change?' I asked.

'It changed,' she said, 'when Jacky got involved with that weird church. She withdrew into herself, became quiet and introspective. It was about four years ago, when I met Alan. Perhaps she was jealous that I didn't give her so much attention. I don't know. Perhaps it would have happened anyway. All I know is, once religion took a hold, she changed and for the worse. It was like a drug, she had to have a fix – either do-gooding or actually being in church. To be honest, in those last four years she was more like a lodger. We hardly saw each other. Alan was completely ignored. He was an angel, he never complained. Just reassured me that one day she would marry and that she would come to her senses. I clung on to that but it wasn't to be, was it?'

I was leaving and Clare was just about to close the front door when she said, 'I've looked everywhere for that pass book. It isn't here. I don't believe she ever had one.'

'Perhaps not,' I said. 'But I'll make every effort to find it if it does exist.'

'Good,' she murmured, and then she added, 'It's sad, isn't it, no one really liked Jacky – except Kevin, I suppose.'

I nodded before turning away. What could I say?

Chapter Eleven

Hubert rang that evening to ask how I was and to give me the news he'd had to suppress all day. His voice sounded high-pitched and excited and he sensed my response was less than enthusiastic.

'Do you want to know what I've found out or not?' he asked testily.

'Of course I do,' I said. 'It's the end of the day and I'm just feeling a bit tired, that's all.'

'It can wait till tomorrow,' he said.

'Be a sport – tell me now.'

'The PM's been done on Ada Hellidon.'

'And?'

'Strange really, they say she was full of Mogadon. That's why she fell down the stairs.'

'You mean the police think she was murdered.'

'Seems like it,' said Hubert. 'A bottle of paracetamol had been replaced with the sleeping pills – although the police seem to think she could have done that herself. They are not quite sure how many she took although the stomach contents contained about two. However, she had very high levels in her bloodstream. She could have been drugged for days.'

Poor old Ada, I thought.

'Are you still there?'

'Sorry, Mr Humberstone. I was just thinking about Ada.'

'There's something else. She was ready for a funeral. An old friend of hers, being buried in Longborough. Only Ada had got the wrong day. Her friend's funeral was the next day.'

Full of Mogadon, Ada had obviously become confused. I could imagine her struggling through the morning, trying to get herself dressed, trying desperately to keep awake, to concentrate, to keep faith with her dead friend. Probably she had just forgotten to change her shoes. She might have lived if she'd worn shoes with more support.

'So it looks like two murders,' I said eventually. 'And I'm not having much luck with one.'

'Give it time,' Hubert said. 'Give it time.'

I'd put the phone down before I realised I hadn't asked if the Mogadons had been prescribed for Ada. If they were, she would either have to go into town to the chemist there, or get someone in the village to go for her. In bed that night, I wished I had both the Mogadons and the paracetamol. My head still ached slightly and I couldn't sleep. Ada had told me something about Jacky and yet I couldn't work out how it fitted in. Someone was missing in Jacky's life and because he was so conspicuously absent, I had failed to realise his importance. I had read through the diary as though I were an MI5 decoder – nothing. Each entry was as dull as a calorie chart. 'Bright morning, glad to be off duty. Going into town. Seeing Kevin tonight. Jesus saves.' If there were clues there I was missing them. I found only one puzzling entry, 'AA', at the top of a page. Alcholics Anonymous seemed unlikely. Knowing Jacky, though, she was probably trying to save a few whisky-drenched souls. I finally slept.

My black eye was definitely a better shade of mottled in the morning and my headache had completely gone. I decided to go to Short Brampton first, then visit the old girl who lived near Kennie at Leys Court. I might even visit Kennie and show him my eye.

Frost covered Short Brampton, sifted like icing sugar over rooftops and gardens. There was little sign of life otherwise. I knocked at both sides of Ada's empty house and was about to give up when a thin woman wearing a red jogging suit that drained the colour from her face opened the door about three inches.

'Yes?' she said suspiciously.

This time I thought honesty was the best policy, 'I'm a private detective on an investigation and I wondered if I might have a few words.'

'Is it a good job?'

'What?'

'Is being a private detective a good job?'

'Yes, it's okay,' I said, feeling wary, now that I could see her eyes. I swear they bulged with desperate interest.

'Do you get abused and attacked physically?' she asked.

'Well, not so far.'

'Good. You can come in then and we'll have a chat.'

I followed her along the hallway into the sitting-room. She hadn't tidied up in a long time. Newspapers and magazines lay as thick as dust. And you could actually see dust. Unwashed cups and saucers decorated every available shelf and had even crept underneath the coffee table, which itself was covered with magazines, papers, and empty chocolate wrappers. Half-written letters lying on the sofa she scooped up and threw on to an overflowing waste-bin.

'Find a seat,' she said. 'I know it's a mess. I'm off sick with depression. I've been off for weeks now. I don't care any more. I'm a teacher, well, an ex-teacher now.'

I lifted a magazine and a ball of knitting wool and sat down on the sofa. I had a strong feeling this interview was not going to run an easy course. Strange, that in all the detective novels I'd ever read the interviewee always keeps to the point with only minor deviations. In real life people want to talk out their problems, seeing life only as it affects them. Murder is still a rarity and for most people it's of interest because they can feel not only a vicarious fear but relief, too. Perhaps some feel envious that murder has removed for the victim the effort of worrying about their own death.

'I'm Gwenda Carey, by the way,' Ada's neighbour was saying. 'I teach at Longborough Comp. Well, I used to. It just got too much for me. You've no idea how awful teaching is. Really awful, especially these days. And the kids! My last day of trying to play sane, this girl brought in a suitcase of clothes, opened it in the classroom and started to hold up various bits and pieces – as if it was an auction. For God's sake, it was an auction! They all started bidding. I asked her to stop, quite nicely, calmly. I didn't let myself get rattled. I suggested she could sell her clothes when the lesson ended. She stared at me for a moment and then said, "You fucking old cow. What you need is a good screw." I could take the abuse – I'm used to it. But she wouldn't stop. She sold all her stuff. I just stood there. I tried shouting, threatening them. Nothing worked. Then I just found myself standing there, tears pouring down my face. I was still standing there when break was over, like a statue but still crying. The deputy head brought me home. That was two months ago. I haven't left the house since. I've been applying for jobs; trouble is, I never finish the letters . . . ' She paused, looking at me carefully as if suddenly realising I was there and I was a guest. 'Would you like a drink – vodka, scotch?'

'It's a bit early for me. I'd love a coffee with a tot, though.'

She left the room, looking back at me once, as if to make sure I was still firmly in place. The coffee took much banging of cupboard doors and clattering and general sounds of confusion, but eventually she reappeared with a tray and she set it before me by sweeping off the paper debris from the coffee table on to the floor in one continuous motion. It wasn't done for effect; I could tell that. It was just less effort. The plastic tray's flowers were covered in old stains and the coffee had slopped into the saucers. A bottle of whisky stood in the middle of the tray.

'I'm a born-again drinker,' she said, smiling at her own joke. 'I've taken to it like the proverbial duck. Oh, fuck the duck. You were going to tell me about your job. Could I do it?'

'I'm sure you could,' I said. And as I spoke I could see her eyes glimmering with frantic hope. A desperate sort of madness. I would have to keep hold of her self-interest if I wanted to find out anything abouts Ada's last days. 'I'll give you a hypothetical question and you see if you can glean any more info on it or give me a new angle.'

'Fire away, I like puzzles,' Gwenda said with her hands cupping her face and leaning forward slightly.

'An old lady dies after falling downstairs, seemingly an accident; she's dressed for a funeral. She lives alone, is a little eccentric and lonely but otherwise in average health for her age. She has few visitors but would probably invite anyone in. She has a tenuous link with a much younger neighbour who was murdered three months before. The post-mortem reveals she has been taking sleeping pills from a paracetamol bottle. I suppose you could say she was either committing suicide at a snail's pace or being murdered, equally slowly, by an optimist . . . ' I paused. 'How would you begin to deal with that?'

She stared at the floor for several seconds and then grinned at me without humour. 'I'd interview the neighbours, first of all. The police did interview me. I told them I saw nothing. Why should I tell them I spend my day watching from my windows? It was all right for Ada, she was old. It's acceptable in the old. I'm still

102

young. I'm only thirty-six. I'm divorced, you know. Three years. He ran off with a shop assistant. Cheerful little thing, made a change from me; I was just practising for misery then. I've perfected it now. Chocolate and vodka, what more could anyone want? I could get better, you know, if I had a job like you.'

'Did you talk to Ada?' I asked, trying to keep her on track.

Gwenda looked down at her hands and began to stroke them lovingly. After a while she looked up. 'Talk to Ada. Yes, I talked to Ada. Sometimes I invited her in for a drink; she liked sherry, large glasses of it. She was kind to me. Sometimes she helped me to tidy up. She had a lot of arthritic pains but that didn't stop her doing things. Occasionally I went next door to her. She missed having the district nurses but she did have one nurse who came to see her now and again. I think she came the day before Ada died but I didn't actually see her.'

'What did she look like?'

'I don't know. I'm not always watching at the windows. Anyway, she always came along the path at the back. I'm usually at the front of the house. But I used to hear her.'

'Going in the back door, you mean?'

'No. I used to hear the wheels of her bike. She always came on her bike.'

'Did you tell the police about her?' I asked.

Gwenda frowned angrily. 'No,' she said. 'I did not tell them. I've already said. I didn't want them to think I was some sort of window-watching moron. Anyway I've only ever seen her from the back view. She was cycling away in the pouring rain. I couldn't tell you what she looks like. I do know that Ada didn't like her very much.'

'What makes you think that?'

She smiled then, slowly with a hint of malice or delight, I wasn't sure which. 'I'm helping you, aren't I? You didn't know about this woman before, did you?'

I agreed that I didn't.

'Good. You'll be one up on the police, won't you? Have a drink, I'm going to have another one.'

I declined. 'I'm driving. Do you know this visitor's name?' I asked as casually as I could.

Gwenda didn't answer at first; she pulled out a vodka bottle from behind a cushion and poured some into a used coffee cup.

Then she took a large gulp. 'Never told me her name. Just called her "my friend".'

'But she didn't like her?' I pressed.

'I told you that. No, she didn't like her. I think this woman had even offered her a home. Ada had laughed at the suggestion. "She'd kill me with kindness," she said.' Gwenda paused then, realisation flooding her face. 'Oh, my God . . . You don't think that she did, do you?'

'I really don't know, but it is a possibility. What I do need to discover is what happened about the tablets. Was Ada ever confused about what she had to take?'

'No, I don't think so. I knew she took paracetamol quite often. "Helps to get me moving in the morning," she used to say. As the day went on she eased up. And I knew she took sleeping pills because one evening she knocked on the door with one in her hand and asked me to check that there was "5" printed on the tablet. It looked like a paracetamol but it did have "5" on it. She couldn't see too well and I did tell her to be careful.'

She gulped again on the vodka. 'It wasn't my fault, you know. That was a few days before she died. I could see she wasn't well and I did tell her to see the doctor but she thought all doctors were suspect, especially that lot at the Health Centre. Really it wasn't my fault . . . You won't tell anyone, will you, not the police or anyone.' Her voice tailed off miserably.

'Please don't worry,' I said. 'You've really been a great help. And in my job I have to rely on other people all the time. I use my discretion and I certainly wouldn't break a confidence, especially of people who have nothing to do with the crime. It's up to me to pick up on the things people don't tell the police.'

Gwenda Carey began to cry then, silent, unwrenching tears that simply flowed. I handed her a tissue from my pocket, put an arm round her and said, 'Why didn't you tell the police?'

Eventually she wiped her eyes and her face. 'He reminded me of a boy at school. This boy was six foot tall, handsome, he never cheeked me or answered me back but there was something about him, something that scared me and the CID man was like him . . . just like him.'

'I understand. You've told me now. So with any luck I'll be able to find this woman and if she had anything to do with Ada's death I'll get the evidence and pass it on to the police.'

'How will you get evidence? Fingerprints, that sort of thing?'

'Criminals aren't always so helpful. Fingerprints and fibres are the stuff dreams are made of. Forensic science is good PR material, makes the public feel less vulnerable. In reality it's talking to people that really counts, talking and listening. It's harder than it looks. Words can trap criminals just as solidly as fingerprints . . . ' I tailed off. 'At least that's the theory.'

I said all this with a confidence about as steady as a sapling on a windy day. But I liked to think Gwenda was convinced I knew what I was doing.

She nodded. 'What I want is a quiet life. I don't think detecting is for me. What do you think I should do?' Ada seemed forgotten already.

'How about being a library assistant? It's not well paid but it's quiet, dignified, and you get to read all the good books first.'

'That really might suit me, you know. Thank you for suggesting it.'

As I was leaving I said. 'Did Ada ever mention Jacky Byfield at all?'

'Oh, yes. Thought she was a little madam but she didn't explain what she meant. Once she said, "If that girl doesn't look out, she'll come to a sticky end." She was right, wasn't she?'

I nodded in agreement. 'And that was all?'

'Well, yes . . . except that one day she came back from the town and said, "I saw a ghost from Jacky's past today." And when I asked her what she meant, she laughed and said something about bad pennies and selling a chamberpot to a man with a funny name. Does that make any sense to you?'

'Not at the moment,' I said. 'But it might be important. I just wish I could get into Ada's house to have a look round.'

'No problem,' said Gwenda. 'I've got a key.'

My surprise must have shown.

She smiled. 'Ada was always giving keys to people. She lived in fear of falling. She wanted the neighbours to be able to get in. I didn't tell the police I had a key. I didn't want to be suspected of anything.' She offered to come with me. 'It's really quite exciting, isn't it?'

'Very,' I murmured, hoping that an exploration of Ada's house would reveal something. The trouble was I had no idea what to look for.

The house still had a vague smell of paraffin and stew and death. And I was convinced Ada still lurked in dark corners. I shuddered. The house felt like a fridge. A dark fridge.

'We'd better not switch on the lights,' I said. 'Someone might see.'

'They're all at work,' said Gwenda. 'And why are we whispering?'

'I hadn't realised we were,' I said, deliberately raising my voice.

First I checked the kitchen drawers. There were only two, both in a formica-topped cabinet that ceased manufacture in the fifties. The drawers stuck, but I managed to yank them open. In one was cutlery, in the other an orderly arrangement of scissors, matches, tin tacks, string, Sellotape, a book of stamps and a crêpe bandage.

'What are you looking for?' asked Gwenda.

'I'm not sure but I'll know it when I see it. Does that make sense?'

In reply she shrugged. 'I'm bloody cold and I could do with another drink. Mind if I go?'

'Not at all,' I said, wondering why she had wanted to come with me in the first place. 'Thanks for your help.'

She raised her eyebrows as if to say 'rather you than me' and walked out, her slippers making slap slap noises on the linoed hall floor. And then she was gone and I was alone. And I was scared . . .

Chapter Twelve

So scared, that although I forced myself to stand at the bottom of the stairs, all I could do was stare up into the darkness and the closed door at the top.

Once when I was a student nurse working on the private wing I'd gone into a room to check on a patient at two a.m. The bed was empty, the window open and the curtains fluttered. I had rushed to the window dreading what I would see. And then the door had closed behind me. And behind the door a bald woman laughed maniacally. In her hand she held a wig, waving it in the air. I had thought it was a severed head.

I climbed the stairs slowly, each footstep a creak as loud as a whiplash. I don't believe in ghosts, I told myself, I don't believe in ghosts. And I didn't. But there always comes a time, just like not believing in God, when you say – I could be wrong.

At the top of the stairs there were four closed doors. I opened each door quickly and loudly, letting the doors bang against the wall and standing well back – just in case. But the emptiness of the rooms stared back at me, an emptiness that was strangely disappointing, like being given a large chocolate Easter egg and opening it carefully and finding it hollow.

Two of the rooms contained beds; in the smaller room the bed was simply a bare mattress on a divan bed. But in the larger front room, Ada's, a double bed covered with a maroon bedspread dominated the room. On the bedside cabinet a paperback novel lay open, jacket up, showing a handsome couple locked in an embrace. *Dream of Love* it was called. I had been in this room before, but it was as if I were seeing it for the first time. Ada alive in the house had lent the room life, had given the room its persona. Now the room and the house were as dead as Ada.

I crouched down to search the bedside cabinet. There were two shelves, the top one stacked with romantic novels, the bottom one with pain-relief sprays, and a writing pad and envelopes – new and unused. As I stood up my arm caught *Dream of Love*. I was about to put it back when I noticed she'd used a book-mark. A slip of paper, a receipt. On the top in bold black script was the name Adam Angel – Antiques of Quality; beneath, it said, Chamberpot – £50. I knew immediately I'd found what I was looking for. Thank you, Ada.

I folded the receipt carefully and put it in my jacket pocket. I closed all the doors as quickly as I'd opened them and it was only at the front door that I paused. I breathed in fresh air that was warmer outside than in and then I slammed the front door hard. As if in final salute.

Gwenda Carey watched from her front window but came out as I walked into her front garden. She staggered slightly and her voice slurred. 'Did you find it?' she asked.

'Yes, thanks.'

'Will you come again?'

'I might. Will you try for a job in the library?'

She smiled. 'I might. Good luck.'

'And you.'

The morning had unsettled me but I drove to Leys Court accompanied by a gardening programme on the car radio. It was about growing tomatoes, which wasn't a pastime I'd thought much about before. Anyway, it made me feel cosily domestic.

I called at Kennie's house first. His mother answered the door. With no make-up she looked older and tiny blue veins showed on her checks like thin strands of a spider's web.

'You come to see Kennie, dear?' She didn't wait for my reply. 'He's not in. He's in the General. Ever so bad he is. Static Asthmaticus they call it.'

I didn't correct her – it's Status Asthmaticus – but whatever it was called it's serious. 'May I come in?'

'Course you can, dear. I'm just getting ready to go and see him. Come on in.'

I sat and watched her lose five years in five minutes as she put her make-up on.

'There, that's done,' she announced, closing her compact with a flourish. 'I'm ready now. Will you give me a lift?'

'Of course. When was Kennie taken ill?'

'Last night. I'd been out and when I came back he was sitting in the chair gasping for breath. Terrible colour he was, all blue in the face and white round his lips. I called an ambulance straight away and they were here ever so quickly. The ambulance men were marvellous, they really were. Blue lights, siren, oxygen, everything . . . ' Her voice tailed off and I knew she was desperately trying to keep in control.

'He's ever so poorly, he's struggling for every breath. Poor kid. I think he lost his inhaler in the hospital grounds. It wasn't in his pocket. Funny that, he's never lost it before. We've got spares in the house but I think he was too ill to look. If I'd been here it wouldn't have happened. It's all my fault . . . ' She began to cry then, her mascara leaving black smears on her cheeks like bruises.

In the car she chain-smoked but by the time we reached the hospital she had repaired her face.

'Can't go in to him looking a mess, can I?'

The hospital corridors stretched in front of us like a maze and as we walked Renée clutched at my arm for support. We found Kennie in a side room; intensive care was full. He lay propped on pillows with oxygen being given by nasal tubing, his eyes wide open and full of fear. The red patches of colour had gone from his face, and his skin was as white as the pillow his head rested on so uneasily. A student nurse, young and timid-looking, stood by his bedside checking his intravenous infusion.

'Kennie, it's your mum,' she said. 'You'll soon feel better.'

But I knew that he wouldn't. At the sight of his mother he pulled frantically at the sheets as if trying to pull himself higher in the bed. His face showed not only the exhaustion of struggling for every breath but the characteristic white pinched nostrils of the dying.

'Mum, Mum . . . ' he managed to say in a hoarse whisper, the effort of which caused him to slump against the pillows in an agony of breathlessness. It was as agonising to watch.

Renée, though, was composed; she took his hand. 'Don't you try to talk, love. Just take it easy. You'll soon feel better. I'm going to stay here until you do. Now just close your eyes, pet, and try to get some sleep.'

Kennie obediently closed his eyes. And we sat in silence for a long time.

Eventually Renée looked away from her son and turned to me. 'You don't have to stay,' she said. 'Thanks for giving me a lift. I'll be staying till he's breathing okay.'

'I'll stay on for a bit,' I replied. 'I can stay while you go out for something to eat.'

'More like a fag break,' she said. 'I'll go outside and have one now while you're still here.'

When she'd left the room I glanced at the student nurse questioningly. She shook her head in a 'no hope' motion.

'Has the consultant seen him recently?' I asked.

'He's coming again soon.'

I nodded. Kennie began to stir then, as if knowing his mother had left the room. His sunken eyes focused slowly but the fear came quickly. His mouth opened and closed soundlessly and I knew he had recognised me.

'Sh . . . sh . . . ' I said, putting my finger to my lips. 'Go back to sleep, Kennie.'

But again his mouth opened and he gasped, 'I . . . I saw . . . '

'It doesn't matter. Just rest.'

Again his eyes held mine, and again he struggled to find enough strength to speak. 'I know who . . . I saw . . . it was her.'

I longed to say 'Who did you see?' but even the few words he had said seemed to have worsened his breathing. His eyes had closed and his chest rose and fell as though devils fought in his lungs. He wouldn't be answering any questions now. The student nurse felt his pulse and pressed the emergency bell by his bed and within minutes a doctor had arrived with the ward sister. Renée came back then, her face becoming ashen as she saw Kennie and heard the doctor murmuring about trying more hydrocortisone, more aminophylline.

'I'll wait outside, Renée,' I said.

She sighed. 'He's not going to make it, is he?'

'Have a word with the doctor,' I mumbled as I patted her arm.

I stood for a while in the corridor and then a passing nurse brought me a chair. I sat for what seemed like hours and then with the shout 'Cardiac arrest' all hell broke loose. The door flew open and I could hear the panic in the voices.

'Where's the board? Get him on the bloody floor then!'

And then the crash team arrived, hurtling along the corridor with their trolley, which in so many cases could just as well have been the mortuary trolley. Renée was bundled out shaking and sobbing and I put my arms around her and cuddled her and knew that poor Kennie would never be a trouble to her again.

The team tried for half an hour to resuscitate Kennie and then eventually one of the doctors emerged to tell us they had done everything humanly possible and would his mother like to see him now. We walked in, huddled together. The paraphernalia of defying death had been removed and all that was left was death itself. Kennie was at peace, a half-smile on his lips as if he was telling everyone how much better it was not to have to struggle any more.

Renée became more composed once she had seen him. 'He's out of it now, isn't he.' It wasn't a question, it was her consolation.

We left the hospital then and walked to a nearby pub. Renée drank two gins and I drank a single whisky.

'I've got a friend,' said Renée. 'I'll stay with him.'

'I'll drive you.'

'Thanks for being with me, dear.'

'Will you be all right? Do you want me to call your doctor?'

'No, thanks. I'll be fine.'

I drove Renée to an almost derelict terraced house in the back streets of Longborough and a tall unshaven man answered the door and immediately put his arm around her. Before going into the house she turned to me and waved as if to say, 'I'll be all right, don't worry.'

It was too late now to visit Mrs Tonbridge; I felt hungry, exhausted and miserable. Perhaps going to the office would cheer me up. That was optimistic.

Hubert, looking worried, met me at the door. 'The police are here. They insisted on waiting in your office. Don't say too much, will you?'

'Mr Humberstone,' I said. 'I'll be as tight-lipped as a driving examiner. I'll not divulge a single family skeleton even when they start on me with their rubber truncheons.'

'You should take life more seriously,' he said as he watched me go up the stairs.

Two men in plain-clothes took up most of the space in my office. They looked me up and down with the neutral expression they no doubt reserved when they found something that looked rather nasty. Private detectives I know are viewed by the police as a lower form of life, with as much status in the crime world as an unsuccessful pick-pocket. A female detective, though, no doubt had some novelty value.

'How's business?' said the more senior-looking of the two.

'Booming,' I replied, giving him what I hoped was my most friendly smile.

I noticed he wasn't handsome, he looked a bit grey and slightly dusty for that, but he was attractive if angularity and greying hair were any criteria.

'I'm Hook, Inspector – CID. This is DS Roade. We've come to ask you what exactly you were doing at Mrs Ada Hellidon's house on the fourteenth. It seems you found the body.'

Before I could answer DS Roade said, 'Mind if we sit down?'

Roade had acne and looked about nineteen. He also seemed to have the permanently anguished frown of a chronic indigestion sufferer.

'Would you like tea, coffee, a Rennie?' I asked.

Roade's mouth opened slightly; I could see he was impressed. 'Yeah,' he said. 'I'd love a Rennie.'

I smiled at Hook. 'And you're more a migraine man.'

He didn't deny it but replied with a gruff request for tea.

It was quite cosy sitting there drinking tea. I had to admit to them, of course, that I was investigating Jacky Byfield's death. They exchanged glances at that, but when I explained I hadn't had much luck they both smiled knowingly. Just as long as I wasn't ahead of them; that seemed to be their attitude.

'It's a pity about Kennie Litchborough,' I said.

They nodded as if they knew, but Roade couldn't contain his curiosity.

'What about him?' he asked. 'We still keep a watch on him. Nasty little pervert.'

'Not any more,' I said. 'He died today, in hospital.'

Hook sighed and muttered, 'Shit' under his breath and then asked me about Ada again. 'Why do you think she had any connection with Jacky's death?'

'Just a hunch,' I said. 'Just a hunch.'

Hook stood up as if to leave and gave me an avuncular pat on the shoulder. 'You just watch yourself. We think Jacky's killer may well strike again. He's probably got a fetish about nurses.

Hanging about that hospital could be dangerous. We do have a suspect there. He's got a criminal record – all we need is a bit more evidence.'

'Do you mean Mick O'Dowd?' I asked.

'That's him.'

'I'll be careful,' I promised.

Hook asked me a few more questions about Ada's state of mind and if I knew of any friends. I said very little in a helpful way and he seemed satisfied. He didn't say a word about the PM result.

As they left I wondered why the police still stuck to the theory that Jacky's murderer was male. She hadn't been raped and the stab wound in the back was more indicative of a killer who perhaps wasn't strong enough physically to face the chance of a fight. A cowardly male perhaps? Kevin had an alibi and poor Kennie . . . I couldn't believe he'd had that streak of viciousness in him or, for that matter, a motive. As soon as I worked out why, I reasoned, I'd know who. Perhaps, too, I should tell the staff at the hospital who I was and what I was doing.

When I told Hubert he didn't agree. 'You could be next in line. There's been two deaths already.'

'Three,' I said. 'Kennie Litchborough died in hospital today. A natural death, he had a severe asthma attack.'

Hubert raised a questioning eyebrow.

'It *was* natural,' I said. 'It must have been.' But suddenly I wasn't so sure. Why didn't he have his inhaler with him and who had he seen? And why was it so important to tell me on his death-bed? Perhaps my murderer was not only far cleverer than I had imagined but also far more dangerous. I'd have to start acting like a detective, take a few risks, start asking awkward questions. Make myself a target.

Chapter Thirteen

The next morning I drove to Leys Court to see Mrs Tonbridge. The house outside had mean council house-type windows but the paintwork was fresh and a potted shrub stood guard by the front door. I knocked and waited. Then I heard the click, click, shuffle, of someone walking with a Zimmer frame. The door was eventually opened by a tall grey-haired woman with matching eyes and a stoop. She stared at me for a moment.

'My daughter's in bed,' she said. 'She's asleep.'

I smiled. 'I'm from the Church of the Second Coming. I've come as a replacement visitor for Jacky.'

She seemed neither pleased nor surprised to see me. 'Come on in.' She shuffled and clicked into the living-room and sat down heavily in an armchair by a coal fire.

'How lovely,' I said. 'A coal fire.'

She gazed into the fire for a moment. 'The Lord's blessing,' she said. 'I can't keep it going myself, I have to get Margaret up to put on more coal. She never puts enough coal on. Where did you say you were from? You can sit down.'

'From the church, instead of Jacky,' I replied as I sat in the high-backed chair opposite her.

Mrs Tonbridge stared at me for a moment and I felt conscious I probably didn't look the part in my red and black skirt and make-up and costume jewellery.

'Jacky was a nice girl,' she said, her whiney voice hinting that perhaps I wasn't. 'I went to the funeral. Lovely service. Nothing was too much trouble for that girl, she had lovely manners too. Always took an interest in old people. Not like most young people nowadays.'

I nodded. 'Is there anything you'd like me to do?'

'Well,' she said, 'I'm trying to think what Jacky used to do.

Sometimes she went on errands for me, to the shops. She'd go straight after work. Not like Margaret. All she wants to do is go straight to bed. She's got no go in her. Now Jacky, she was full of energy. And she was always willing. Margaret didn't know how lucky she was. Didn't appreciate how lucky we were to have Jacky. When Margaret wanted to go out Jacky would stay with me. Mind you, Margaret does take me to church. Not that she comes inside, she leaves me in my wheelchair just inside the door. She doesn't hold with religion. She goes off for a walk or sits in the car. Probably goes to sleep – she's always complaining she's tired. I'm nearly eighty and I don't complain I'm tired.'

'How often did Jacky come?'

'Every two weeks, more sometimes. We were always glad to see her. Margaret doesn't have many friends, she's very reserved, likes to keep herself to herself. Never been much for boyfriends either. The ones she did bring home when she was young were scruffy and no good. I said to her, "Margaret, you'll be better off with me than with a lazy good-for-nothing man." Anyway she took my advice. She couldn't have coped with children, she hasn't got the patience. Now poor Jacky would have made a lovely mother, she had lots of patience. And she had good taste.'

'What do you mean exactly – good taste?'

Mrs Tonbridge looked round the room, her eyes resting ad-miringly over the spotless but old-fashioned decor. The chairs with antimacassars, the oak table with a potted fern resting on a crocheted runner, a glass cabinet full of neatly arranged crockery. My eyes followed hers.

'You have a lovely home,' I said, feeling like a real creep.

'Jacky appreciated it. She was always admiring my lovely things. I gave her one or two presents over the years. Just little things. She offered to buy them, of course, but I wouldn't hear of it. You can't take it with you, can you?'

I agreed that you couldn't.

'Will you stay for something to eat? I wake Margaret up about twelve and she cooks and we eat at one. If I don't wake her she'd sleep all day and it's bad enough when I'm on my own at night. It's terrible being old. I just pray I'll be with the Lord in paradise soon, although I don't know what Margaret would do without me.'

Start to live, I thought, but I smiled, asked if there was anything I could do for her and got up to leave.

'Well, I have enjoyed your visit,' she said. 'Perhaps next time when you come Margaret will be up. Not that she talks much. Mostly just sits and sews.'

Mrs Tonbridge followed me slowly to the door, rested on her Zimmer frame for a moment and then waved me goodbye. I forced a farewell smile and a wave. The Tonbridge house had felt oppressive; discontent hung in the air as strongly as if it were the smell of fresh paint. Margaret had all my sympathy. In keeping with her whiney voice, Mrs Tonbridge had the taut downturned mouth and pinched expression of a person who rarely laughed, and who had been rarely satisfied. Jacky had flattered her, had no doubt talked about the joys of everlasting life. Encouraged her to believe that God handed out compensation as surely as an insurance company and that she would be one of the few to benefit. Margaret, on the other hand, merely slaved in this life without hope and with a lot of criticism.

As I drove along the High Street I saw Hubert going into the Swan. I pulled into the forecourt and then had misgivings. He could be meeting someone, his wife perhaps? I peered cautiously round the door, not wanting to intrude, but he was alone. The pub was empty and he sat in one of the booths staring into a full pint with the air of a man who'd lost yet another funeral to the Co-op.

'Mr Humberstone,' I said, 'just the person I wanted to see.'

He looked up and smiled. 'I'll get you a drink,' he said and in his haste to get to the bar his beer spilt on the table. He shrugged, as though one more blow in life's struggle wouldn't make any difference. By the time he bought my drink I'd mopped up the table.

'My wife's met someone else,' he said and he looked about to cry.

What could I say? From then on I just kept buying him strong ale, while I sipped shandies wishing I could talk about the case.

After four pints he began to verge on the maudlin. 'Why don't you call me Hubert?' he said. 'That's my name. No one calls me Hubert any more. My wife, she's the only one to call me Hubert and she's found herself a toy-boy. Well, he's over forty but he's younger than me.'

I sympathised and bought yet another round.

'Hubert,' I said, 'try to concentrate. I'm making headway with the investigation.'

He gave me a beery smile in return for calling him Hubert. 'So who dun it?'

'I'm not quite that far advanced but I think I know how Jacky made her money.'

Hubert propped his head up with one hand and made an obvious effort to listen.

'Jacky may have made her money with antiques, admiring the most valuable pieces in old ladies' homes and gradually being told, "You keep it, dear, if it means so much to you." Then she sold them to antique shops or maybe to only one shop.'

'Who killed her, then? Not one of the old ladies. They didn't rise up out of their graves, did they?'

Hubert's tone had changed, from the maudlin to the aggressive. It was time to leave. I appealed to his sense of chivalry by suggesting I was more drunk than him.

'I'll take you back to the office, my duck,' he said. 'You lean on me and we'll be there in no time.'

I took his arm and together we walked down the High Street, shoppers having to stand aside for us. Halfway to the office Hubert began to sing, 'If you were the only girl in the world'. He sounded as if he were choking. Brazen it out, I told myself as I joined in.

Once we were back at Humberstones, Hubert had reached the dizzy, silent stage and I handed him over to the receptionist.

'He can't drink much, can he?' I said.

'It's not like him. He's a two-pint man at most,' she said, taking his arm and helping his slump into a chair.

'He was led astray. He fell into bad company.'

'Don't you worry, dear,' she said. 'I'll look after him.'

My telephone was ringing as I started up the stairs so I managed to run up two at a time and picked up the receiver sounding as though I'd just run a marathon.

'Are you okay? You're not ill, are you?'

At first I thought Pauline Berkerly was genuinely concerned. Then all became clear. St Dymphna's needed a staff nurse on Harper Ward – tonight. She was sorry it was such short notice but would I?

Of course I would.

But first I had to see Adam Angel about his antiques. I found the shop in a back street on the outskirts of Longborough. I walked there, my car still being in the Swan's forecourt. I'd drunk too many shandies to risk driving. The shop, in a row of terraced houses, had once been just a front room; now, it had the quiet elegance of a thriving antiques business. Through the window I could see a middle-aged man flicking a feather duster over his treasures. He obviously didn't specialise, for crammed into the ex-front room were grandfather clocks, tables, chests of drawers and, on all surfaces, plates, saucers, porcelain figures, silver ware. The walls were decorated with paintings and miniatures and apart from the man and his wares the shop was empty.

He smiled as I walked in. 'Good afternoon,' he called. 'Looking for anything special?'

I shook my head. 'Just browsing.'

The shop smelt of lavender polish and coffee and the clocks ticked away in resonant accord and I was mesmerised by the peace. The room contained so many lives. Ex-lives mostly, I reminded myself. Lives probably dominated by the ticking of clocks and the chimes of the hour. One clock in particular interested me. A plain-faced grandfather that I thought I had seen before, but that had stood silent. I just couldn't remember where.

My browsing had become embarrassingly long and the owner had begun to watch me. He was a short, thin man, in his fifties I supposed, with gold-rimmed glasses, unusually heavy eyebrows and wearing a grey pinstripe suit. He would have looked more at home in a jeweller's. He had given up dusting and was now sitting at a child's desk sorting through a stack of papers. He looked up as I approached.

'I'm looking for a chamberpot,' I said.

'Very popular choice at the moment, madam. They make a wonderful setting for plants. I've only got one in stock and it's not in perfect condition. I'll fetch it for you.' He disappeared into a back room and returned in seconds with a grimly dark green pot with a broken handle.

'Lovely glaze on this one,' he said, caressing it with as much finesse as if it had been a woman's rump.

'I was really looking for a . . . more floral one.'

'This one's a bargain at a hundred pounds. I really don't get many in. Snapped up by Americans usually. You could decorate it yourself, of course.'

Of course. Why didn't I think of that!

'I did have a particular one in mind. A friend of mine brought one in recently. You paid her fifty pounds for it. I wanted to buy it back as a keepsake.'

'I see,' he said. 'And it wasn't this one?'

'No, hers was floral.'

'I'll check the incoming book. The name?'

'Ada Hellidon.'

As he began checking through a large bound ledger I managed to look over his shoulder.

'I'm surprised Jacky didn't bring you a few things in.'

'She did,' he said and in that instant he knew he'd been trapped. His mouth tightened and paled at the corners.

'Who the hell are you?' he demanded. 'How did you know Jacky?'

'I'm a private detective investigating Jacky Byfield's death. And you, I presume, are her father?'

Chapter Fourteen

It was a guess of course. But the slight tremble of his hands on the ledger and blinking of his eyes convinced me that he was indeed Jacky's father.

He closed the ledger and sighed. 'How did you find me?' he said. 'Jacky swore never to tell a soul.'

'I wasn't looking for you. You were noticeable by your absence. And you do look rather like Jacky – especially around the eyes and brows.'

'Oh, God! My wife doesn't know about me, does she?'

I could see the muscles of his jaw twitch in agitation and at that moment a customer came in.

'Go into the back room,' he murmured. 'We can talk in there. I'll deal with the customer.'

I sat on a rocking chair in the storeroom cum kitchen, and waited and thought out the questions I needed to ask him. I needn't have bothered, for when he came back he launched into an explanation after getting me to promise I wouldn't tell Clare that he was in the area.

'But surely you're taking a risk that you'd pass each other in the street or that she'd come into the shop?'

'That's a risk I have to take,' he said. 'In the antiques game it pays to move around. This shop came up for sale and business is good so I've stayed for a while. I've had businesses all over the country. Jacky came across me in the Cotswolds about four and a half years ago. She was on holiday and we recognised each other. I was as pleased to see her as she was to see me, and she promised not to tell anyone we'd met. After that, we kept in touch, usually by phone. And when I worked nearby she'd come and see me. Then she became a born-again Christian, involved in all sorts managed to meet up. I'm an atheist so I suppose I was a bit of a challenge— '

'And the antiques,' I interrupted. 'She gave you some to sell.'

He frowned. 'She didn't give me them. I paid her a good price, over the top mostly. Guilt, I suppose. She'd paid for them anyway, so we weren't making a great deal of profit. Usually she brought me small bits and pieces, snuff boxes, a few nice plates, porcelain, the odd picture.'

I signalled with my head towards the shop. 'And the grandfather clock, second on the left?'

'The plain one?'

'That's the one.'

'Came from an old lady around here. Jacky told me she had a few larger pieces she wanted to sell. A Miss Holcot, I think. I can always check.'

'Did you pay Miss Holcot direct?' I asked.

'Well, no,' he replied. 'Strange that, she said to give the money to Jacky. I gave Jacky something for her trouble of course. It was good stuff. Only the clock left to sell now.'

'Over the past few years, then, Jacky provided you with quite a fair stock of antiques?'

'Well, yes,' he said. 'But what's wrong with that? You're not . . . you're not trying to say that I had anything to do with her death, are you? I couldn't . . . I mean I wasn't a good father, I know, but I was fond of her. I wouldn't have hurt her.'

'Relax, Mr – it isn't still Byfield, is it? But I don't think you had any connection with your daughter's murder.'

He sighed with obvious relief, removed his glasses and wiped a hand over his face. 'No. It's Angel now. I changed it by deed poll. It goes well with antiques. I thought it had a ring to it.'

'There's no other reason for the change of name, then?'

'If you must know,' he said, peering at me with his now naked eyes. 'If you must know, I wanted a new identity – Clare has been after me for maintenance for years and years. I didn't want children. I hate children. Why should I pay for something I didn't want? I got out and I wanted to stay out. I wasn't going to give her a penny. So I changed my name, my appearance, my job and I never looked back. And I never remarried. Jacky recognising me was a shock I can tell you. Coming here was chancy but Jacky found me these premises and she was self-supporting so

I came. It was our little secret. She liked secrets. She was the secretive sort.'

'She was indeed,' I said. 'So much so that she's managed to take you for a ride.'

'What's that supposed to mean?'

'Jacky never bought those antiques. She was given them. She may even have stolen them, I don't know. But you paid her for them, fenced for her if you like. And you must have paid her well, because in her deposit account she had twenty-five thousand pounds. In fact you paid for them twice. It must have knocked your profits somewhat.'

I'd expected some kind of angry reaction but instead he smiled. 'Who'd have believed it?' he said. 'Crafty little bitch. She was a chip off the old block after all. And I thought she was . . . '

'An angel.'

'Very funny,' he said, not in the least amused.

'You haven't asked yet who could have murdered Jacky?' I said.

He shrugged. 'The papers said it was a psychopath, a nutter on the loose.'

'I don't agree. Psychopath just means a sick mind and people with sick minds aren't just roving around looking for someone to kill. They live in houses, with people, go to work, have hobbies. In situations you or I could cope with, they can't. And then those with criminal tendencies are compelled to steal or kill. It cures their immediate problem. Psychopath or not, I think she was sussed by someone. Someone who realised Jacky was no angel. Someone who had lost something or someone or who was threatened with loss— '

'Look, I'm telling you it wasn't me,' he interrupted. 'She was bringing me business. Even if I was overpaying her I was still making good profits. Nowadays if something's old, whatever it is, some fool will pay the earth. Anyway she wasn't about to shop me – was she?'

'Oh, no. I found you, via a receipt for a chamberpot.'

I got up to leave, the rocking chair moving backwards and forwards on its own in a slowly dying motion.

'It's a pity you didn't keep in touch with your daughter when she was a child. Her fate might have been different and you would have made a great team.'

To a more sensitive soul that remark would have caused a moment's anguish, a pang of regret for what might have been. But not to Adam Angel. He smiled fleetingly as though I'd paid him a compliment. Somehow I could imagine Jacky smiling that way on her way to the bank, relishing the moment when she handed over the money. She probably justified her actions as divine retribution. And somehow it made me like her.

It was late afternoon when I arrived at the cottage, growing dark, and beginning to snow. All I really wanted to do was curl up on the sofa and watch something cheerful and trivial on TV. Instead I sat in the kitchen for a while, planning supper and dreading the night ahead. Night duty is like that, like work in general I suppose. The worst part is thinking about it. Perhaps premeditated murder was like that, too, planning and dreading and scheming and then actually doing the deed. Thinking, it's over now. It's done. Forget it. Pretend it didn't happen.

I ate sardines on toast, followed by marmalade on toast, followed by half a chocolate bar. I'd used a knife to cut the chocolate bar, cutting with careful precision down the middle groove, and I was admiring the neatness of my work when I began to think about the murder weapon never having been found. Where would I hide a knife if I had just used it to stab someone? I definitely wouldn't throw it away – I might need it again some time. Oh, God! Surely not? But if it wasn't needed again, where would I hide a knife in hospital? In a geriatric hospital? Somewhere no one would look, somewhere no one would want to look. And then I knew. Soon, I told myself, I'm going to crack this case. But my optimism quickly gave way to apprehension, for if I was right, one of the people I was working with had murdered not just once but twice, and possibly three times. Could I be sure Kennie's death was totally natural? Had he lost his inhaler or had someone stolen it and then literally frightened him to death? 'I saw her,' Kennie had said and he'd recognised her. A woman perhaps; definitely more clever and a damn sight more deadly than the male.

The drive to St Dymphna's didn't help my nerves. Huge snowflakes drifted against my windscreen as though they had a personal vendetta against drivers mad enough to be out on such a night. The snow clumped at the sides of my windscreen, making me feel as if I were driving through a tunnel and, worst of all, the snow had covered the white road-markings. I felt disorientated as though I were driving in an alien land. As if I were the only driver left in an alien land. For not a single car passed me.

By the time I arrived at the hospital gates I felt comforted and not disconcerted by the night ahead. Murderess or not on the premises, it was preferable to driving in such conditions; the hospital would be warm and dry and there was less chance of being murdered than there was of going into a skid and ending up in a ditch.

Sister was on duty on Harper. She smiled in relief as I arrived. 'It's a foul night, isn't it? I'm so glad you could get here.' She made it sound as if I were a guest at a party. Then, smiling again, she said in her whispery voice. 'We're short again tomorrow night, will you be able to do another night? We are desperate – please?'

'Yes, I'll do it,' I said.

Margaret Tonbridge walked into the office then, the shoulders of her raincoat spattered with fast-melting snow. On her head she wore a navy blue knitted beret.

'Sorry I'm late,' she said. 'Mother's not too well. She couldn't get comfortable. I managed to sort her out in the end.'

'Don't worry,' said Sister Barnes. 'All that matters is you're here. Let's hope your mother's better soon.'

The report was brief and to the point.

'It's all in the care plans. Two falls today. Both seen by the doctor, no obvious injuries but keep a close eye on them. Otherwise it's fairly quiet, no poorly ones. The new patient, Edith Hunsbury, is inclined to wander. We found her outside today looking for her garden. Just make sure you lock the doors.'

Margaret gave me a knowing look and I winked at her. Were we likely to leave the doors unlocked?

When Sister had gone we checked the windows and locked the doors and then began the drinks round. All was calm. Margaret's experience with her mother made her an excellent nurse. Efficient without being bossy, she made the work seem easy. She lifted well and by ten most of the patients were sound asleep. Apart from Edith Hunsbury.

'I should be out in my garden. All my plants will die. All that work. It's not right keeping me a prisoner here.'

I made the mistake of telling her it was snowing.

Her voice rose in an anxious whine of despair. 'You stupid woman. Of course it's not snowing. You're a liar. Let me out of here and I'll do it myself.'

Her thin arms threw back the bedclothes, followed by equally thin legs. It was Margaret who came to the rescue. I hadn't heard her walk to the bedside but she was there by my side holding a plastic watering can used for indoor plants.

'Now then, Edith, I'll water your plants. Shall I do the roses first?'

Edith laid back on the bed 'Well, thank you, dear. I'm glad someone's got some sense here. Yes, dear, do the roses first and then the pansies and the lilies. I can go to sleep now, can't I?'

'Yes, of course,' replied Margaret. 'I'll report back when I've finished.'

There was no need. We had returned to her bed within minutes to reassure her that her roses were fine, but she was asleep.

Margaret smiled down at her. 'I wish my mother was as easily satisfied,' she whispered.

Later when we'd had tea and Margaret had begun sewing some sort of floral square, I said, 'Is that for your mother?'

'It's a new bag for her Zimmer frame. She keeps her bits and pieces in it. Glasses, tissues, mints, that sort of thing. I make pockets for most of her clothes, saves me hunting for things she's lost. Look,' she said, standing up to take her cloak from the hook on the door, 'I've even put a pocket in my own cloak. It's useful for putting scissors and pens in, so I don't forget to bring them from home.'

There was silence for a while as Margaret concentrated on her sewing.

'I met your mother today,' I said. 'Did she tell you?'

I'd hoped that she might have been surprised or at least thrown off guard; she wasn't. 'She did say a redhead had come from the church. I thought it might be you, although I didn't know you were a churchgoer.'

'I'm not. I'm a private detective.'

The needle paused mid-stitch but Margaret's expression remained impassive, apart, that is, from a fleeting suggestion of a smile.

Chapter Fifteen

Margaret continued to sew, bending her head over her work so that I couldn't see her face.

'Why are you working here?' she asked, keeping her eyes focused on the needle. 'What are you hoping to find out?'

'I'm hoping to find out who murdered Jacky and . . . ' I paused, for dramatic effect, 'and Ada Hellidon.'

This time Margaret did look up, her eyes reflecting the look you see in sheep just before they're sheared. A look of puzzled apprehension mixed with excitement. 'But she fell, I read it in the papers. Surely that's death by natural causes?'

'Did she fall or was she pushed? Or she could have been drugged.'

'Who on earth would want to kill poor old Ada? That's ridiculous.'

'Oh, you knew her then,' I said. 'I didn't realise that.'

Margaret paused to rethread her needle. 'My mother knew her, they went to the same school. Longborough's not a large place. Those born and bred here are bound to know each other.'

'Yes, of course,' I agreed. 'So she was your mother's friend, not yours.'

'She certainly wasn't a friend of mine and she wasn't exactly a friend of my mother's either. They knew each other, that's all.'

'But you didn't like her?' I asked.

Margaret turned her sewing and checked the seams before answering. 'I didn't really know her. I might have met her in the town occasionally and she'd always have some gossip or other to tell me. But, as I've said, I didn't really know her.'

'And you never visited her house?'

'No. Why on earth should I?'

'No reason,' I said. 'No reason at all.'

Margaret folded her now completed sewing carefully and placed it in front of her on the desk. 'I'll check the patients, shall I?'

'Please.'

Her footsteps on the wooden ward floors only made the slightest sound and she returned in a few minutes.

'It's all peaceful,' she announced as she came back into the office. She sat down and took a newspaper from her bag. 'I don't have time to read much in the day. I get more peace at work. Do you want to ask me any more questions? Or can I just read for a bit?'

Was that meant to make me feel guilty, I wondered? 'I'll leave you in peace for a while,' I said. 'I'll go over to Melba and have a chat there.'

'Have a good snoop, you mean.' She spoke in that laughing sort of way people use when they're trying to cover up a bitchy comment.

'That's right. A good snoop.' I smiled weakly, knowing that I'd probably gone too far, then rang the ward to tell them I was coming.

'Kettle's on,' said Claudette. 'Want some toast?'

'Love some.'

I was just unlocking the door when Margaret called out from the office. 'Borrow my cloak if you like, it'll be warmer than your jacket. You'll need a brolly.'

I'd forgotten about the snow. The ward temperature was always about 75@F, always perpetual summer. Margaret came out then, with the cloak and brolly.

'Thanks.'

She flashed me a tight smile. 'Be careful.'

The freshness of the air was quite invigorating at first, but then I began to feel the cold seeping up from my feet to my legs and as I crossed the grass, the snow splashed at my ankles and I began to shiver. The trees and bushes had that white, silent eeriness that falling snow seems to dredge over them, as though snow itself had the power to create silence. A silence that was only broken by the wet splash of my feet on the grass. I held Margaret's cloak tight around me with my free hand and with the umbrella lowered to protect my face I walked on, only looking up occasionally to avoid colliding with the trees.

Linda opened the ward door. 'It's enough to freeze a pawn-broker's balls, isn't it?'

'Brass monkey weather,' I agreed, as I shook my cloak and brolly in the porch.

'Put your cloak on the radiator,' suggested Linda.

I draped the cloak over the radiator and placed the umbrella in the corner and watched for a moment as the water began to run in tiny rivulets on to the floor. For some reason it reminded me of blood; slow, trickling blood . . .

'Don't worry about that,' said Linda. 'It's only a drop.'

In the office Claudette had a tray of tea and toast ready. 'How is it on Harper?' she asked as she poured out the tea. Her hands were the colour of minced beef and when she saw that I'd noticed she tried to hide them.

Linda, perhaps sensing the awkwardness of the moment, began to chat, about the patients, about her 'lazy git' at home, about how she was going to run away before Christmas because she couldn't face another year of her mother-in-law.

'Guess what we have every year for Boxing Day dinner? Go on, guess.'

We tried turkey, pork, beef. In the end we gave up.

'Spam!' she said. 'Bloody spam salad and apple pie. And every year she says the same thing, "Lovely pastry this is. The first slice is the best." Can you believe it? And every year I say never again. And the kids don't stop giggling because they think they're barmy. Which of course they are. This year I'm doing a runner. I'm definitely doing a runner.'

Linda managed to make her moans so funny I was sure that when she was depressed, no one even noticed. Could she be a murderess, I wondered? Do killers have a sense of humour? I was prejudiced enough to believe they did not. Linda was also too well-adjusted to commit murder. Or was that just another prejudice? Is maladjustment necessary for the ultimate act of violence? For premeditated murder I thought it was. And I had no doubt that both Jacky's and Ada's murders had been planned very carefully indeed.

'And holidays, that's another thing,' Linda was saying, but I stopped listening and concentrated on Claudette. She had taken a small fruit knife from her bag, removed its leather cover and was painstakingly peeling an apple. Round and round in a circle moved the knife in one continuous motion. It was clearly important that the peel should remain in one piece. When she'd finished she pushed the circle of red peel to one side of the plate and began to section the apple. She did this as carefully as a surgeon performing micro-surgery. Finally she ate the pieces of apple, nibbling delicately, savouring its taste as though it were the world's finest truffle.

Could a killer be that fastidious, I wondered? Even though Jacky hadn't bled much, there had always been the chance that she might. Even planned murder contains a certain random element; the victim might have chosen a different route, might have turned and fought, someone might have disturbed them. Could Claudette have coped with that . . .

'Kate – more tea?' Linda asked, lifting the pot above my mug. 'You've been away with the fairies.'

'Sorry. I was thinking about murder. I'm a private detective. I'm investigating Jacky's death.' I blurted it out before my better judgment persuaded me otherwise.

Silence then. Linda paused with the teapot still raised, then lowered it slowly to the table. 'But you're a nurse!' she said. 'Do nursing in your spare time, do you?'

'I do both,' I replied.

Claudette swallowed her last piece of apple and stared at me. But not before I had noticed both their startled expressions. Their faces had shown surprise, yes, but also fear and suspicion.

'I'd be very grateful if you could tell me in detail about the night Jacky was murdered.'

'We told the police everything,' said Linda wearily. 'You don't think we did it, do you? No one liked her very much but that doesn't mean we'd stab her in the back, does it?'

'No, of course not. But I think a member of staff did kill Jacky.'

Claudette stood up then. 'I've got to wash my hands,' she said. 'And then I'll check the patients.'

When she'd gone Linda rounded on me angrily. 'She's not bloody Lady Macbeth, you know. She might be fussy but she's had a lot of problems in her life. All that washing she does, just stops her thinking and worrying; it's only like turning to drink, isn't it?'

I agreed that it was. 'Calm down, Linda,' I said. 'I don't

think Claudette is a killer. Germ killer maybe, the scourge of bacteria but nothing more sinister. But I do think you're both lying about what happened that night. I think you are covering up for someone, in all innocence of course. The information I want needn't go any further.'

'Huh! Not till the police start following your tracks. Then it will all come out.'

'What will come out, Linda?' I asked softly.

'The truth,' she answered miserably.

At that moment Claudette returned; she had obviously heard some of the conversation. She looked at Linda briefly and shrugged. 'We'll have to tell in the end, won't we?' she said as she sat down and inspected the hands that she'd just washed. I got the distinct impression she wanted to wash them again but she was resisting the urge.

'Tell me,' I said. 'What happened when you came on duty?'

Linda spoke first, slowly and reluctantly. 'Jacky had turned up early on Harper Ward, before me. She seemed the same as usual. The ward was quiet, we had three empty beds and no one all that ill. But as usual we were late settling everyone down, it was after eleven thirty by the time we turned the lights off— ' she broke off. 'Is this the sort of thing you want to know?'

I nodded. 'You're being really helpful, thanks. Just go back over that night as it happened.'

Linda glanced at Claudette as if to say, 'I'll have to tell the truth,' and Claudette smiled in resignation, and after removing her white paper cap and placing her hair clips in a row she stretched herself back on the office chair.

Linda and I sat upright, wary, and I think we both felt surprised Claudette should have suddenly managed to appear so relaxed.

'Tell me why it was "usual" for you to finish late?' I asked Linda.

She smiled. 'If you'd ever worked with Jacky you'd understand. Luckily we get changed from ward to ward every so often. So we didn't always work together but when we did she faffed around, talking to her favourites. They were the posher patients or the religious ones. Sometimes she'd stop and say a prayer with them. It annoyed me because some of the others were desperate for sleep. Anyway, I remember it was warm early on that night, but by the time we'd finished it was quite cool. The heating wasn't on, so we

130

closed all the windows and doors. Even the French windows in the day room were still open. We had tea in the office, I had some toast but Jacky didn't want anything. We chatted for a bit; well, I talked and she listened, and then, about quarter past twelve, Jacky told me she was going over to Melba for more incontinence pads. We had a few left, but she said she'd rather we were well stocked. She rang you, didn't she, Claudette, to say she was coming over?'

Claudette nodded. 'Yes. She came over. But she didn't stay long, about five minutes. She collected the pads and said on the way back she would see if Dr Duston was in his room. She told me not to bother to ring Linda because she wouldn't be long. So I didn't.'

'How long did you wait before you began to get worried?' I asked Linda.

Linda crossed her legs and looked down at her feet. 'Ages. Some of the patients were calling out and I tidied the ward and started to get things ready for the morning. Then I sat and read for a while. And then . . . '

'And then?'

'Well, I noticed how late it was and I had begun to feel tired and wanted to go to my break, so I rang Claudette to ask if Jacky was still there. When I heard she'd gone to see Robert Duston – I thought . . . '

'What did you think?'

'If you must know, I thought, sanctimonious little cow. He's supposed to be gay but he could be bi, couldn't he? And so I waited a bit longer. She'd been gone for more than two hours. I rang Claudette again and she asked if I could ring Mick O'Dowd so he'd look for Jacky. Margaret was still on her break and you were busy with a patient vomiting everywhere, weren't you?'

Claudette nodded, frowning. 'I feel guilty now I wasn't more worried about Jacky but I was so busy, I suppose I just put the patients first.'

It wasn't hard to imagine that night, Claudette wearing gloves, mopping up after the patient, changing the sheets, the nightie, offering a mouthwash or a drink. Jacky being late would be the last thing on her mind. And of course there would be the washing of hands afterwards.

'There's one thing I really don't understand,' I said. 'Why on earth didn't you just fetch Margaret from her break?'

The awkward silence that followed seemed to fill the small office, made it seem claustrophobic. Linda shifted uneasily on her chair and I sensed both women were trying to keep in their minds, even now, not Jacky, but the minutiae of ward life as if by hanging on to ward routines they could forget that Jacky had gone missing.

'I suppose you'd find out sooner or later,' said Claudette, finally breaking the silence. 'Margaret wasn't on the ward. She pops home in the break to check on her mother. Always has done. We don't get paid for our two-hour break but it's a sort of gentleman's agreement we don't leave the ward for it. If we had a fall or some sort of emergency, like a fire, it wouldn't be fair on the one who was left. Margaret had gone home about twenty to one. When Linda phoned she wasn't back but I knew she wouldn't be long. Just occasionally she was late, when her mother played up. We just pretend she's on the ward, you see. She has a really miserable life and she needs this job, for her sanity as much as the money. But we couldn't tell the police that, could we?'

'And Mick? Did he find the body?'

It was Linda who answered this time. 'Yes. He came running on to the ward. I couldn't believe it. These things happen in the papers, don't they, but you don't expect it in real life. I just left the ward, it wasn't that far and the ward was quiet, so I followed Mick and he ran to fetch Claudette and then Margaret followed up the rear . . . '

'So you were all there?'

'We panicked I suppose,' said Claudette. 'And Mick was in a terrible state saying he didn't want to have to tell the police he'd found the body and Margaret asked us not to say she'd been at home. It was a nightmare. We covered her body with a cloak and rang the police. Before they came we had to get our stories straight. We didn't want to admit Jacky had been missing as long as she had. There was at least an hour and a quarter's difference between the time we said and the time she was actually found. Instead of just after twelve we said she came over to collect the pads at about one fifteen. We couldn't be that accurate, we said, because we were so busy on the ward . . . '

Claudette paused and looked towards the door as if planning to make a run for it but she merely said, 'I'll make some tea,' and left the office. I knew she would take her usual time and I

132

tried to work out the basic flaws in the events of that night. The main one as far as I could see was Dr Robert Duston. Jacky had visited him about twelve twenty-five. The time of death is never very accurate, it was August and her body had been covered for a while. She was young and fit and the weather not cold; an hour and a quarter discrepancy wouldn't be abnormal. But what about the doctor?

'Why did Robert Duston agree to lie for you?' I asked Linda.

She didn't seem surprised by the question. 'We rang him, straight after the police and he agreed to saying it was later when she turned up.'

I was still puzzled 'But why on earth would he deliberately lie? He had nothing to hide.'

Linda smiled at what she must have considered my naïvety. 'I thought you used to live with a copper? You ought to know what some of them can be like. Doc Duston hated the police. He was always having rows with them in casualty. It got round that he was a gay left-winger and I think they gave him a hard time.'

'I see,' I murmured and I remembered how Dave had told me tales of the 'gay baiting' that some of his colleagues engaged in. Somehow I had believed it was a rare occurrence, confined to a few obviously camp victims. I didn't think such things happened to doctors.

The arrival of tea seemed to indicate a change in tactic.

'I'm really grateful that you've confided in me,' I said. 'Only a few more questions about police procedure on the night.'

'Thank God for that,' laughed Linda.

Her pretty face had resumed its cheerful look and her cheeks had once more a pink sheen as if relief had opened up her capillaries and allowed the blood to flow once again. Claudette, on the other hand, still looked pale and anxious. Confession hadn't had such a liberating effect on her and I saw a trace of blood on her hands where she had scrubbed again at the raw patches.

Could she have left the ward, done the deed and returned to the ward to dispose of the knife, I wondered? With Margaret off the premises she could have opened the curtains, watched Jacky leave the main building after seeing Robert, followed her, stabbed her, and been back on the ward within minutes. And then she would have washed and washed. If this was true, there still remained the question of motive. And how could it possibly be proved?

Claudette poured out the tea but she couldn't control her trembling hands and she handed me my mug with two hands as if it were a chalice. She held my gaze with her pale grey eyes glistening with the desire to speak, like an eager child in class with a hand held up and the last one to be asked.

'What is it, Claudette?' I asked softly.

'I want . . . I want to . . . confess.'

Chapter Sixteen

'Confess?'

Claudette sat down, smoothed her blue uniform dress over her thighs and stared at me miserably for a moment. 'I've wanted to talk about Jacky ever since it happened. You see, that night when we found her body . . . I didn't feel anything . . . no real emotion at all. I looked down at her lying there and I thought . . . I thought . . . thank God it wasn't one of us. But she was one of us! But she was apart from us, if you know what I mean.'

I nodded. 'I understand.'

'Do you? I don't think so. She wasn't bitchy or even a gossip . . . she was creepy. She smiled a lot, not a friendly sort of smile, but the sort of smile that said, "I know a secret." But it wasn't just that she felt superior because of her religion, it was as if she could tell your innermost thoughts, knew your weak spots and if she chose she could somehow expose you . . . '

Claudette's voice trailed away and she lowered her head and then in a whisper said, 'I was glad she died. I was glad someone had killed her. I don't know who did it but if I did, I'd know that they had good cause. That makes me as bad as the murderer, doesn't it?'

I moved my chair nearer hers and put my arm round her shoulders. 'Wishing someone dead and putting wishes into action are quite different. It's like fancying the milkman – how many women do anything about it?'

She smiled then. 'I suppose you're right— '

'Of course she's right,' Linda interrupted. 'I've fancied my milkman for years and I've still got no nearer than asking for an extra pint.'

Claudette half smiled and shrugged her shoulders. Emotionally she seemed in that limbo land somewhere between laughter and tears.

But I couldn't leave it there, so I said, 'Talking of fancying people – was it you who was seeing Mick?'

'Do you mean . . . ?' she asked, her thin eyebrows arching in disbelief.

'Yes. Were you having an affair?'

The honest surprise that showed in her face didn't need any explanation to convince me, and after the initial shock she laughed briefly. 'Do we look suited?' she asked. 'He wouldn't say no to anyone, but give me credit for a bit more taste. Did you think that was my big hang-up? Why I didn't like Jacky? You've got it all wrong. I'm living with someone. I have a child, not his, in an institution. My son is blind and deaf and brain-damaged. An infection in utero. I couldn't cope, you see. I try and wash my guilt away. It doesn't work of course. I've been told it could have happened to anyone. Since he was born I suppose I've tried to wage war on germs. I do know what I'm doing is abnormal and doesn't make sense, but it makes me feel better. It's a sort of punishment, isn't it?'

It was a question which I sensed she didn't want me to answer. Some people need their obsessions to survive. I'd seen people 'cured' of one sort of compulsive behaviour only to acquire another. Better, I supposed, to have a withered natural leg that supports you, than the discomfort of a perfect artificial one.

I looked at my watch then; I couldn't expect Margaret to cope on her own any longer. Both Claudette and Linda were on duty the next night and I already had some idea of what the police did at the scene of crimes. What I wanted to know about that night could wait.

'I'll go back to the ward now. Thanks again for your help,' I said.

'Want me to ring Margaret to let her know you're on your way?' Linda asked.

'Okay,' I said. I had planned to speak to Mick O'Dowd but he could always come to the ward when Margaret had gone on her break.

It had stopped snowing, and the dark moodiness of the sky had cleared, like chalk wiped from a child's slate, allowing the stars to shimmer and the quarter moon to shed some light on the dripping branches of the trees. Branches that shed their snow in soft and irregular splashes as though the trees themselves were shaking an unwanted guest from their domain. Underfoot the ground snow seemed harder and crisper and my footsteps sounded loud in the early morning quiet.

I took my time on the walk back. There were two routes Jacky could have taken that night. The shortest and more isolated passed old closed wards and then into the wooded area. The longest was via the covered walkways and out on to open grass and the back of the ward. I could only guess why Harper and Melba Wards had been kept open and the others closed. They were in the best condition. Their roofs were still intact, they weren't damp and they were spacious. As I passed the empty wards their windows stared back at me like sightless eyes and the only reflection in them was mine. Someone cried out, not in sudden and unexpected fear but with the chronically agonised cry of the demented. I started to walk faster; that cry could well be coming from my ward.

Margaret seemed unhurried and in control when I returned.

'It was only Eva shouting for attention,' she said when I asked her who had screamed. It remained peaceful after that and when Margaret went for her break I rang Mick O'Dowd.

'I'll be about three-quarters of an hour,' he said. But he didn't ask what I wanted and I had the feeling from his tone of voice he knew already.

When he did arrive, though, he seemed cheerful enough and he stood in the doorway of the office looking me over and smiling. 'I hear you're a private detective,' he said. 'Wouldn't have believed it. Well, well.'

Something in his tone seemed to suggest he now placed me in the same category as a mud wrestler and with as much sexual innuendo. 'No need to get excited, Mick,' I said. 'Sit down and you can give me the benefit of your life's experiences. Criminal experiences.'

'What's that supposed to mean?'

'Just what it says. I want to know why the police suspected you and why they still suspect you of Jacky's murder.'

His jaw tensed as he clenched his teeth but he took his black jacket off and hung it carefully over the back of a chair. Then, sitting down, he crossed his legs and undid the first three buttons of his blue shirt. I could see the thick gold chain of his medallion, and the black hairs curling into his neckline. Once he'd settled down in the chair his brown eyes flicked tongue-like over my breasts.

'Now then, young Kate, what do you want to know?'

'I want to know what crimes you committed in the past,' I said.

He laughed. 'No need to be so serious,' he said. 'I wasn't in for murder, you know. I'm not the violent type. I stay clear of that sort of thing. I prefer women and fast cars.'

'Come on, Mick. I've got to check the patients soon. What was it? Robbery without violence, kidnapping women drivers?'

'Under-age sex, if you must know, and taking and driving away. Big stuff, eh?'

'Tell me about it.'

'I was twenty,' he began. 'Painting and decorating. I met this girl at a disco. Not very tall but was she stacked! Make-up, tight skirt, low-cut blouse, long blonde hair to her shoulders. She told me she was sixteen; she looked older than that. Anyway we went out for three months until her father saw us together. He laid one on me and next thing the police were round my place saying this girl was only twelve! Twelve! It was funny really, I nearly passed out with shock. They decided not to prosecute when they saw some photos I'd got of her. I only saw her once after that, going to school. She only looked like a well-developed twelve in her uniform. I learnt my lesson, though. I found out I liked older women. Which was just as well.'

'And the taking and driving away?'

'Ah, that! Just a little hobby of mine. Did a spell in the old Borstal system for that. When I got a car of my own I stopped. I haven't been in any trouble since, or I wouldn't have got this job. When the police found out, you'd think they'd found the Moors murderers. They made enough fuss. I thought they were going to dig up my bloody garden. They kept me for hours trying to make me confess. Then they latched on to Kennie, the peeping Tom. Questioned that poor little sod too, over and over.'

'And the nurses?'

'The police were hardly bothered with them. The ex-boyfriend got a grilling but it seems he had a watertight alibi. They even questioned one of the doctors, got no joy there.'

'And by that time the trail was cold,' I said.

Mick nodded and expanded his chest with a good stretch, 'Well,' he said. 'That's all I can tell you.'

'Not quite. If you had stabbed Jacky, just an if, but if you had, where would you have hidden the knife afterwards?'

Mick passed a hand through greased hair and frowned. 'Not sure, probably down a drain. I wouldn't have just tossed it away. The police went all through the grounds with torches; I watched them fan out in a line searching everywhere.'

'What about the mortuary?'

'Locked. Not in use. Undertakers do the job.'

'Rubbish bins?'

He shrugged. 'Dunno. Maybe.'

'You wouldn't have kept the knife on you?'

'No. They might have searched me. I had to turn out my pockets anyway. Well, they didn't force the issue but suggested that it might be in my own best interests. And they searched the porter's lodge. Found nothing of course. I didn't have anything to hide, did I?'

'I don't know, Mick. What about the woman?'

'What woman? I don't know what you're talking about. I haven't got a woman, not here anyway. I know someone down south but not up here— '

'You're protesting too much, Mick,' I interrupted, with what I hoped was a warm but knowing smile. 'It would be strange if you hadn't. You're in your prime, good-looking, probably virile. A man like you surely wouldn't have any problems attracting women.'

Not quite knowing if I was totally sincere, but perhaps hoping I was, he said, 'That's true. There is a woman but I can't tell you who. She's— '

At that moment the telephone rang. Mick saw his chance, picked up his coat and made for the door.

'I'll see you tomorrow night,' I mouthed as I picked up the telephone. He smiled, a tight mean smile, and I knew it masked an obscenity.

Night sister's call was brief, interrupted by one or two shouts from the ward, and when I went to investigate I found one extremely large patient half out of bed and a slim one wedged between the cot side and the bed. I wondered wearily how I would manage, and I'd just started to ease their legs back into bed when bed when the day room door opened and Margaret appeared. She walked slowly towards me, her primrose-yellow dress fresh and uncreased. In the dim light she looked younger and I noticed for the first time the fullness of her breasts and the trimness of her waist. A shape Mick would say was 'well stacked'. I knew at that moment Margaret and Mick shared more than just an initial.

From then on the ward just seemed to erupt. As we got the large patient out of bed on to a commode we heard a thump and guessed someone had fallen. At first I couldn't see the patient at all and I switched on the anglepoise attached to the wall.

'She's under the bed. Silly cow,' called Alice from the next bed.

'Don't worry, Alice,' I said. 'We'll soon have her back to bed.' But I was wrong. I knelt down on the floor and peered under the bed. The old lady lay flat on her back, eyes wide open, her rose-red brushed-nylon nightie at knee length and her left ankle awkwardly rotated. She blinked as though coming to life.

'My leg,' she wailed, 'my leg.'

I didn't hear Margaret approach, just saw her feet in their regulation lace-ups and the shapely ankles above.

'Shall I ring the doctor?' she asked, trying not to smile at my position.

I nodded. 'Tell him, probable fracture left leg and that she's ninety-something with severe osteo-arthritis.'

'Will do,' she said.

I could hear her soft voice on the telephone but not what she was saying. Then her final words resounded. 'Well, thanks,' she said, her voice heavy with sarcasm.

'What's wrong?' I asked, as she knelt beside me on the floor.

'He won't come. Says give her two paracetamols and she'll be seen in the morning. He said if we couldn't get her back to bed we could nurse her on the floor.'

'Oh, well. We'll have to do what we can.'

'How can you take this so calmly? It's a disgrace.'

'I agree, Margaret, but they won't pin and plate her; they may try traction or plaster of Paris but a few hours won't make that much difference. If she'd appeared in casualty she'd have had to wait hours on a hard trolley.'

She shrugged dispiritedly as though she knew I had a point.

'Come on,' I said, trying to encourage her. 'We'll pad her

and splint her as best we can and lift her on the bed. She's not heavy.'

We had no problems doing that, except our patient, Aggie, insisted on trying to hang on to the underneath of the bed and we had to prise her fingers apart and offer her various inducements. Finally, she agreed on a brandy.

Once Aggie was on the bed, given her well-deserved tot, she began to relax and close her eyes.

'Strange isn't it, how the really old don't feel as much pain as a younger person.' Margaret spoke softly as she stood by Aggie's bed, looking down at her.

Margaret's voice held a trace of wistfulness as if she couldn't wait for a time when she too would feel less pain. And as she stood there in the glow of the anglepoise, with her shoulders slumped as if in defeat, and with her dress the colour of sunshine, she reminded me of a daffodil that had wilted early. Full of promise, verging on beauty, but destroyed by – frost? too little sun?

'I'll make some tea,' she said. 'It's nearly morning.'

Back in the office I opened the curtains, and although it was still dark, lighter patches of grey showed in the black, the snow still covered the ground and the birds had started singing. And soon it would be light and the night would be over. It was one of those moments which pass so quickly, you just have time to register the emotion as happiness, and it's gone.

'Look,' I said, pointing to the sky when Margaret came into the office, 'it's nearly dawn.'

'I prefer the night,' she said. 'I've always preferred the night.'

Chapter Seventeen

I had several letters that morning. Hubert handed them to me at the bottom of the stairs. 'One from Australia,' he said. 'Old boyfriend?'

I shook my head. 'My mother.'

He stood watching me expectantly, but I was too tired to explain. My early morning euphoria had vanished as I'd driven along roads made treacherous with snow and ice, and I'd only returned to the office because I couldn't face the even more exposed roads to Farley Wood.

'I'll see you later,' said Hubert. 'Do you want to be woken?'

'Only if Prince Charming is available,' I said, feigning cheerfulness.

Hubert smiled his slightly crooked smile. 'We could go to the pub. I'll buy you lunch.'

'The last time in the pub, Hubert, I practically had to carry you home.'

'Whose fault was that?'

'I blame your wife. Any news on that front?'

He shook his head. 'Have you found the murderer yet?'

I shrugged. 'Sometimes I think I know who, sometimes why, but not both together. Let's just say I'm looking sideways at most people.'

Hubert's eyes shone with interest and although I did want to discuss progress, my concentration was at an all-time low.

'We'll talk later,' I promised. 'My brain is on shutdown at the moment.'

A wash and three chocolate biscuits later I lay on the sofa-bed and read my mother's letter. She had found a job waitressing near Sydney and if I had any spare cash would I please send it. She had met a man, a Crocodile Dundee type, but he was only thirty-five and although she had made a play for his body, he seemed more interested in the outback. 'Men are such a disappointment, Kate,' she had written. 'What's happened to all the randy ones?'

A stranger reading the letter would have thought it written by a worldly-wise teenager, not a fifty-year-old widow who once did meals on wheels. Not that my mother looked fifty, she looked older. Three years of world travel takes its toll, I supposed. And perhaps the photographs lied.

Her letter – marked Letter One – ended mid-sentence. Disappointed and dejected, I snuggled under the covers and tried not to think how much I missed her, how much money I could afford to send, and how much she infuriated me. Why, I wondered, couldn't my mother live up to my expectations? I was drifting off to sleep when I realised I hadn't opened the rest of my mail. It looked like junk mail, so that I could happily ignore it. Probably yet another lucky number win on some car or a credit company offering me one more facility for increasing my debts.

I slept then, dreaming my mother had been bitten by a funnel spider and was being flown home, in a wheelchair, by hot-air balloon. And I would have to look after her for ever.

It seemed only minutes later I woke up worried and apprehensive; the dream still a reality. I peered bleary-eyed at the alarm clock and it took some time for my brain to decode the message from my eyes – it was twelve thirty.

I dressed in peach blouse, long purple skirt, purple cardigan, black beads. I looked like a fortune-teller, but I felt comfortable and the dream had just been a dream and soon I was about to crack my first case. One day perhaps I'd be able to afford to go to Australia to see my mother, and perhaps find my own Crocodile Dundee.

I drank three coffees and stared into space for a while, then I went downstairs to find Hubert. He was just putting on his coat and arranging a red scarf by tucking one end into the front and tossing the other end over his shoulder. He cast himself a glance in the glass of one of the landscapes that lined the main hall, smoothed his remaining hair and then gave me a look as if to check my presentability.

'I don't approve of mirrors in funeral parlours,' he said. 'Our customers don't want to see their grief staring them in the face.'

That was something I'd never thought of. I smiled and took

his arm. 'Let's walk to the Swan,' I said. 'The sun is trying to shine.'

'Not trying very hard, is it?' he said glumly.

The view up the High Street towards the Swan was depressingly empty. Although the sun shone feebly, the wind blew at our faces with icy preciseness. The snow had turned to grey-black sludge and passing cars churned it over until the gutters and the edges of the pavements were banked on either side as though it were a defensive sea wall. The shop windows shone with the lights and shiny red and gold paper of early Christmas decorations but the empty street seemed to mock the effort to be jolly. Occasionally one or two shoppers appeared from shops and scurried away quickly with their collars up and heads bowed to avoid the chill wind. Hubert tried to linger at the shoe shops, but I yanked him past, complaining that I was cold.

As I opened the lounge door of the Swan the beery warmth of the inside hit me. A log fire roared with fierce orange flames in the open fireplace and as we entered, one or two faces I recognised as regulars turned to us and smiled. Here, they seemed to be saying, is sanctuary.

Hubert got the drinks and we sat near the fire, removed our coats and began roasting our cheeks and warming our hands and staring into the flames. Then, when I felt warmer, my hands cupped a rum and blackcurrant, hot on the stomach but sweet in the mouth, and Hubert stayed with his usual ale which I supposed was neither.

'Do you think the female is deadlier than the male, Hubert?' I asked.

Hubert stared into the fire, his face pink and childlike in its glow. He'd probably been an ugly little boy, bullied or shunned because his father was an undertaker. I wondered if, as a teenager, he had lied to girls about his job, dreading the moment they would find out that the hands that caressed them also caressed corpses.

'No,' he said at last. 'Women make better liars. Their brains work quicker because they are shorter. The messages don't have so far to travel. I think it's also something to do with electromagnetic fields.'

'You're joking!'

'I'm not. I believe it. Some very sound research has been done on it.'

'Well, I've never heard . . . that before,' I said, not wanting to upset him.

'There's always exceptions, I suppose,' said Hubert graciously.

'Would homosexuals be an exception?'

Hubert looked a little worried by the question. 'How do you mean?'

'I was wondering if homosexuals had more female attributes than male. The main difference being their physical strength . . . ' I tailed off. Robert Duston was strong physically and he had a caustic tongue. If Jacky had been so much of a nuisance surely he could have dissuaded her from her frequent visits. Perhaps he had – the ultimate dissuader!

'That's because the police are prejudiced,' Hubert was saying in a line of thought I must have missed. 'They expect murder to be a male crime. If she wears a nurse's uniform she must be okay. Suspecting a nurse would be like suspecting one of their own.'

'What about a doctor?'

Hubert shrugged. 'I still think the police are more likely to suspect outsiders.'

I knew Hubert was right but I thought it careless of the police not to suspect everyone. In all the murder films I'd ever seen detectives always kept an open mind until the final reel, and the camera managed to hover suspiciously over everyone from the baby-sitter to the butler. Not so in real life, though.

'How do you think the knife was disposed of?' I asked.

Hubert smiled. 'Perhaps it wasn't. Perhaps the murderer just took it home.'

My mouth opened to argue the point and then closed. He was right. It was so simple. Why does anyone who isn't a suspect have to get rid of a weapon? 'You are a genius, Hubert,' I said, laughing. 'I shall buy you another drink.'

Although he looked pleased, he said, 'The closer you get to this murderer the more likely they are to start plotting your end – let's face it, you are a rank amateur.'

'Thanks, Hubert. You do wonders for my confidence.'

Hubert shrugged. 'I'm only worried about your welfare, Kate.'

'Well, you needn't worry, Hubert,' I said, patting his hand. 'I won't take any unnecessary risks.'

'You never turn your back on anyone then?'

'Well, of course I do but we're not talking homicidal maniac. are we?'

Hubert raised an eyebrow and drained his glass. 'He or she will be getting desperate. You might be the only obstacle in their way. Our killer might feel the need to get rid of you. Kate, I'm telling you to take care. You ought to stop working at the hospital now.'

'Tonight's my last night,' I said, and only realised how ominous that sounded when Hubert sighed, loudly.

By the time I went on duty the snow had mostly disappeared but patches of ice had remained on the roads, malignant and black, waiting to catch the unwary. But tonight I planned to be wary. Hubert's misgivings must have got through to me because when I knew that I was working with Linda I felt a great surge of relief.

We worked well together and by eleven all the patients were asleep and the ward tidy. We sat in the office and Linda put her feet up on a chair and chatted about her family and we laughed about my mad mother chasing men in Sydney.

'Talking of mothers,' said Linda, 'Margaret's mother has had a stroke, quite a bad one. Margaret's off on unpaid leave to look after her. That poor girl doesn't have much luck, does she?'

I agreed that she didn't. 'Do you think she'll ever come back to work?' I asked.

Linda shook her head. 'She might. Mind you, she'll probably have to wait until the old girl dies.'

Linda had brought in eggs and bacon for our evening meal and we both stood in the ward kitchen watching it sizzle in the pan.

'Tell me about Margaret and Mick,' I said.

She flicked over a rasher of bacon before she answered. 'Tell you what?' she said, but there was no surprise in her voice.

'Did you know they were having an affair?'

'We only guessed. Mick was mad about her. But Margaret . . . well . . . you could never be sure.'

'Did Jacky know they were seeing each other?'

'I doubt it. With Jacky we only talked about work or the church. Sex wasn't something Jacky showed any interest in. And if she had found out about Mick she would have made Margaret's life a misery.'

146

Linda served up the egg and bacon and we'd just sat down to eat when a plaintive cry echoed down the ward.

'Typical!' said Linda. 'Bloody typical!'

By the time we came back to our meal the eggs were cold and splashes of fat had congealed on the plate. We looked despairingly at each other and burst out laughing.

Later, over toast that we managed to eat hot, I asked Linda about the police on the night of the murder.

'What do you want to know?' she asked.

'Just tell me what happened.'

'Mick stayed with the body. We went back to our wards and rang the night sister, she rang the managers and they arrived in force, creating havoc. The police cordoned off the area and took photographs and then a bit later they moved into the main building to interview people. One by one they talked to us all. And that's it really.'

'Did they act as if they suspected anyone?'

'Only Mick. To the nurses they said not to worry, to go back to our wards and lock ourselves in. They assured us the boys in blue would soon catch him.'

'And they didn't search anyone?'

'Not that I know of.'

'Thanks, Linda. I'd like to have a word with Mick also if he's on duty.'

'He's on tonight. I saw him as I came in.' She looked up at the office clock. 'He's late coming round. I haven't heard him, have you?'

I shook my head. 'Perhaps he's on Melba.'

'Yeah. Probably talking to Olwen, they always chat for ages.'

'If he's not here soon I'll go over to the porter's lodge to see him on my break.'

At one thirty there was still no sign of Mick so I rang the staff on Melba Ward, but they hadn't seen him either.

'I bet he's asleep,' said Linda. 'I've had to wake him up several times. He does too much overtime. He often works twelve nights in a row. Night porter isn't a popular job. They have to get a day man in to relieve Mick and he hates doing it.'

I borrowed Linda's cloak, unbolted the door and stood for a moment breathing in the night air and watching my breath white against the dark outside.

'I won't be long,' I promised.

My footsteps echoed along the boards of the walkway and from there it was through the archway, past the one bike in the bike shed and under the second archway. Here it reminded me of stabling yards, a section of low wooden huts, sealed and windowless and at the end of the row the porter's lodge, like a cricket pavilion long unused. The white paint had become grey and peeled with age and the six wooden steps leading to the door were warped and cracked and my first step on them sounded, in the silence, like treading on a dry stick in a forest. A light shone inside from behind thin green curtains that didn't quite meet, and the gap cast a shimmery arrow of light on to the ground. The steps remained in darkness. I walked carefully upwards, holding on to the single handrail. It wobbled in response.

At the top I knocked loudly. 'Mick,' I called. 'Wake up.' I called again. No answer. There was no handle or latch on the door, just an empty keyhole. I pushed open the door. The room inside smelt musty; a central light bulb hung naked and moving slightly as the door opened and underneath it were a trestle table and two chairs. A half-empty bottle of milk, a mug, an unopened packet of biscuits and a newspaper lay on the table. In the corner of the room on a mattress covered by a red hospital blanket lay Mick. I could just see the top of his head, his black hair peeking out on to a white pillow. I could hear him snoring. Loud and very slow and deep . . . like a . . . oh, my God!

I moved forward. 'Mick!' I shouted. I heard the footfall on the bare boards behind me but I wasn't quick enough. The crack on my head felled me. I knew I was going to be hit again. But I didn't feel a thing.

Chapter Eighteen

I was awake before I opened my eyes, and just for a moment I wondered if I was hung over. My head felt encased in a vice and my hearing seemed supersensitive. I could hear feet moving over solid floors, hear coughs and whispers, a trolley rattling along, keys jangling. Footsteps approaching, cold fingers forcing my left eye open and shining in a great light and then assaulting my right eye. And it seemed as if someone was trying to invade my head, see my brain. I tried to speak, but all that came out was a feeble 'Don't.'

'Welcome back,' said a young voice from above me. 'Open your eyes – you're in the General Hospital.'

She said it with such pride you'd think I'd somehow acquired the best suite at the Ritz.

'Go away. Leave me alone,' I said ungratefully, my eyes still tight shut.

I heard the slight rustle of her plastic apron and then the sounds of rubber soles moving away and when I felt sure she'd gone, I opened my eyes. My ears had deceived me, I wasn't in an open ward. I was in a single room and by my bed sat a woman in blue – not a nurse, a policewoman. A young woman, pretty, wearing red shiny lipstick and with blonde curly hair that stuck out from under the front of her cap.

'Hello,' she said, smiling. 'How are you feeling?'

'Lousy.'

'Like some tea?'

It seemed like a big decision at the time and I took ages to answer, 'Yes. Thank you.'

When the policewoman returned she brought the same nurse back and together they helped me to sit up and banked me against pillows and I couldn't avoid once more facing the world. A world of beige walls and pale green curtains and counterpanes. I ran my fingers over the embossed leaves of the counterpane; it seemed familiar, and then I remembered – during my nurse training the beds had been covered identically.

The nurse smiled and left.

'Feel like talking?' said the policewoman. 'I'm Angela.'

I didn't, but I'm quite polite, especially to the police, so I attempted to nod. It was a mistake. My head still belonged in the vice and raising my hand I moved it gingerly over my scalp. My hair was still there, although at the back of my head I felt a prickly shaved patch and round the edges the matted, unmistakable feel of dried blood. I felt the patch again; the prickly bits were sutures, seven in all. I wondered if I'd bled dramatically.

'Tell me what happened,' said WPC Angela.

I told her about finding Mick on the mattress snoring. And then realising he wasn't snoring but dying.

'A bit like the poem,' she said.

I didn't catch on but I smiled as if I had. 'And then I heard something behind me and, wallop, I was downed but not quite out.' I began to shiver then, at the memory of waiting for the second blow, knowing it would come but not knowing if it would be the last thing I ever felt.

'You didn't see who it was, then?' she persisted.

'No,' I repeated. 'I did not.'

She wrote that down and I asked, 'How's Mick? Did you get to him in time?'

Shaking her head she said, 'He was rushed here, and the doctors tried very hard, but it was too late.'

'What had happened?'

'An overdose of insulin. He was a diabetic.'

'A diabetic?' I echoed stupidly.

'Yes. Since childhood, it seems. The doctor said something about him being a very unstable diabetic and even though the dose was large if he'd eaten plenty of glucose he could have survived. It seems as if he wanted to die.'

'Rubbish!' I blurted out. 'Why on earth would he want to kill himself?'

'Miss Kinsella, please don't upset yourself. It does seem, though, that he did kill himself. His fingerprints were the only ones found on the syringe and the bottle of insulin. And the

CID have got no reason, at the moment, to think anyone else was involved.'

'What about the crack on the head? My two cracks on the head. Or have I imagined that?'

Angela's red mouth broke into a smile that was no doubt meant to be soothing. Then, to make matters worse, she patted my hand as if I was an old lady in need of reassurance. 'I'm sorry to have upset you. Try to get some sleep. I'll leave you in peace for a while and perhaps when you wake up you'll remember some more about what happened.'

She carried a chair outside and closed the door behind her. I lay back on the pillows feeling defeated and suddenly very alone. A mad killer was managing to bump people off, as easily as a ball knocking down skittles, and was getting away with it. I appeared to be the only failure. But what if I developed complications, a sub-arachnoid haemorrhage, a severe infection, a clot on the brain? I'd be on one of Hubert's slabs, tucked away in his freezer with a certificate stating that death, by person or persons unknown, was due to complications following a head injury. And I'd never manage to grow tomatoes – ever. And why hadn't Hubert come to see me? Tears of self-pity began to well in my eyes. Private detectives don't cry, I told myself, but they do, and I did.

I felt better when I woke up. The vice around my head had been replaced by a band and another nurse brought me in a plate of sandwiches and more tea.

'You've got a visitor,' she said.

'Could I eat first?' I asked, feeling like a real pig, but I was unused to the sensation of being hungry. I always eat before the pangs begin.

'I'll send him in in about fifteen minutes,' she said.

Five minutes would have been enough, they were very small sandwiches, and once I'd eaten them, I watched the clock until the time was up and the door opened. But it wasn't Hubert, and I felt childish disappointment well inside me. It was Dr Hiding.

As he strode towards me I fluttered my eyelids as I believed this would make me look sweetly vulnerable. It didn't work.

'My dear,' he said as he took my hand, 'you're looking remarkably well. I expected you to be at the very gates. I'm so glad you are on the mend.'

I smiled weakly, trying to suggest I was being brave and grateful.

Dr Hiding sat down and adjusted the crease in his cavalry twill trousers and pulled down his toning brown cardigan. I gazed past him to the door, desperately hoping Hubert would come in to rescue me. Dr Hiding still held my hand and I tried hard not to squirm.

'I had hoped to come yesterday but you were still semi-conscious. I prayed for you very intensely, Miss Kinsella. And my prayers were answered. Here you are, fully restored.'

'Praise be,' I muttered.

'Amen to that.'

He let go of my hand then and his face assumed the look of a headmaster about to deliver a beginning-of-term pep talk. 'I do hope that this has been a lesson to you. You should be leaving this investigation to the police. The fact is, I don't think you're quite cut out to be a private detective. I'm sure you'd be much happier if you simply found a permanent job nursing.'

'Dr Hiding,' I said, trying to keep icy cool, 'thank you for your concern, but I happen to think I've been making headway in this case . . . ' I paused, trying not to laugh. 'Well, perhaps "headway" is the wrong word but I am making progress and I'm confident my future lies not in nursing but with medical and nursing investigations. I may not be Sherlock Holmes but— '

'Quite. Quite. Please don't upset yourself,' interrupted Hiding. 'I do understand. I'm sure God will help you if needs be. He works in mysterious ways and I'm sure if you are righting wrongs, prayer will be the only inspiration you need. Now be a good girl and get some rest and you'll be out of here in no time.'

As he left I cursed him under my breath in a variety of expletives. 'Good girl' indeed!

I'd barely had time to recover from his visit when Linda rushed in, bearing a bottle of wine and a sad-looking spider plant. 'Sorry I haven't got any flowers,' she said. 'No time. Anyway this will perk up with a drop of water.'

She slipped off her coat and laid it on the bed. She wore a pink mini-skirt with a tight, tucked-in matching shirt and several gold chains. She looked cheerfully tarty and after Dr Hiding she was as welcome as sunshine after rain. Linda covered the usual patient/visitor questions; my state of health, the food, the nurses, were the doctors dishy?

I asked her if she had found me in the porter's lodge.

'I couldn't really miss you,' she said. 'You were sprawled all over the floor and the blood! It was flowing in rivers. I did the right thing, though, got you into the recovery position and applied pressure to your head. Mind you, it was bleeding so much I couldn't see where it was coming from. But I did my best.'

'You saved my life, Linda. There aren't any words that can quite cover the thanks I owe you.'

Linda shrugged and laughed in nervous embarrassment. 'I didn't help poor Mick much, did I? He was on his last legs when I got there. I knew there wasn't anything I could do.'

'Did you know he was a diabetic?'

Linda shook her head. 'He never let on. Never seemed fussy about his food either. You'd think he'd have taken a bit more care with his dose, wouldn't you?'

'I think someone gave him that injection. Someone he trusted.'

'You can't mean? Not Margaret . . . I don't believe it. She wouldn't . . . would she?'

'I think she might, Linda, or Dr Duston. Mick would have trusted a nurse or a doctor.'

Linda frowned but she didn't seem particularly surprised. 'You're just guessing, though. What about evidence?'

'Good point. I haven't got any real evidence, it's all circumstantial. I'll have to rely on a confession.'

Laughing, Linda patted the bed with her hand and then tried to inspect the counterpane as if that would stop her laughing.

'Why are you laughing, Linda?' I asked.

She stopped after a moment and composed her face into a thoughtful expression. 'I can imagine Robert Duston in a jealous rage but . . . over Mick?'

'You were the one who said Dr Duston could be bisexual – perhaps it wasn't him but Mick who was bi?'

'But he seems – seemed, so macho,' said Linda, bewildered.

'So does Robert Duston. Appearances can be deceptive. Perhaps Jacky was blackmailing one or both of them.'

'And do the police suspect him? Couldn't you just tell them your suspicions and let them get him to confess?'

'I could,' I said. 'But I'm not going to. I've done a lot of work on this case; why should they get the credit? Anyway, they seem to think if there isn't a knife sticking out between the shoulder-blades or a bullet lodged in the brain, it can't be murder.'

Linda put her head on one side and gave me a long warning glance. 'You just be careful. The murderer might be panicking now. He could be planning his next one.'

I nodded. 'I'll take care. I don't want to be snuffed out on my first case, do I?'

As she left Linda handed me her phone number. 'Give me a ring,' she said. 'We could go out on the razzle sometime.'

'Thanks for coming, and thanks for the first aid.'

'No need. It was the most exciting moment I've had since my cat fell down an uncovered drain. See you.'

And she was gone. Night was falling and Hubert still hadn't visited and I didn't want to sleep; I hoped a police person would stay all night, just in case Robert Duston decided to visit me and finish me off by tinkering with my treatment or just bashing me again.

At just after ten, another policewoman arrived, chatted for a while and then sat outside the door. I found that very reassuring; it appeared the police were taking the threat to my life seriously. But as Mick and Kennie, their prime suspects, were dead, I wondered who they suspected now. If he was a strong suspect, I didn't want to be wasting valuable investigating time in hospital and find when I came out it was all over. Could I do a runner? Tomorrow, I resolved, if I wasn't discharged I would take my own discharge. It was simply a question of signing a form.

Two nurses came to give me a hot drink and settle me down for the night and just as they had finished, a young houseman turned up. Thin and tall with the sallowness of someone who rarely sees the sun, he said, 'Glad to see you're awake. No fractures, just cuts and contusions. Your head will be sore for a while.'

'When may I go home?' I asked.

'Probably tomorrow after the Big Chief – Mr Hadley-Royes – does his round. Usually about twelve.'

'Midday?' I asked, smiling.

'Yes,' he said solemnly. A sense of humour wasn't his strong point but I supposed working a hundred hours a week would knock the smile off anyone's face.

'About Mick O'Dowd?' I ventured as he was about to leave.

'What about him?'

'Did you know him?'

He shook his head. 'Hardly likely, I'm the surgical houseman.' I felt stupid not realising that. 'Sorry,' I mumbled.

'It's okay,' he said and left.

I tried to sleep then but I kept watching the door, still half expecting Hubert. Did he even know I was in hospital? Did Robert Duston know I was still alive? More to the point, I thought, does anybody even care?

I padded in bare feet to the door and opened it to check the policewoman was still there. The chair outside the door was in place. The policewoman wasn't. The corridor was empty.

Chapter Nineteen

I stood in the silent corridor moving from one foot to another in an agony of indecision. Should I go back to bed or search out a nurse? And where the hell was the policewoman? I had two choices, of course: go back to bed and try to sleep, or find a nurse and ask what had become of the policewoman. At that moment, in the distance, I caught a glimpse of a white coat disappearing into one of the rooms leading from the corridor. Just a flash of white, but it registered high on my fear score: spiders rated nine out of ten, homicidal doctors a mere eight. I'd just decided to make a cowardly return to my room when the policewoman appeared. She walked towards me, tall and elegant with an eye-catching way of swinging her hips. She would have looked at home on any catwalk.

'I thought you'd gone,' I said feebly.

'I went to the loo. Policewomen have to occasionally. Did you want something?'

'No. Thanks,' I said, feeling like some scruffy mongrel caught sniffing in the wrong place. 'I'll try to get some sleep now.'

I left the door of my room open, got into bed and tried to sleep. But it wasn't easy. The corridor that had seemed deserted minutes before suddenly became a thoroughfare, with nurses passing my door as if they were managing a full-scale evacuation. I'd never been a patient before and the amount of noise came as a surprise. The scraping of beds being moved, the dull thud of rubber-soled shoes, the swish of plastic aprons, the insistent call bells, the running taps and flushing water. There was no way I could sleep. I put on the bedside light and then remembered I had nothing to read. I stared at the spider plant, for something to do; it was still drooping, its leaves, brown at the tips, spilling out like entrails on to the bedside locker. Plants and flowers are all very well but you can't read them.

The policewoman came in to investigate why my light was on. 'You feeling okay?'

'Fine. I can't sleep, though. I've got nothing to read.'

Her expression seemed to say 'that's the least of your worries,' but she offered pleasantly enough to fetch one of the nurses.

I felt strangely guilty then. I'd quickly acquired the 'I don't want to be a nuisance' patient mentality and when a student nurse did arrive I made an effort to strike the right note of humble gratefulness.

'No problem,' she said. 'We've got a big stack of mags in the day room.'

When she came back she had her cloak over one arm, the magazines on top and in her other hand she had a packet of sandwiches and a banana.

'I'm off to my break,' she said, handing me the magazines. Then she put the food under her arm and threw the cloak around her shoulders, pulling it tight.

'You could do with a pocket in your cloak,' I said.

'Don't read too long,' she warned me with a smile.

I tried to concentrate on some of the triumph over tragedy articles or 'Mustn't Grumbles' as I called them. Titles like 'My baby was no bigger than a bag of sugar', 'I gave my kidney to my best friend' and 'I lost half my brain but can still enjoy life'. What would a murderer have written, I wondered?

Eventually I began to drift off but instead of counting sheep I went over the details of murder. Choosing the method, the timing, the weapon, disposal of the evidence, the alibi, feigning surprise, mixing truth with lies to be extra convincing. Duston's article could well have been 'I murdered for ???' I had no answer yet, but with pre-sleep optimism I had no doubts that by the morning all would be revealed.

Morning comes early in hospital. It was still dark when a thermometer was thrust under my tongue, my wrist held for seconds and a cup of anaemic tea thrust in my hand.

'Oh, by the way,' said a weary-looking student nurse I'd never seen before, 'a Mr Humberstone rang yesterday evening. 'We've just found a message from the day staff. He'll be visiting this morning. He wished you well.'

By seven thirty I had bathed and, without bothering to ask, washed my hair. The first rinse was the colour of iron filings but gradually the water ran clear. I wandered around for a while, wearing a towel turban, until a nurse found the ward's ancient hair-drier and I managed to dry my hair properly. I'd had my make-up with me the night of the attack so I made myself up. Once I had a face on, I felt quite glamorous, although the effect was spoilt by the thousand-times-washed, once blue hospital nightie that hung voluminously on my body like some discarded parachute. My uniform and duty shoes and underwear had been removed, probably because they were covered in blood.

And then I waited and waited. Between breakfast and lunch, time seemed suspended. An announcement could have been made about it: THE TIME NOW STANDING AT THE GENERAL WILL STAND UNTIL FURTHER NOTICE.

Lunch was fried fish with soggy, tasteless chips and tinned peas. Even so, eating was something to do. I was debating with myself whether to finish the chips or not when Mr Hadley-Royes arrived. He was not alone, of course; several people crowded into my room and stood with expectant deference by his side. Being in such a crowd made it less likely that Mr Hadley-Royes would ever experience rudeness or ingratitude. There was definitely safety in numbers.

Dapper and thin, he wore those half-glasses that I think always manage to look more like an accessory. He made a promising start. 'Ah,' he said. And then there was a pause while the ward sister, who had so far managed to avoid me completely, handed him my notes.

'Ah, yes. Miss Kinsella. Head injury.'

I nodded.

'Feeling dizzy? Sick? Headache? Double vision?'

I shook my head.

'Good, good.' Turning to Sister he said, 'Any temperature? Loss of memory?'

She decided I hadn't.

'Fine, fine,' he said. 'Home today then. Come back to have the sutures removed. Nice to have met you, Miss Kinsella.' He nodded at me, and as if on cue the entourage followed the turn of his heel.

It seemed I'd been pronounced well, discharged, and I hadn't been examined nor had I managed to say a single word.

I turned to my dessert then, congealed custard covering some sort of sponge pudding. No one is that hungry, I thought, well, no one who is already a size fourteen. I paced up and down for a while, then watched from the window, not that I could see much, mostly just a brick wall and a huge chimney that sent grey smoke into watery sunshine. It could have been either the crematorium or the laundry. Then I lay back on the bed and watched the door for Hubert.

He came just after two o'clock. He walked in clutching two plastic carrier bags and smiling.

'I thought you weren't coming,' I said, feeling like a whingy child.

'You look better.'

'Better than what?'

'Better than when you came in. I thought you were a gonner.'

'You were here before?'

'Of course.'

That surprised me but I didn't want to hang round chatting so I said, 'Have you brought my clothes?'

'A nice selection,' said Hubert.

I wondered vaguely how long he had spent over choosing my shoes.

'I'll wait in the corridor,' he said.

He'd forgotten to pack a bra and tights but he'd remembered everything else, including a pair of stockings, which were no use at all without the suspender belt, and the only pair of high heels I had at the office. It felt strange being dressed again; the shoes felt like stilts and pinched without tights. The dress he had selected was one I save for that special occasion which rarely comes. The only reason it was in the office was that it had been dry-cleaned. In shades of creased purple, black and gold, sans bra, I looked like someone who had been to a party and had to leave in a hurry.

I emerged from the room with my black jacket over my shoulders, trying to appear nonchalant.

Hubert stood outside in the corridor. 'You look nice,' he said, glancing at me from the shoes upwards.

'Wonderful,' I snapped tersely.

Outside in the car park more embarrassment lurked, in the form of a smart shiny black hearse.

'Had to bring the Daimler, my car's being serviced,' explained Hubert. 'It's a lovely smooth ride.'

I didn't say a word. The fresh air had made me feel dizzy and my brain had turned to foam. I held my chin in cupped hands and stayed silent. If I talked I was sure my head would fall off. I hoped it was only a passing phase.

The cottage looked different. The living-room seemed smaller and the colours brighter. I sank down on the sofa and Hubert kept muttering that I didn't look as well as I had done in hospital.

'I'll be fine,' I said. 'It's just that fresh air came as a shock.'

He didn't seem convinced but he made tea and after a while my head began to feel more normal.

'You get some sleep and I'll stay here for a while,' suggested Hubert.

I was about to protest, when I realised that I didn't want to be alone. Someone might come calling.

'I'd prefer you to stay,' I said to Hubert, who stood awkwardly in front of me like a man whose wife has just brought their baby home and is waiting for instructions.

I didn't have any instructions and there was a long pause before Hubert said, 'Some reflexology would fix you up a treat.'

'Do you really think so?'

He nodded eagerly and I didn't feel up to arguing, and I didn't have to bother to take tights off, so it couldn't do me any harm, could it?

Hubert took the process very seriously, raising my feet on to a cushion covered with a towel and then sitting at the end of the sofa and beginning to massage my feet with heavy concentration. He was right, it was a treat. It was more than that, it was heaven.

'How was it?' he said when he'd finished. He looked very pleased with himself.

'How was it for you?' I asked, but he didn't seem to understand and I felt ashamed at teasing him. So I said, 'That was great, Hubert. You could make your living at that. You've got a real flair for it.'

He smiled self-consciously. 'You'll feel really tired now, and sleep like a top.'

160

He was right. I felt exhausted and when he went off to wash up, I curled up on the sofa and slept.

When I woke up I'd been covered with my duvet and there was a pillow under my head. Hubert was closing my red velvet curtains against the blackest of skies. It was six p.m.

'I'll make some toast,' he said.

He came back in a few minutes with a tray of tea and toast. 'You don't keep very well stocked, do you?' he complained. 'What do you live on?'

'Rubbish mostly. Anything that can be put on toast or eaten from the packet.'

We ate in silence for a while. I suddenly felt awkward that Hubert was having to hang around playing nursemaid to someone who had only had a bit of concussion. 'I'll be fine on my own now, thanks. I felt a bit jittery earlier on, but I'm over it now.'

Hubert looked up at me, his brown eyes bright, and frowned. 'Who did it?' he said. 'I'd like to break a neck or two.'

I laughed in surprise at Hubert's intenseness. 'He's only got one neck. But I've got ideas and I'm sure I can get him to confess.'

'I don't want you trying any more stupid stunts on your own.'

'Does that mean you'll come with me?'

Hubert's eyebrows raised in surprise. 'Where?'

'I'll explain tomorrow.'

'You're getting to be a worry to me,' said Hubert wearily.

'Now, now, Hubert, you're beginning to sound like an anxious father.'

'Not bloody surprising, is it?'

'It was only a minor head injury,' I said. 'I wasn't on life-support.'

'Very nearly. You were semi-conscious for twenty-four hours.'

That still surprised me. It was only one day in my life but its loss had managed to disorientate me.

For a while we watched television, and although it flickered in the corner I couldn't concentrate and neither could Hubert. He fell asleep, snoring, and I watched him guiltily. He looked thinner in the face and paler. He slept until ten and when he started to stir I suggested he should go home to bed. He didn't argue.

'You just make sure you lock all the doors and windows,' he said. 'And at the slightest sound, phone the police.'

'If I hear so much as a creaking floorboard,' I assured him.

'There's no need to be flippant.'

'Sorry, Hubert,' I said and kissed his cheek. 'Thanks for everything.'

His pallor lifted a shade then and he moved his shoulders in an embarrassed shrug and grimaced slightly. 'See you tomorrow,' he mumbled as I closed the front door.

I decided to sleep on the sofa that night. Downstairs was more cosy and I could watch television until I slept. With Hubert's reassuring snoring gone the house seemed quiet. I turned up the television and lay on the sofa.

It was a buzzing sound that woke me up. The BBC had finished for the night. Getting up, I switched off the set and removed the plug and then in the silence I could hear it. A soft, shuffling noise, a bird or an animal, or . . . or shoes on gravel. There was someone outside.

Chapter Twenty

The silence that followed frightened me more than the footsteps. I stood still in the middle of the room, my breathing fast and shallow, my throat dry. Don't panic, I said to myself, but I wasn't anyway, I was moving and thinking in slow motion, telling myself what to do. Go to the window, I told myself. I moved to the window, pulling the red velvet aside in a minute crack. I could see the front gate and the shaft of upward light of the spotlight outside the church. And the two trees with bare gnarled branches reaching wide, like giant claws.

I replaced the curtain and listened again. Could I have imagined the footsteps? Now there was no sound. Then suddenly in the silence, loud rapping on the front door. I couldn't see who stood on the porch from the front window and even if I went to the front door I had no spyhole.

I rang the police.

'There's a murderer on my doorstep,' I blurted out. 'He's here, please come quickly.'

'Calm down, Miss . . . ?'

'Kinsella.'

'Now, Miss Kinsella. What's the address?'

I gave him the address.

'You stay put, miss, and we'll be there as soon as we can.'

Stay put! I thought, what else could I do and what did 'as soon as we can' mean?

The rapping became more insistent. I walked out into the hall.

'Go away,' I yelled. 'The police are on their way.'

'I am the police,' came the deeply masculine reply. 'It's Constable Spratton from Great Yearby. Open the door, madam.'

Even then I wanted to be sure. Anyone could say they were a policeman. I got down on my hands and knees and lifted my ridiculously low letter-box. Huge, black shoes that shone to perfection and above them a glimpse of black socks were, I thought, identification enough.

'You're nervous,' said Constable Spratton, as I opened the door. He must have heard me lift the letter-box.

'Just eccentric,' I said, smiling weakly. Even with his helmet on he was handsome. Broad-shouldered but with lean hips, he looked athletic and in my rush of relief, even intrepid.

'May I come in?'

I showed him through to the sitting-room and asked him to sit down. He sat in the spare armchair, his long legs taking up much of the floor space and as he removed his helmet, although he lost inches, he gained in charm. With his helmet off, and by the light of the lamp, I could see his eyes properly: deep blue eyes and the ability to stare without seeming rude. I was disconcerted by his eyes and the fact that for a while he didn't say a single word. It was as if he'd taken a course in counselling that recommended staying silent and letting the client wade into their tale of woe. So I started. I'd just launched into what would have been a detailed description of events when I noticed him smiling.

'Was it you creeping round the house?' I asked.

'Not creeping,' he said. 'That's difficult in size twelves. I made as much noise as possible. I was asked to keep an eye on your house— '

'I called the police a few moments ago,' I interrupted. 'They won't be pleased to come out on a false alarm.'

'I'll give the station a call on my two-way, and explain the situation.'

I mouthed 'Tea?' as he began speaking into his radio. He nodded. As I came back from the kitchen I heard him mumbling about me. It seems I was a neurotic spinster. I wouldn't have bothered with my best china mugs if I'd known.

I stayed silent then, and after a few sips of his tea, he said, 'I don't approve of women private detectives.'

'Have you known any?'

He shook his head, his close-cropped dark hair moving slightly like burnt stubble in a high wind. I was rapidly finding him less attractive.

'A dangerous occupation,' he continued. 'You seem a bit too nervous for any rough stuff.'

'It's brain more than brawn you need,' I answered defensively. 'I do medical investigations. There shouldn't be too much rough stuff attached. Anyway, I'm tougher than I look.'

He smiled patronisingly and I felt my face grow hot with embarrassment.

'Thanks for coming,' I said. 'I'm fine now. The crack on my head must have made me a bit wary of receiving another one.'

'I'll stay for a bit,' he said. 'You can tell me who you think is trying to murder you.'

I gave him a baleful stare. Now I no longer found him attractive I didn't want him to stay, but he lounged in the armchair as if sitting there was a whole lot better than hanging about on my front doorstep.

'I prefer not to discuss my cases with the police. I'd be quite happy, though, if we talked about something else,' I said. 'And anyway, I've been having terrible bouts of nausea. You know the type of thing – great heaving waves – I can't control it at all. Talking murder would just make it worse.'

He grimaced, passed his hand through his hair, realised his helmet wasn't on, and, snatching it from the table, was on his feet and walking towards the door in seconds. 'I'm okay with haemorrhage, fire or flood but I can't cope with . . . illness,' he said, opening the door. 'I'll check the house again later.'

I stood at the front gate as he walked the few yards up the road to his bike propped against a wall. I was smiling. I'd got my own back. I watched his rear light disappear into the darkness and I stood for a few moments, pleased with myself, until I realised I was still wearing my best dress and little bits of toast had stuck to it.

I slept badly after that; the sutures pricked like slivers of glass and by seven I'd bathed, had breakfast, and decided to get to the office early. I was just leaving when the phone rang. It was Hubert.

'Thought I'd better let you know, Kate, CID want to interview you today.'

'When did you find out about this?' I asked.

'When you were in hospital,' said Hubert. 'They questioned me for quite a long time.'

'What about?'

'Your sanity.'

'My sanity!'

'They seem to think you could be a nutter.'

'I banged myself over the head, is that it? Why didn't you tell me they wanted to see me before?'

'Didn't want to cause a relapse, did I?'

'I'm coming into the office now.'

Hubert cleared his throat. 'Are you well enough?'

'No. I'm nuts.'

'Don't upset them. They seem a bit edgy.'

'I shall play it by ear, Hubert. Just because the police here are so incompetent they couldn't catch measles, doesn't mean I've got to act like a dumb blonde.'

'Redhead,' corrected Hubert.

'It's dyed.'

'It looks natural,' he said, obviously disappointed.

'Bye. See you at the office.'

At ten a.m. the CID arrived, ushered in by Hubert, who gave me a warning glance as he was about to leave the office. In return I gave him a quick salute, which didn't go unnoticed by Inspector Hook. The expression on his face seemed grim, slightly antagonistic. Detective Sergeant Roade, still spotty, managed a half-smile.

'You two friends, are you?' he asked, tossing his head at Hubert's receding back.

I was about to say no, he's my landlord, but Hubert was a friend and a good one. 'We're friends,' I said firmly.

'Have you got many friends, Miss Kinsella?' He seemed to infer I didn't deserve any.

'No, not many. I've only recently moved here.'

'From London?'

'Yes.'

'Ever been in trouble with the police?'

I paused, watching his eyes flicker with interest. 'Yes,' I said, 'I have. Why don't you both sit down.'

Hook sat on the corner of the desk; he was much too shrewd to sit in the armchair.

'Ever been in trouble with the police?' he repeated as though I hadn't quite understood the question.

'Yes,' I said again.

166

'Crime?' he asked eagerly. His expression of mere surprise had changed to one of excitement, his greenish eyes glistening like sun shining on dewy grass.

I didn't answer immediately.

'Crime?' he persisted.

'Living with a drunken copper. I got three years solitary. He was always in the pub.'

'Very funny. We are trying to establish . . . '

'My sanity.'

DS Roade sniggered. He stood by the door, his elbow propped against the wall in a pose he probably thought was worldly-wise. He wore a smart pale grey pinstripe but it gave the impression that it was his first ever suit, like a young footballer just into the first division, who thinks he should make it obvious that he's a success. Inspector Hook, in contrast, wore a well-worn, light brown number with shiny patches on the lapels and the air of a man who was long past worrying about the impression he made.

'We have to be careful about private detectives in these parts,' he was saying. 'We're not used to them. And as I've just been trying to say, we do want to establish that we're not overlapping in this investigation.'

'I thought you were trying to find out who attacked me?'

'Of course, we've already spoken to most of the staff at St Dymphna's,' he blustered. 'And we've got a good idea who did it. You mustn't underestimate us, Miss Kinsella – we do use modern police methods.'

'Of course.'

He frowned, seeming to indicate he'd noticed the insincerity in my voice.

'Right, Miss Kinsella,' he said, 'let's start to take things seriously, shall we?'

He was rattled now, I could tell, so I suggested coffee. Only Roade accepted. While I waited for the kettle to boil Hook drummed his fingers on the desk and I couldn't think of a thing to say.

Once the coffee was made and poured, Hook sighed loudly. 'Perhaps now we could move this interview along,' he said. 'What exactly happened the night you were attacked? I want to know times, reasons – the lot.'

The moment he asked the question my mind went blank.

'I . . . ' I paused and swallowed. 'Inspector,' I said. 'I can't remember.'

He pursed his lips, in annoyance or disbelief; I couldn't be sure which.

'I'll try to refresh your memory,' he said caustically. 'You were found unconscious in the porter's lodge. Why were you there in the first place?'

'I wanted to talk to Mick O'Dowd.'

'Why?'

'That's personal.'

'So was the crack on your head. You could have died. Now come on, Miss Kinsella, let's go back over events, shall we?'

Yes, let's go back over events, shall we? And that gave me my first good idea in ages. A reconstruction. I could do my own reconstruction. In the grounds at night. If I could solve Jacky's death, then the other deaths would . . .

'Miss Kinsella!'

'Call me Kate.'

Hook grimaced, 'Kate, then. We're waiting. And I warn you now, I'll do you for wasting police time.'

He forced me to lie. I told him I was visiting Mick because I suspected him of killing Jacky.

'Foolhardy, weren't you? You suspect him of murder and yet you go to see him on your own in the middle of the night.'

'Put like that it does seem a bit chancy, but I felt I could handle it if I was diplomatic enough. Anyway, Mick wasn't a danger to me, was he?'

'You quite sure about that?' asked Hook, raising one quizzical eyebrow.

'What's that supposed to mean?'

'I mean, are you so sure that it wasn't Mick himself who hit you?'

Was the man mad? 'How could he? He was lying down, as near to death as anyone can be.'

'You're sure of that? With your memory being so impaired.'

'Only a momentary loss, I can assure you. I wasn't brain-damaged by the blow.'

'I'm sure you weren't,' said Hook with a hint of a smile. 'Now just tell me what happened from the moment you left the ward.'

I thought back, trying to remember the details, the minute

details. 'I left the ward,' I began, 'just after one thirty. It was icy cold so I borrowed Linda's cloak and I went straight over to the porter's lodge— '

'What was the ground like?'

'Wet, but the snow had gone. There was a light on in the lodge and a crack in the curtains. I knocked and called out, but of course there was no response.'

'So you made plenty of noise.'

I shrugged. 'Yes,' I agreed. 'The stairs creaked on my way up.'

'And then what happened?'

'I opened the door— '

'How did you open the door?' asked Hook.

'I just pushed it open and walked in. Mick was lying on a mattress on the floor in a corner of the room. I thought at first he was asleep but then I realised he was Cheyne-Stoking— '

'He was what?'

'Cheyne-Stokes, it's a type of breathing. It's a sure sign that someone is dying. It's like loud snoring but the pauses are extra long; so long that each one seems to be the last. At first I didn't recognise it but as soon as I did I moved forward and then, wallop!'

'You didn't hear any footsteps?'

'Not exactly. In the split second I did hear a noise I didn't have time to turn.'

'What about the door?'

'The door?' I echoed.

'Yes, the door! Did you close it or leave it open?'

I tried to think back. I pushed the door, noticed the table and the blood-red blanket, heard the groaning snores, walked across three paces . . .

'No,' I said, remembering, 'I didn't close the door.'

'So he could have been waiting for you,' said Hook triumphantly.

'He?' I was finding Hook's line of questioning rather baffling.

'Your attacker.'

'But why should it have been a he?' I said and even as I spoke the words I knew I should have followed my instinct all along. My attacker was female. A male would have finished me off.

169

Hook shrugged and shifted uncomfortably on the corner of my desk.

'You should try the chair,' I said, but ignoring me he stood up for a moment to ease himself and then sat down again. I was longing to ask who he had in mind but I controlled myself. I didn't think Inspector Hook was too impressed by my answers so far.

'It seems, then,' he said slowly, 'that your attacker was waiting for you.'

'That's ridiculous. Only Linda knew I was going to see Mick that night.'

'She had a phone call after you left the ward. She told someone where you were. Didn't she tell you that?'

I shook my head. I was surprised but I didn't want to show it. 'Who was it who rang?' I asked, trying to sound casually unconcerned.

'That's confidential. I'm sorry.'

He wasn't sorry, of course, he was pleased to have a secret.

Hook smoothed down his green striped tie with one hand and gave me a glance that suggested mere private detectives couldn't match the sheer expertise of the police no matter how hard they tried.

'Who do you think attacked you, Kate?'

'I was about to ask you the same question.'

'Let's just say we have someone under surveillance,' he said.

'And you're not going to tell me who?'

'We think it better that you don't know at this stage. We don't want our investigation hampered by . . . '

'An amateur?' I suggested helpfully.

'A well-meaning amateur, I was about to say.'

He stood up then. 'Come on, Roade,' he said, gesturing with his head. Roade straightened himself up ready to leave.

'Just one thing before you go,' I said. 'What about Mick's girlfriend?'

'You mean Margaret Tonbridge?'

I nodded.

'What about her?'

'She couldn't be a suspect?'

Both Hook and Roade smiled in unison, patronising unison. 'No problems there. Very fond of each other by all accounts.

Mick had been a bit depressed lately. Perhaps he wasn't careful enough drawing up his insulin . . . '

'You mean you still think it was an accident?' I said incredulously.

'Or suicide. Happens all the time.'

'But what about my attacker, Jacky's murder? Couldn't Margaret have been responsible?'

It was Hook's turn to look surprised. 'Nice woman like that? A devoted daughter. What motive would she have? Anyway she had alibis for both Jacky and your attack.'

'Where was she then?' I asked.

Hook moved towards me as I sat at the desk and patted me on the shoulder. 'She was with her mother, of course.'

'Of course,' I said weakly. 'With her sick mother.'

'In my experience of caring unmarried daughters it's the old mother who gets murdered, not a virtual stranger.'

'Jacky wasn't a stranger,' I protested. 'They worked together.'

'They weren't friends, though, were they?'

'No, they were . . . ' I had been about to say enemies but that hadn't been apparent. Disliking someone doesn't necessarily make them an enemy.

'I think you'll have to think again on this one, Kate,' said Hook, clearly relishing his professional one-upmanship. 'Miss Tonbridge seems a well-adjusted, caring person, certainly not murderess material at all.'

'Murderers have to be a special type, do they?'

'Most are, in my experience. They are different from normal people.'

'I'm glad you told me,' I said.

He didn't seem to notice the sarcasm in my voice.

Chapter Twenty-One

I rang Linda immediately. She told me that yes, there had been a phone call that night, just after I'd left the ward. She'd simply said that I'd popped over to see the security man and I'd be back in a few minutes.

'Honestly, Kate, I was dead casual. He was talking about sending us an admission and I had to say where you'd gone and that you'd give him a ring when you got back. He wasn't a bit pleased, I can tell you.'

'Dr Duston?'

'Yes. Sorry I forgot to tell you, hope I didn't drop you in it.'

'Not at all, Linda. Bye. Thanks.'

Hubert came up just after the phone call, looking remarkably cheerful. 'How did it go?' he asked, standing in the doorway.

I shrugged and looked heavenwards. 'Not well,' I said. 'The Inspector patronised me and the Detective Sergeant propped up the wall as talkative as a stuffed parrot, and my chief suspect, it seems, has an alibi as solid as my suet dumplings.'

'I like suet dumplings.'

'You would, Hubert. Are you coming in?'

He walked in, frowning slightly, 'Do I have to sit in that chair, Kate?'

'Please yourself, Hubert.'

Hubert smiled weakly and sat down. 'I've got some news,' he said. 'A bit of info.'

'Make my day, Hubert.'

He really did try. It was another triumph for the coffin grapevine. It seemed Mick O'Dowd had tested his blood the night of the murder – the pricking of his thumb had been freshly done. He had also had very recent sexual intercourse. Hubert had stuttered over those words. Shortly after that, he had either injected himself with four times his dose of insulin or someone else had done it for him.

'What does your informant think happened?' I asked.

'He thinks Mick did it himself; there were only his fingerprints on the insulin bottle and the syringe. The equipment was found beside him in the bed as if he were tired after . . . after . . . '

'I understand, Hubert. But why? That's what I don't understand.'

'Perhaps we'll never know,' said Hubert. 'People do commit suicide on the spur of the moment.'

'And murder,' I said.

'You don't think he just made a mistake with his dosage?' asked Hubert.

I shook my head. 'Years ago, maybe. Then there were several different types and strengths of insulin. Now there is only one strength and one type of syringe. Insulin itself is slightly cloudy so you can see the amount in the syringe; a mistake of one or two units is possible but not four times the dose.'

'His sister . . . ' began Hubert.

'His sister!' I repeated excitedly. I'd been thinking of Mick as being a creature of the night, a loner. I'd been very stupid. 'What about his sister?'

'He lived with her. She's a widow.'

'You don't know her address, do you, Hubert?'

'I could find it out.'

'How soon?'

'Today.'

'Hubert, I think you deserve a pub lunch.'

'I'm not arguing,' said Hubert.

At the Swan we ordered chicken in a basket with chips and I broached the subject of my planned reconstruction.

Hubert nearly choked on one of the chips and he swallowed hard before he answered. 'That's a daft idea,' he whispered, looking round the pub to make sure no one was listening.

I looked round too, and got the impression today was pension day: the young business types were gone and in their place a few elderly couples sat laughing and relaxed in neat, ultra-clean clothes. In the corner near us a small group of elderly men discussed next spring's plans for their gardens; their mortgages by now a long-forgotten thorn.

'No one's listening,' I said.

'It's still a daft idea. The police do that sort of thing. It's all organised and safe . . . '

'Admit it, Hubert. You're scared.'

'No, I'm not,' said Hubert indignantly. 'It's just that things you do either go wrong, or someone dies.'

It was my turn to feel both indignant and guilty, for the thought crossed my mind that if I hadn't been investigating Jacky's death maybe, just maybe, no one else would have died.

'Aren't you going to argue?' asked Hubert.

'Perhaps you've got a point,' I said. 'I may have made things worse. Do you think I should tell the police my suspicions?'

'Didn't you say your suspect had an alibi?'

'They said she has.'

'Well, unless you've got some real evidence, do you think they would take any notice of you?'

'No, I suppose not,' I said, beginning to feel a little less dispirited.

Hubert carried on eating and then wiped his mouth carefully with a paper napkin. 'What do you plan to do for this reconstruction?'

'You mean you'll help me?'

'Why not? I'm not chicken.'

'Do you think you're normal, Hubert?' I asked, remembering Inspector Hook's comments on normality.

Hubert looked only a mite surprised at the question. 'What's normal?' he asked. 'I'm just different.'

I shrugged. 'Exactly, Hubert, exactly.'

'What's that got to do with the reconstruction?'

'Nothing at all really, only I know who the police suspect.'

'Someone who's not normal.'

'A doctor— ' I began.

'Not Hiding?' interrupted Hubert with a grin.

I laughed, 'I agree he's not normal, but it's not him. I think they suspect Robert Duston. In police eyes being a homosexual is an abnormality, and being left-wing as well makes him verge on the outright subversive.'

'Surely not,' said Hubert. 'The police are supposed to be fair and impartial, aren't they?'

'Tell that to a man caught with a friend in a public lavatory. The police can respect a criminal for his daring and bravado. However, it seems that catching gays in the act has less status in the police force than arresting a bag lady for loitering. So some of them compensate themselves by . . . being less than friendly to gays.'

'How do you know about that sort of thing?'

'I used to live opposite a public lavatory.'

'You're having me on,' said Hubert.

'Yes, Hubert. I am.'

We left the pub agreeing to meet outside the hospital at eleven p.m. I still wasn't sure I knew what we were going to do exactly, but I didn't tell Hubert that. I let him think it was as organised as a shopping trip. I don't think he knows quite how disorganised a shopping trip can be.

He promised to ring me with the address of Mick's sister and I drove to the cottage to plan the reconstruction.

I assumed in the peace and quiet of my home I would be able to work out a plan of devilish cunning, instead of which I spent ages removing four sutures from my scalp. They had begun to irritate and I was determined to make it a DIY job. I propped up a magnifying mirror and then angled my head in position. My pointed scissors were a fraction too thick for the job but I managed it in the end, minus a drop or two of blood. Still, it gave me great satisfaction and I'd just finished when Hubert rang.

Mick's sister lived in a hamlet about two miles from the hospital.

'What's the plan for tonight?' asked Hubert, with what I thought sounded like enthusiasm.

'You'll have to wait and see. Don't get too excited, will you?'

'I've still got my doubts, Kate. We could come a cropper.'

'Trust me, Hubert,' I said with my fingers crossed.

The hamlet of Billing-on-the-Water consisted of a cluster of five houses and not a drop of water that I could see. Mick's sister's cottage was of grey stone, built by a man with a sense of humour. Squashed between two more normal-size cottages, it was three storeys high and yet not much wider than a man's outstretched arms. The front garden contained a selection of battered-looking weeds and the front door was painted in a matching green.

The woman who answered the door wore a floral apron over her full body, a green Crimplene dress and a harassed expression. Only her hair reminded me of Mick: most of it was still black.

'I'm Kate,' I said. 'The new liaison nurse from the diabetic clinic. I was so sorry to hear Mick made such a tragic mistake with his insulin. We'd like to make sure nothing like this ever happens again. Could I come in and talk to you about it?'

'Course you can, duck. You come in and warm yourself by the fire.'

There was no hall to the cottage and with one step I was in the front room and practically on top of the fire. The room was cosy but claustrophobically small. The fire roared and spat like an angry animal but my hostess encouraged me to sit within less than spitting distance. The room was so narrow that it contained just the two flimsy chairs, covered with gold Dralon, a round coffee table and in one corner a glass cabinet of china birds.

'You like a cup of tea, duck?'

'Love one, Mrs . . . ?'

'Eydon. But call me Babs, everyone does except Mick. He calls me Sis . . . used to call me Sis.'

From the kitchen, which seemed to be an extension of the living-room, Babs continued to speak to me.

'I do miss him, you know,' she called from the sink. 'I didn't see much of him really, him being out most nights, but he used to get up about one and we'd have a bit of dinner and then he'd do odd jobs or go to the shops for me. He was ever so good like that.'

She carried in the tea on a tin tray, already poured out into her best china cups. On a doily-covered plate sat a pile of home-made biscuits.

'Mick loved my biscuits, he did. Mind you, I didn't let him have too many. Not with his sugar trouble. He was always a bit careless though, always accident prone.'

She paused to chew on her biscuit. I wasn't surprised Mick couldn't resist them; I couldn't either.

'Poor old Mick. He didn't have much luck. The moment he got diabetic, he was about twelve, he went down to skin and bone and then when they said he had to have injections he went a bit wild. Never came to terms with it, see. As for the needles, well! He was a little bugger. Just refused to give his own injections. His mother had to do it and then when she died I did it, or anyone who was willing. As for his schooling, well!'

176

'What happened about that?'

'Didn't go, did he. My poor mum tried everything. If she was lucky he'd go once or twice a week. The times the truant officer called was nobody's business. He left at fifteen, could hardly read or write, but he was quite sharp, he was always in work. Mostly labouring jobs, mind you, but he liked to dress well and have a few pints, so he never saw himself short.'

'Do you think he understood about his insulin?' I asked.

Babs laughed, 'Didn't want to understand, more like. He often had funny turns; I used to give him sugar and he'd be okay then. He wouldn't be told though, he could be a stroppy sod. The last couple of years he improved, though. He had this friend, Margaret, at the hospital, a nurse, took a real interest in him, she did. Even got him library books about diabetes. She taught him quite a lot, did his blood test at night for him and everything. Ever so good to him she was. He was scared of the needles, you see, even after all those years. We were too soft with him. He used to screw up his face and look the other way when he had to have the needle.'

'Did you tell the police all this?'

Babs looked away, frowning.

I waited and moved my chair back as far as I could from the fire. I was roasting down one side of my face.

'You getting too hot?' asked Babs, obviously glad to change the subject. 'I like an open fire, don't you? Nothing like it; mind you, you either get too hot or you ruddy well freeze.'

'About the police?' I ventured.

She shrugged. 'I'll have to tell you, I suppose. Mick was in trouble once or twice with the police – nothing serious, you understand, but when that girl was murdered at the hospital they questioned him ever such a lot. He got in quite a state about it. Once he got drunk and said he knew who did it but he'd take his secret to the grave. He did, didn't he?'

I nodded. 'What did you tell the police about his fear of needles?'

Babs sat forward in her chair and stared at me, the flames of the fire reflected in her hazel eyes. 'Look, love,' she said quietly. 'We're working class and they knew Mick. In my position you say as little as possible. I didn't want them to think he was stupid, did I? If I told them he sometimes had funny turns they might have said he killed that girl and didn't remember doing it. They would think he was a nutter, wouldn't they?'

'What exactly did you tell them?' I asked softly.

She grimaced slightly. 'I told them,' she said slowly, 'I told them he was ever so careful and that he gave his own injections. Well, I didn't want to get that nurse in trouble, did I?'

'Of course not,' I agreed.

'They kept asking me if he could have made a mistake or had he tried to kill himself. Well, I had to say he must have made a mistake, didn't I? He was quite happy, not a bit miserable. He wasn't the type to kill himself.'

'Were they happy with that?'

Babs laughed. 'The police, happy! Huh! They just kept asking if he would let anyone else do his injections. I couldn't go back on what I'd said, could I?'

'You're sure he wouldn't have given his own injection?'

'I'm sure,' she said firmly.

'What if . . . ' I began. 'What if it wasn't a mistake, what if someone had deliberately given Mick an overdose?'

'Don't be silly dear,' she said. 'Who would want to do a thing like that? He should have eaten soon after his injection, he was just careless.'

'But he had four times his usual dose,' I protested.

'Perhaps he needed more. Since he met that nurse he used to alter his dose. She tested his blood, see; it's more accurate than just testing your water. Anyway, I blame Mick. He was always prone to accidents. Broke his leg once and his arm. In a way I wasn't surprised. I knew he'd come a cropper one day.'

'Is there anything the clinic could have done to help him?'

'Bless you, no, duck. Mick was his own worst enemy. It was bound to happen one day. You have to take care with something as dangerous as insulin, don't you?'

'You certainly do. Thank you for your time,' I said, standing up. 'Knowing about someone like Mick helps us to do our job. I think we may have let him down.'

'Now don't you say that, it's not true. People did help Mick, that nurse especially. Too much help, that was his problem. Take a few biscuits with you, duck, and thanks ever so much for coming.'

As I left, Babs waved me goodbye, and I, clutching a paper bag full of biscuits, could have cried.

Chapter Twenty-Two

I drove straight from Billing-on-the-Water to Longborough High Street and the public library. I'd been vaguely meaning to join since I arrived, but now I desperately needed some information.

Although small and with the look of an old-fashioned bank, inside it was modern. The librarians sat at computers and waved wands over the books. As a child I had quite fancied the idea of selecting from and filing away those little tickets into their rectangular boxes. To me the computer didn't seem half so much fun.

'I'd like to join the library,' I said to the young girl who sat, eyes down, at the computer.

'Here's a form,' she said, looking up with a half-smile. 'You can fill it in over at that table. You'll need identification.'

You'll need identification! You'll need identification! Just like opening a bank account using a false name . . .

'Over there,' she repeated, pointing past the turnstile towards the bookshelves, and a round table and two chairs. I'd just started to fill in the form when I felt a tap on my shoulder. I turned, and there stood Gwenda Carey.

'You're looking well,' I said in surprise. And she did. She'd gained weight and her face had lost its anguished expression. She wore a peach-coloured dress, her slim neck adorned by a row of pearls. Clear eyes told me she was off the booze.

'I did it!' she said eagerly.

'Did what?'

'Got a job here, of course. I can't thank you enough for giving me the idea.'

I felt genuinely pleased for her, and for myself. I needed information. 'I'm so glad, Gwenda,' I said. 'Perhaps you could help me.'

'Of course I will, although I'm a real junior. Still, it's lovely not having any responsibility. What can I do for you?'

'I want to find a book on diabetes. Not just any book. A friend recommended it, but I can't remember the title.'

'That's a tall order. What's your friend's name? I could see if any of the librarians know her.'

'Margaret Tonbridge.'

'You hang on and I'll see what I can do.'

Gwenda walked off and I could tell even by the way she moved that she'd gained confidence.

It was about twenty minutes before she came back. 'You're in luck,' she said. 'It's called *Diabetes Made Simple* by Alice Grace. Only trouble is it's out at the moment. Overdue, actually. A reminder note was just being sent.'

'Who to?'

'Your friend, Margaret Tonbridge. I'm surprised she didn't tell you she'd still got it.'

'She's had a lot on her mind lately,' I said. 'Thanks anyway.'

Gwenda smiled. 'You take care.' And then she added brightly, 'I see you've had another injury.'

My hand shot to my head to flick my hair over my shaved patch and the remaining sutures.

'Don't worry,' she said. 'I only caught the merest glimpse when your hair moved. What happened?'

'It's a very long story, Gwenda. Next time I come to the library I'll tell you all about it.'

She walked with me to the door after I'd selected a book called *The Joy of Tomatoes*.

'I think I made the right decision,' she said with a serene smile. 'Detective work seems just as dangerous as teaching.'

'It's just the way I do it.' And I laughed as I waved her goodbye.

Outside in the High Street I stood for a moment gazing at the darkening sky. Battalions of great black clouds were on the march, scudding into ranks ready for the onslaught. Perhaps it wouldn't be war, I consoled myself, just a few skirmishes. And rain or no rain I was going to the hospital tonight. I just hoped Hubert would still be willing.

On the way home I bought fish and chips, the heat from the packet rising like steamy nectar, but by the time I arrived back at the cottage, steamy had become soggy. I ate them anyway, every single chip, because I had moments of slight panic if my next meal was to be more than a few hours away. And tonight, I really didn't know when I'd be through.

I got ready for action early. Dressed in thermal vest, black track suit, never worn before and bought only because it was reduced, and in the belief it might make me look reduced too. Then I sat by the window and watched the sky.

There wasn't long to wait before the black sky jettisoned its ammunition. The rain fell and fell, an unrelenting barrage that hit the ground, bounced up again, drummed frantically on the roof and poured out of the guttering like a flushing loo. Occasionally my eyes strayed from the rain to the telephone. I expected Hubert to ring and cancel. He didn't. I had to admire his courage.

As I put on my green wellies and beige raincoat I pulled the collar up to get me in the mood. A trilby hat would have made me feel more the part, but all I had in the way of headgear was one of those plastic hoods. And I couldn't remember where I'd put it, and anyway it would have looked ridiculous.

The last thing I did before leaving was collect a sharp knife from the kitchen drawer and pick up my pièce de résistance – a condom filled with tomato sauce and tied tightly at the top. I placed both very carefully in my raincoat pocket.

Hubert was waiting for me, parked outside on the main road by the hospital gates. There was no mistaking his car even in a deluge. It was long, wide, white and American. As I parked directly behind it I could see Hubert's straight back. He was wearing a hat. He didn't acknowledge my toot on the horn, so I waited for a while with the engine running and the headlights illuminating Hubert's car. Then I switched off the ignition and as the windscreen wipers died the rain made it impossible to see anything.

I ran the few paces head down, my hair soon plastered to my head, and banged on his car window. Hubert looked at me for a moment as if he didn't quite recognise me and then he leaned over slowly and opened the passenger door.

'I thought for a moment you weren't going to let me in.'

'I thought you'd change your mind when you saw this lot,' he said reproachfully, as he continued to stare out into the murk ahead.

'It's only rain,' I said as I settled myself beside him.

We sat in silence for a while, listening to the rain beating on the car roof, while inside the car our breath condensed like fog on the windscreen, and the light of the lamp outside the hospital smeared like trickles of orange juice in our line of vision.

'Come on, Hubert,' I pleaded, like a mother to her sulky child, 'let's get on with it. We'll be finished in no time at all.'

'I'm not leaving my car here,' he said.

'That's okay. Drive into the grounds, turn left under the arch and we'll be quite near the ward then.'

He drove in slowly without speaking and parked near the bike shed.

'You don't have to do anything at the moment, Hubert,' I said. 'Just sit here and wait for me.'

'Where are you going? If I wasn't needed I wouldn't have come.'

'I shall need you later, really I will. But I want to ride that bike to Margaret's house.'

Hubert's eyes followed my finger to the lone bike. A smile – or was it a smirk – crossed his face. 'I hope it's not far.'

'I want to time myself, that's all. You see if she did murder Jacky I think she biked home first, collected the knife and then rode back to lie in wait.'

'So I've just got to sit here?'

'That's the idea, Hubert.'

'Just hurry up then,' he said. 'And be careful.'

'I like your hat, Hubert,' I said, flattery being the highest form of creeping. It worked. He looked in his overhead mirror, pulled the browny-green hat a touch forward and smiled as if pleased with what he saw.

'All it needs is a feather,' I said, as I closed the car door behind me.

The bike, unchained, was old and black with one of those thick sprung saddles. I didn't want to let Hubert see me ride it, just in case I'd forgotten how. I hadn't ridden a bike since I was a child, and even then I seemed to spend as much time picking myself up and cleaning grazed knees as I did actually in motion. So I walked the bike out of the bike shed and on to the path.

The rain hit me full in the face and although I found my balance pretty quickly I couldn't see very well. I had to pedal with my head down and my eyes squinting. But I rode on past empty dark buildings I'd never seen before until eventually I came to the estate at the back of the grounds. It had taken me five minutes. Without the rain and being more used to the bike I could probably have done it in three.

Kennie's house was in darkness, the curtains wide open; his mother had obviously not returned. Margaret's house was in darkness except for a dull glow in a front bedroom. I stopped cycling just before the house and walked with the bike to the front gate. The bike squeaked even without a rider, but I hoped the swishing of the rain would mask the noise.

I swept my hair back and wiped the rain from my face and looked around at the few other dark houses in the estate. No one was out on such a night but I could hear a dog become aware of my presence. I propped the bike up by Margaret's front gate and then began to walk fast towards the hospital.

Once out of sight of the houses I began to break into a run. But that didn't last long. It seemed like hard work against the force of the rain and by now my jogging bottoms were so wet that I could feel them slipping downwards.

By the time I got back to the bike shed I must have weighed an extra half-stone in water. The walk back had taken ten minutes. Hubert had turned the car round so that the boot was under the roof of the bike shed. As I staggered back he got out of the car and signalled to me to come with him.

'Where's the bike?' he asked.

'I'll tell you in a minute,' I replied, shivering. 'Can't I sit in the car for a while?'

'In that state! Not in my old girl you can't.'

'I'll catch pneumonia.'

'Good!'

I continued to shiver but then Hubert opened the boot and put a blanket around me and handed me a fluffy pink towel.

'Get yourself a bit drier,' he said, 'then you can have a cup of coffee.'

Amazed, I began drying my face and hair while Hubert poured coffee from a Thermos flask.

'Hubert, I'm overwhelmed. Why didn't I think of this?'

He didn't answer for a while, then he said, 'Is that it, then? Can we go?'

'Soon, Hubert. All you've got to do now is stab me in the back.'

He looked down at me. 'Strangling is more in my line,' he said, pulling the blanket tight round my neck.

'Just one little stab, Hubert,' I pleaded, taking the knife from my pocket. When the surprise had registered on his face I pulled out the ketchup-filled condom and waited for that to register.

'Is that what I think it is?' he asked, horrified.

'It's only sauce.'

'Oh, God!'

'There's nothing to it, Hubert. We just go over to the patch of grass where Jacky's body was found and you stab me in the condom and then I take it from there.'

'Take what?' he asked.

'The knife. I want to go over what, I think, Margaret did that night. She had to do something with it. At first I thought she just returned it to her pocket but I'm not sure. Would she have risked being found with a knife?'

'Suppose not,' Hubert agreed reluctantly.

'You'll do it, then?'

'If this goes wrong, Kate, I shall seriously consider getting a new lodger – a dressmaker or a pensioner. Someone who won't give me any trouble.'

'Hubert, you won't regret it, I promise.'

'What about the bike?'

'Oh, yes. Well that's a ploy to get Margaret rattled. In the morning she'll look out of her window and see that black bike standing there like some sinister conspirator to murder. It can't fail to remind her of what she's done.'

Hubert mumbled something under his breath but I didn't catch it and by that time I had begun to shiver again. Even so, I threw the blanket back into the boot of the car and, squaring my shoulders, said, 'Forward, Hubert.'

He swore softly under his breath as he followed me.

We skirted Harper Ward, keeping well down as we passed. Round the back of the ward, the office light glowed but the curtains were completely closed. For a moment I felt a strong desire to be inside in the warm, but I resisted, telling myself that the rain was good for both skin and hair and the back of my neck and my thighs and . . . I was as miserable as hell! 'Come on, Hubert.' I urged in a whisper. 'It's not far.'

In the patch of ground surrounded by trees and bushes it was far darker than I had thought.

'Have you brought a torch?' I asked Hubert.

'No, I bloody well haven't. You're the girl scout. Just get on with it. What am I supposed to do now?'

I peered down at the mud. 'It was about here,' I said.

'Where's the knife?' he demanded.

Close up to his face I could see the rain dripping off his already soaking hat, and his eyes squinting against the downpour. 'It's here, Hubert. Don't get carried away, will you?'

I handed him the knife and explained I'd put the condom down my back and when it was in place he could have a stab at it. As I eased it down beneath my thermal vest, I shivered uncontrollably – it felt as cold as ice.

'Okay, Hubert, stand behind me and feel the lump and then put the knife in.'

I could feel Hubert holding the condom in the middle of my back, and then, nothing happened.

'Now, Hubert!' I urged. 'Do it now!'

'I can't,' he groaned. 'I can't, I might stab you.'

'You don't have to use any force,' I said. 'Just pierce the rubber.'

Whoever had stabbed Jacky didn't have this much trouble, I thought, no layer of clothes, no rain – hardly any effort at all.

He held me gingerly by one shoulder and poked at the condom. The sauce came out in a slow trickle, sliding revoltingly down my back. I turned to Hubert who stood staring at the knife as it gradually lost its sauce to the rain. I took the knife from him and saw splashes dark against his hands. That night there would have been no rain to wash the blood away. What the hell did she do? Where did she wipe the knife? What did she have with her? And then I remembered. It was what *Jacky* had with her that mattered. Jacky had the packet of incontinence pads with her. Margaret had been lucky. And then I knew what she had done. All I had to do was prove it.

'You satisfied?' demanded Hubert. 'I'm too old for this sort of caper.'

'You go on ahead, Hubert. I just want to look round the back of the ward.'

Hubert strode off and I was following on behind when I heard a dog bark and a man's voice shouting, ''Ere you two, what the 'ell?' and then, 'Stop or I'll . . . '

Before he'd finished I screamed, 'Run, Hubert, run!' And he did. I knew I'd made a mistake when the Alsation tore after him and soundlessly held on to his sleeve until poor Hubert was dragged to the ground.

'Don't move!' I yelled. 'Stay perfectly still.'

The dog's owner had by this time appeared, fat and lumbering and wearing a peaked cap. He was still saying ''Ere you' as he approached.

'Call that dog off,' I shouted imperiously. 'I'm one of the nurse managers and that' – I pointed to Hubert lying in the mud with the dog tugging excitedly at his sleeve – 'is the general manager.'

'Here, King – come!' called the owner. The dog let go of the sleeve with some reluctance and Hubert struggled slowly to his feet, totally covered in mud.

I turned to the man. 'Are you trespassing in hospital grounds?' I demanded.

'Me? No, lady, I'm the security guard.'

'Are you indeed? Well, I'm not very impressed. We're here checking, on this foul night, that you are doing your job properly. It took you an inordinately long time to spot us, didn't it? More frequent checks might be in order in the future. And next time you see a suspicious person I should issue a warning before you let your dog loose.'

The dog looked at me, all wet and bedraggled, and hung his head as if in shame. The man looked as shamefaced as the dog.

'Right you are, miss. Sorry about the mistake. I've had a terrible night; someone nicked the hospital bike.'

'That's unfortunate but security is all; just see it doesn't happen again,' I said, waving a finger at him.

As man and dog moved briskly away, I turned to Hubert who was by now standing by my side.

'My arm, my arm,' he moaned pathetically.

His sleeve was in tatters and in the dark I couldn't see if the dog had broken the skin.

'We'll go to Melba Ward and get it looked at.'

'Why did you tell me to run? You nearly got me killed.'

'It seemed like a good idea at the time.'

'You're a bloody menace.'

I didn't argue. I was soaked, cold, miserable and tired. And anyway, Hubert was right.

We stood outside Melba's glass doors and rang the bell.

Claudette was on duty and at first reeled back slightly at the shock of seeing us. She opened the door, looking us up and down with her mouth slightly open. 'Good God,' she said at last. 'What on earth has happened to you two?'

'This is Mr Humberstone, my landlord— '

'Erstwhile landlord,' interrupted Hubert.

'He's not happy, Claudette; the guard dog chased him.'

'Only because you told me to run . . . '

'But whatever were you doing? Oh, never mind, just wait there. I'll be back in a tick,' said Claudette and she was gone.

Hubert looked straight ahead, his hat sitting limply on his head, his mackintosh sleeve torn to the elbow and his face covered in mud. If I'd felt more attractive myself I could have laughed.

As good as her word Claudette came back in seconds with towels, and dressing-gowns. She had donned a plastic apron and gloves.

'Is that blood?' she asked anxiously when we had moved into the light of the corridor.

'No,' I said. 'It's only tomato sauce.'

'Of course,' she said calmly. 'What else would it be?'

A hot bath had never felt so good. I emerged from the bathroom feeling quite wonderful although I had to wear a hospital nightdress under the dressing-gown.

'I've put your clothes in a plastic bag. You'll have to go home in what you're wearing,' Claudette told me and I knew she was longing to laugh.

'Perhaps we could hang on for a while, it might stop raining.'

'Sure. No problem,' she said. 'I've made some tea. And I've checked Mr Humberstone's arm – the skin's not broken. He'll live.'

Hubert was still reviving in the bath so Claudette and I sat in the office and I explained a little about our activities of the night.

'Was it worth the hassle?' she asked.

'It might be,' I said. 'If you can tell me about the incontinence pads and the rubbish.'

'What do you want to know?' she spoke calmly, almost as if this sort of thing happened to her every night. I had expected Claudette to be nervy, if not outright hysterical, but perhaps curiosity had got the better of her.

'The night you found Jacky's body, had that packet of pads been opened?'

'Does it matter?'

'Yes, it does. Please try and think back. Did you hand her a full packet when she came over?'

'I think so,' she said uncertainly. 'I went to the cupboard and reached up . . . yes . . . yes it was a full packet, the plastic handle was still intact.'

'And when you found Jacky?'

She shook her head. 'I can't remember, really I can't . . . '

'Close your eyes,' I suggested. 'See her body lying there and the pads beside her. Were her arms out in front or by her side?'

Claudette closed her eyes and sat silent for a moment. 'They were out in front,' she began. 'I remember that, it was as if she had fallen flat on her face and the pads . . . the pads were still in her hand. She was holding on to them . . . and one of them was sticking out . . . just a corner.' Opening her eyes Claudette smiled. 'Fancy me remembering that.'

'Thanks, Claudette. Just one more thing. The rubbish bags, with the soiled pads in, what do you do with them on this ward?'

'Tie them up and put them outside. Usually that's done by the auxiliary.'

'And on Harper?'

'There's a rubbish skip there at the back. So the black bags get thrown in there.'

'Then what happens?'

'About seven thirty the porter collects it all and takes it to the incinerator.'

'And when Margaret's on duty she takes out the rubbish?'

'Well, yes. About eleven, after the evening change.'

'What's all this about, Kate?' asked Claudette.

I started to reply when Hubert walked in. My hand flew to my mouth to stifle the laughter. His nightie came below his knees and his pastel striped dressing-gown way above.

'Don't you dare laugh,' he said. 'I've never been so humiliated in all my life.'

That did it. Claudette, no longer able to keep a straight face, started first.

'Call yourselves nurses,' stormed Hubert. 'You're a disgrace!' The angrier he got the more we laughed, but I did notice that after a while the corners of his mouth began to twitch just a little.

Chapter Twenty-Three

Hubert sulked all of the next day or, if he wasn't sulking, it seemed like it, because he managed to avoid me. So the day after, I'd gone out early to buy cream cakes to sweeten his mood and went down to his office.

He sat behind a large, highly polished, mahogany desk, a potted fern at each side of him, and in front of the desk two dark brown leather chairs. The slatted blinds were closed and in one corner a standard lamp sported a puce shade, its red glow giving the room a cosy womb-like feel. It was an office, but without any impediments, no filing cabinet, no typewriter, no stacks of files, and no telephone.

'You don't look busy,' I said without tact, and regretted it immediately.

'This room isn't meant to look busy,' he said. 'It's so that grieving relatives can talk to me in restful surroundings.'

'You're quite a psychologist, Hubert. I didn't realise funeral directing was such an art.'

'No one ever does,' he said, giving me a wary glance, as if wondering what I was up to.

Before he could ask I said, 'I've come to creep and grovel, Hubert. I've bought cream cakes to prove it.'

'Well, we can't eat them here – too messy. I'll come up to your office. Yours is always a mess.'

I ignored the insult and Hubert followed me up. I'd worn my highest heels especially, but he didn't comment, although I was aware of his appreciation.

'I'll sit at the desk,' he said. 'You can sit on that chair for a change.'

I smiled. 'Landlord's privilege,' I said. 'Because I'm still grovelling.'

I sank down into the chair and experienced instantly the feeling I might never rise from it again. Hubert's responding smile showed he knew exactly the thought that crossed my mind.

Halfway through a cream slice, as I paused to lick the cream from my fingers, I asked Hubert how he thought I could get Margaret to confess.

'Take her out with you on a cold, wet, dark night, she'd confess to murders she hadn't even done,' he said.

'Be serious, Hubert. I have apologised. I'll never ask you to do another reconstruction again . . . '

'Reconstruction! Huh! It was a complete fiasco.'

'I know,' I said soothingly. 'You don't have to help me ever again if you don't want to.'

A worried frown creased his forehead, 'I didn't say I wouldn't help you. I'll just be a bit more choosy about the weather next time.'

'You're a real sport, Hubert,' I said, and his cheerful smile told me his usual humour was once more returning. I tried to capitalise on that by asking him again how he thought I should work the confession angle.

'Well, if you are sure it's her, it's no good sitting there on your backside eating cream cakes. You'll have to go and see her. She won't confess by post, will she?'

'I'm still not absolutely sure, that's the point, but unless I go to her house I'll never be sure . . . anyway, Hubert,' I said, surprised at his tone, 'I thought you'd forgiven me?'

'I have, Kate. But I think you should get on with it before the police move in.'

I nodded. He was right, of course, but I didn't like admitting it. I swallowed the rest of my cream cake hurriedly and struggled to my feet. 'I'm going this very minute, Hubert,' I said, taking my coat from the hook.

'I didn't mean . . . ' he began.

'It's okay, you were quite right.'

At the door I turned back dramatically. 'It's a far, far, better thing I do now than I've ever done before.'

'You make sure it's not a far, far, better rest that you'll be going to.'

I waved my hand in salute. 'Clever clogs!' I called as I shut the door.

* * *

I stopped on the way to Margaret's to buy a clipboard and paper and one of those pens you hang round your neck, which I always think look businesslike. But what business was I supposed to be on? I had to have a pretext, otherwise I had the feeling she would give me very short shrift.

Margaret took so long to answer the door I had time to think something up and to look round for the bike. It had obviously been returned to the hospital.

'Yes,' she said coldly, when she eventually came to the door. She looked exhausted; her dark hair hung limply from her head as though just washed, and on her forehead tiny beads of sweat glistened.

I had been about to explain I was doing a survey of home carers, but I could see something was wrong. 'What on earth's the matter?' I asked.

'You'd better come in,' she said reluctantly. 'Mother's fallen out of bed and I can't lift her back in. I've been trying for ages.'

I followed Margaret upstairs. On her feet she wore pink mules with a high wedge heel. They seemed like an act of defiance, because otherwise she was dressed drably in a navy jumper with frayed sleeves and a navy skirt which looked a little less than clean.

Mrs Tonbridge lay on the floor, a pillow under her head and covered up to her chin with a rug. Like Margaret she had changed greatly since I last saw her. Her face had grown gaunt and her tongue protruded slightly from a lopsided mouth. When she saw us she began to make grunting noises.

'It's all right, Mother,' said Margaret, kneeling down on the floor to pat her mother's hand. 'Kate will help me to get you back to bed.'

Mrs Tonbridge's eyes flickered with either fear or distaste at her daughter's touch, but somehow the slight retraction of her hand from Margaret's indicated distaste.

For a slim woman she was remarkably heavy but together we lifted her on to the bed.

'There, Mother, you'll feel better soon. I should have put the chair by the bed, shouldn't I? It's all my fault. I'll make you a nice cup of tea now.' As Margaret spoke she tidied the top sheet, pulled up the pink eiderdown and smoothed a stray grey hair from her mother's forehead. Again at her touch there was that flicker of emotion reflected in the pinched expression and the eyes like mean, flat pebbles.

Margaret signalled to me to go downstairs and then turned to look down at her patient. 'Don't worry, Mother, I'll bring Kate up again before she goes,' she said.

Mrs Tonbridge's mouth moved slightly as if in response but again the sound was strangled by the useless tongue that lay between her thin lips like a growth.

At the bottom of the stairs Margaret turned to me and spoke in what I think was meant to be a whisper but sounded more like a hiss. 'Why have you come here today? Haven't I got enough problems without private detectives snooping around?'

'I haven't come to snoop,' I said. 'The nursing agency asked me to do a survey of carers in the area, with a view to loaning out private nurses to social services. I've been asked to assess needs in general. Just a few questions about how you're coping and exactly what sort of help you need.' What an awful lie! If I wasn't careful I'd be the one to break down and confess.

'I suppose that will be all right,' she said after a protracted silence. 'It can't do any harm.'

'No, of course not, and it may bring you some benefits,' I said quietly.

We were interrupted at that moment by the nerve-jangling noise of a bell being rung. Margaret shuddered at the continuing trill.

'It's her hand-bell. She keeps it beside her in the bed. I expect she wants her tea. You sit down in the front room, I've lit the fire. I'll be ages, she can't hold a cup properly. And then I'll have to take her to the loo. There's no end to it, you know, not since she had the stroke.'

I nodded. 'Give me a shout if you need any help.'

When I heard Margaret go upstairs with the tea I began to have a proper look round. The fire flamed feebly, as if in this weary, tired house, it too had trouble staying alive. A bookcase in one corner of the room interested me; perhaps I would find the overdue library book. There were a few elderly nursing textbooks, several historical novels and romances, but nothing on diabetes. One of the nursing books stuck out a little bit more than the others, and as I removed it, something wedged at the back fell with a metallic tinkle: an inhaler – Kennie's inhaler. At least I assumed it was. I stared at it for a moment, not wanting to get my fingerprints on it and wondering how to pocket it without actually touching it.

I didn't hear Margaret come into the room. She was nearly by my side, her face angry, her eyes glittering.

Before she could speak I said, 'Oh, there you are! I was a bit bored so I picked up one of your nursing books to read. They haven't changed much really have they – when was this one printed?' I flicked open the cover to find the publication date. In my haste I had opened it to the very front page. There was a sticker inside, inscribed in gold relief:

PRESENTED TO

MARGARET TONBRIDGE

PRACTICAL NURSING PRIZE

ST MONICA'S GENERAL HOSPITAL

1962.

'Give it back,' she said, snatching it from me and holding it to her breasts.

'I didn't realise you had done your nurse training, Margaret.'

'I didn't finish,' she said sharply. 'I completed two years.'

For a moment Margaret still clutched the book, then she straightened up, moved over to the bookcase and, without seeming to hesitate at the sight of the inhaler, placed the book back.

'What happened?' I asked.

'Happened?' she echoed. 'Oh, yes. My father died. My mother became ill and I had to come home to look after her.'

'How did you feel about that?'

'How was I supposed to feel? Resentful, I suppose. But that was a long, long time ago.'

'What about now?'

'Now? What about now?'

'Do you still feel resentful?'

Margaret stared at me warily for a moment, then, as if realising what she was saying was innocuous enough, said, 'Sometimes I do. But everyone has a cross to bear, don't they?'

I shrugged. 'Some seem lighter than others – depends on how well you cope.'

Passing a hand through her greasy hair Margaret pointed to the armchair. 'Let's sit down, shall we, before we fall down.'

We sat either side of the fading fire. Margaret sighed as she eased herself into the chair. I guessed her back was aching and she closed her eyes for so long that I thought she was dropping off to sleep.

Presently though, she said, 'I really miss work. I don't see a soul, you know. The day seems to last forever. Mother wakes about five; that is, if she's slept at all. Since the stroke she moans a lot in the night. Sometimes I guess what's wrong, sometimes I don't. She misses the church of course. When she used to go I'd take her in the wheelchair and leave her there and then I could have a walk on my own. That was a real treat. But now . . . there's no break from it and whatever I do, doesn't please her. It's always been the same. I've spent my life trying to please her. She doesn't like me very much, you see.'

'I'm sure that's not true, Margaret. When I came to see her, she said how hard you worked and how much she appreciated it.'

A sudden smile animated her face. 'Did she? Did she really?' she asked with pathetic eagerness.

It was a lie that I felt was more than justified. 'Yes, she did. Why are you so surprised?' I asked gently.

Margaret grimaced. 'I've tried so hard to make my mother happy. Everything I've done has been with her in mind. Sometimes I've wondered if it's all been worth it.'

'You've done your duty,' I said.

'Duty! Oh, I've done my duty,' she said bitterly.

From upstairs the bell sounded again. Shuddering, Margaret's face contorted with anxiety. 'I can't take much more,' she said. 'That bloody bell never stops . . . '

'I'll go,' I said.

In the bedroom Mrs Tonbridge lay groaning. I went through the nurse's litany: pain? thirsty? toilet? too hot? too cold? Finally, I worked out what she wanted was a cardigan around her shoulders. There was no smiling response when I'd done as she required, just a cold stare, but her eyes seemed slightly brighter, as though she enjoyed the discomfiture of those struggling to understand her.

When I returned, Margaret was gazing into the feeble flames of the fire and tears ran down her cheeks, slowly and effortlessly. She brushed the tears away with her hand as if they were as irritating as flies.

'I don't think I can go on,' she said. 'I'm so tired, even crying is too much trouble. I thought things would improve when I— '

'When you killed Jacky?' I said bluntly.

The surprise in Margaret's face was only momentary. 'I was going to say, when I killed my father.'

It was my turn to be surprised. 'What did you say, Margaret?'

'You heard,' she said. And then she laughed. A chilling, hollow laugh and as she laughed she continued to stare at me. And I felt fear creep up my spine like a centipede with cold feet and I knew I had made a mistake, a terrible mistake, in coming here alone. 'You're surprised, aren't you?' she asked, as her laughter died, to be replaced by a tight, hard smile.

'I am. Do you want to tell me about it?'

'What's to tell? I killed my father . . . the drunken bastard.'

'How did you kill him?' I asked.

'It was easy. He was drunk. He'd gone upstairs to vomit in the bathroom and when he came out I just gave him a little shove. I didn't expect it to be so easy. He lay at the bottom of the stairs, vomited again and within minutes he was dead. A mixture of fracturing his skull and alcoholic poisoning. I was so pleased with myself. I thought Mum would be free and she wouldn't get beaten up any more. I'd finish my training and move back home and the two of us would be happy. What a joke!'

'What went wrong?' I asked.

Margaret sighed. 'Everything went wrong. My mother, it seemed, loved him; can you believe it? We got on so well when he was alive. We were sort of friends. When he died all that changed. She got depressed, seriously depressed, almost suicidal. Then she had one physical illness after another. I gave up my nurse training and came home, but from then on I think she wished I'd been the one to die.'

'I see,' I murmured.

'Oh, no, you don't. How could you possibly understand? When I was younger I so longed to marry, to have children. All I got was my mother's misery and fault-finding. My job was all I had and now I've lost that too.'

'Why didn't you leave years ago? Make a fresh start.'

She looked at me incredulously.

'You just don't understand, do you? I love my mother. I thought that one day she'd love me as she used to. And now I can see that nothing will ever change. I have to stay with her to the end. The very end.'

'Where did Jacky fit in?'

Margaret smiled slyly. 'Strange survey this. You didn't have to lie to me. I know why you came here today. As for Jacky, she didn't fit in, did she? The little bitch. She tried to take my place. My mother was always praising her. And then . . . and then . . . ' Margaret's voice began to crack with threatened tears. 'She admired them you see, came in one day and admired my mother's porcelain figurines. They sat on top of the television. Two of them, china children with a puppy beside them. I'd bought them in my first year of nursing, took me months to save up for them. And Mother was so pleased. She hugged me and said they were the prettiest ones she'd ever seen. Every time my father went out drinking she hid them away so that he wouldn't smash them. They survived all that, and then little Miss Perfect comes along. "You have them, dear," said my mother. "I'd like you to have them." And she took them.'

Margaret paused and stared at me as if trying to judge the effect on me.

I nodded. 'Go on,' I said softly.

'She's stolen something from me so I stole something from her. One night when she went for her break I searched through her bag. And then I found it . . . '

'Found what?'

'The pass book.'

'I see.'

'Do you? Do you? I don't think so. Can you imagine the shock I got? I sat there looking at the figures – twenty-five thousand pounds! Imagine what that sort of money could have done for us, for me. And suddenly it was all mine . . . '

'I don't understand, Margaret. How could it be yours?'

She grinned then in triumph. 'You're not as clever as you thought, are you?'

I shrugged. 'Explain it to me,' I said.

'The pass book . . . was in my name. Margaret Tonbridge.'

I felt my mouth open in silent query.

'Clever, wasn't she?' said Margaret. 'Months and months before, things were misplaced, letters, bills, even library tickets and then for a whole week Mother's pension book was missing. We blamed each other of course. I thought Mother was getting forgetful, she thought I was careless. Gradually, though, we found our bits and pieces and I forgot all about it. Until I found the pass book. Then it all clicked into place. So much for saintly Miss Byfield! She had used our personal things to open a bank account in my name. I could have killed her that very night. But I waited and waited. I made plans. I had to wait for the right time, didn't I?'

I nodded dumbly.

'And then the night before, I'd come home as usual on my break and Mum had said, "I think we should give those nursing books of yours to Jacky, don't you? After all, she's a proper nurse." A proper nurse! She was a lousy nurse. All smarmy to the ones she thought had money or religion. I knew her little game. She didn't even like old people very much. If she could get by without actually touching them, she would . . . '

Margaret abruptly fell silent, as though realising her outburst had gone too far. 'I'm not saying any more. No one can prove anything, not you or the police. You haven't got a shred of evidence against me.'

'That's true,' I agreed. 'But I do have some circumstantial evidence.'

'Such as?'

'Your connection with all four of the victims, the fact that you gave Mick his injections quite frequently, the fact that you were the only person to hear a car the night of the murder, the fact that you are light on your feet and can creep up on people, and, lastly, you were the only person not to have a coping mechanism.'

Margaret smirked. 'What's that supposed to mean? I cope. You call that evidence, do you? That's just guessing. What about real clues, fingerprints, forensic, witnesses?'

'How do you cope, Margaret?' I asked and when she didn't answer I said, 'A coping mechanism is something people choose unconsciously to help them cope with the stress of life. For some, it's food or drink or sex or smoking or friendships or hobbies— '

'I've got my sewing,' she interrupted. 'I enjoy that.'

'Yes,' I agreed. 'But was that enough? You couldn't cope with your father, so he had to die— '

'I want to talk about proper evidence. Not your stupid theories,' she interrupted, her voice high and petulant.

'Very well,' I said. 'There's the inhaler, the pass book – I'm sure you still have that, the library book – no doubt Mick's and your fingerprints will be on it. I expect the figurines will turn up in court too. Jacky sold them, you know. She had a lucrative little racket going.'

Margaret didn't answer immediately, and I knew she was searching for a way out. Eventually she said, 'I only picked up that inhaler. Kennie was watching Mick and me. I saw him looking through the crack in the curtain. I ran after him. The inhaler dropped out of his pocket. I shouted to him but he just ignored me and ran home.'

'And you didn't think to put it through his letter-box? He lived almost next door.'

Margaret dropped her eyes. 'I didn't wish him any harm. He shouldn't have kept watching me.'

'And Ada, what did she do wrong?' I asked.

'That was an accident. I didn't mean for her to die. I wanted her to come and live with us. She would have been company for Mum. She wouldn't come. She'd seen those figurines for sale but she said she wouldn't tell me where she'd seen them and when I said I wanted to buy them back, she laughed and said I shouldn't have sold them in the first place. When I told her my mother had given them to Jacky she became suspicious. I swopped her tablets so that she would get confused and people wouldn't believe what she was saying. I didn't plan for her to fall downstairs. The three of us could have been happy living here.'

'And Mick? Where did Mick fit into your plans?'

'Poor Mick,' she said. 'He only thought he fitted in. He wanted to marry me, you know. I made a mistake, though, I told him about Jacky. I had to talk to someone. After I'd told him . . . he . . . '

'Threatened to tell the police?'

'No, that was when he offered to marry me.'

'Then why kill him?'

'Surely you can understand that!'

199

'No. Tell me.'

'He would have been able to use what he knew as a threat against me. I didn't love him anyway. He was kind, but stupid. And what about my mother? He wouldn't have wanted her as well. I couldn't have left my mother, could I?'

'How did you do it, Margaret?' I asked softly.

'Kill him, you mean? It was easy. I tested his blood and the blood sugar was really low. Because of that he was already getting a bit aggressive, being hypoglycaemic can affect people that way. We began to make love and I said I'd give the insulin afterwards. I gave him a huge dose. He didn't even look as I gave it, and then I told him to have a sleep. I knew he wouldn't wake up.'

Margaret slumped down into her chair as if confessing had further exhausted her. She closed her eyes again and at that moment I would have loved a coffee laced with brandy. I wanted to escape from Margaret and the house and her awful mother. I moved in the chair, uncertain about staying but feeling I ought, when Margaret opened one eye.

'Stay where you are,' she said. 'I haven't finished yet.'

Chapter Twenty-Four

'I wasn't going,' I said. 'Just getting stiff.' If things hadn't been so dire I would have laughed at that. I had a firm idea that Margaret might have had plans for me anyway. I could imagine her saying, 'It was easy.'

She sat forward and put a few lumps of coal on the fire using the tongs and then raked the remains of the fire with a poker. Grey smoke belched out, the flames doused by the coal. But Margaret continued to poke at the fire as though she could resuscitate it.

'Tell me about the night you stabbed Jacky,' I said casually as though we were discussing a recipe.

'What do you want to know?'

'You left Claudette, saying you were going for your break. Then what happened?'

She stared ahead into the wisps of grey smoke still trailing from the fire embers. 'I put some plastic gloves and a plastic apron in the pocket of my cloak. I knew Jacky had gone over to see Dr Duston in the main building. It was a question of timing. I had to be ready. My plans could have gone wrong. She might have been back on the ward by the time I returned. I had to be lying in wait for her, didn't I?'

I nodded. 'But why,' I asked, 'did you have to go home at all?'

Margaret raised an eyebrow at my stupidity. 'I had to check on Mother, didn't I? And I didn't have a knife.'

'Of course,' I murmured.

'I went home as I told you,' she continued, 'and then I waited in the bushes for her . . . '

'What knife did you use?' I asked.

'Oh, yes, the knife,' she said absently. 'It was a Kitchen Magic one, really sharp and long.'

'And you went home on the bike and came back on the bike?'

'Yes. I left it in the bike shed. Strange about that bike. Someone left it outside the other day. Children, I suppose.'

'Then what happened?' I prompted.

'I just waited in the bushes, she always came that way if it wasn't raining, and then suddenly she was there in front of me. I told her I knew about the pass book and she laughed at me. She said religion had given her everything and then she laughed again, saying how easily people were conned. "Just a little kindness," she said, "and they would give you anything." She told me she was planning to leave Longborough and go into business. And then she turned and started to walk away. I crept up behind her . . . ' Margaret paused and thrust the poker deep into the dead coals. 'Like that,' she said, demonstrating again. 'Just the once, though, once was enough. I knew exactly where to aim. She fell down straight away, I think death was instantaneous . . . '

'And then?'

'What do you mean?' she asked, as if that should have been enough.

'What did you do with the knife?'

'I had to think quickly. I'd worn surgical gloves and there was blood on those and on the knife— ' She broke off. 'You'll never find the knife, you know, so what does it matter?'

'Just interest, that's all.'

She paused, still holding the poker and smiling as she played the poker tip over the coals. 'I thought I managed things quite cleverly,' she said. 'I removed one glove and held that in my hand and then from my pocket I took a clean glove and with that hand I removed a pad from the packet. I couldn't afford to get any blood on the packet, could I? I laid the pad on the grass, pulled the knife from her back and placed it on the pad with the used gloves and apron. I then stuffed it all into my pocket.'

'And then you went back to the ward?'

'Yes. Outside the ward I planned to put the package at the very bottom of the soiled rubbish bag. But I thought the police might search there so I went back into the day room, through the French windows, and once I was in the ward I simply slipped the lot under a patient's mattress. I knew the police wouldn't search there. Later, after I'd been questioned, I retrieved it and put the stuff in my bag underneath my sewing and brought it home and put it with the rest of our rubbish. It was . . . '

'Easy?'

'No, I was going to say, over. And it was, until you came snooping and raking over the past.'

'Talking of raking, Margaret, the fire's gone out.'

'Oh, yes,' she said. 'So it has.'

For a moment she stared down at the poker and then after she had replaced it in the brass coal-scuttle, she looked at me with dull, defeated eyes.

'What happens now?' she asked.

'That's up to you. The police do have another suspect at the moment. I'm sure you wouldn't want an innocent man to go to prison in your place.'

'No, I suppose not,' she said slowly. 'What really made you suspect me? I thought I'd been so clever, so careful.'

'That pocket in your cloak was odd. It worried me. You didn't need it. You had your sewing bag, why should you need a pocket in your cloak? And I thought Jacky may have been blackmailing you about Mick, perhaps threatening to tell your mother.'

We sat in silence for a moment and then the bell rang upstairs. This time it was me who shuddered at the sound.

'Come and say goodbye to Mother,' she said, which sounded ominous, so I followed Margaret up the stairs, reluctant to turn my back on her. Each step I took was a slow and measured one, as if each leg had suddenly been weighted and needed to be dragged along by pure effort of will.

I stood by the bedroom door while she approached her mother's bed and began to stroke her mother's hand. The old lady's mouth moved and her tongue slicked out as she tried to communicate.

'Come and say goodbye to Mother,' said Margaret as she beckoned me with one finger, a finger that now seemed as compulsive as a snake and twice as deadly.

Slowly I moved to the top of the bed, feeling for the high wooden bedpost and holding on to it for support. 'Nice to have met you again, Mrs Tonbridge,' I managed to mumble. 'I've just come to say goodbye.'

Margaret leaned over her mother as if to kiss her on the mouth and I looked away for a second in sickly embarrassment. From the corner of my eye I saw a flash of blue, the raised arm, and then the flash of red. As I turned and moved forward the spurting fountain of blood stopped. The room seemed to swirl in a mass of red and I saw the head on the pillow of blood: the blood on the ceiling, on Margaret's hands, on the eiderdown.

'I went for the carotid,' she said. 'I got it right, didn't I?'

Her arm was still raised, the blade of the scalpel glinting like a diamond in its pale blue holder.

'You certainly did,' I managed to say, as I swallowed hard and tried to ignore the haze of red and the smell of blood and concentrate on the position of that shining steel blade. 'I should put that scalpel down now, Margaret,' I said, aware that my voice had become high and squeaky with shock. 'You might cut yourself.'

'Yes,' she said, smiling. 'But cutting doesn't hurt – look.'

The blade flashed again – downwards – slicing at her arm, the blood seeping through the navy sleeves and running over her forehand and through her fingers and dripping on to the floor. She too seemed hypnotised by the blood, watching the relentless drip, drip, drip, on the floor.

I took my chance then, trying to grab her arm but she was too fast and she stepped back, the scalpel high in the air, too high for me to reach. And she was laughing.

'You don't think you're going to get out alive, do you? This is the house of the dead. We're all going to die!'

She slashed at her other arm then but this time I had moved back, trying to edge my way to the door. And I knew I had to keep talking if I wanted to live. God help me, God help me, I prayed over and over again as waves of nausea began to torment me and my stomach twisted in agonising knots.

'Please don't, Margaret,' I croaked. 'Think of your mother – think of the mess. She wouldn't have approved, would she? She liked a tidy, clean house, didn't she?'

Margaret paused to watch the blood of her fresh wound and said nothing but I didn't wait for her answer. I turned and ran to the door. Even as I slammed the door she was behind it. I held on to the doorknob, my arms and neck and back straining in my desperation to keep the door closed. My strength wasn't enough, she won. As the door opened, her hand clutching the blade appeared through the crack in the door, slashing and cleaving the air and my upper arm. I managed to hold on to her wrist and pull her thumb back viciously. The blade dropped to the carpeted floor without a sound. As it did so I lost the momentum of my hold and she yanked open the door. Abruptly my fear became rage and I grabbed her arm, pulled her from the room into the hall and hurled myself into the bedroom, leant against the door and locked it.

With my shoulder still pressed to the door I waited. My breath rose and fell in judders and I tried desperately to breathe more normally so that I could hear what was happening outside the room. Margaret and the blade were still there, but now I was at least locked in. She couldn't get to me, not for a while anyway.

There was silence for a while in the hall and then I could hear Margaret begin to whisper tearfully, 'Mummy, Mummy, Mummy,' over and over again. I stood for a long time, my ear pressed to the door listening to that pathetic lament, and then I left the door and walked over to the bed.

Mrs Tonbridge's head lay back on the pillow; her eyes were closed but her throat was open, wide open, cut from ear to ear. There was no doubt that she was dead.

My stomach began then to tighten and twist and I could feel the saliva rise in my throat. I swallowed it, but my mouth was dry and I could hear a buzzing noise in my head. I stood for a while trying to breathe myself calm. Telling myself that I must do something.

I went back to the door and listened again. Margaret was quiet now and I could hear water running. I unlocked the door and opened it a fraction; there was a pool of blood on the carpet and smeared blood on the walls, but no Margaret. I didn't hesitate. I ran past the open bathroom door without looking, down the stairs and into the hall. Dreading Margaret's reappearance I watched the stairs hawk-like as I dialled Hubert's number, trying as I did so to control my trembling fingers.

'Please come quickly,' I whispered, frightened Margaret would hear and come out of the bathroom. 'I'm at the Leys. I'll be standing in the road. It's at the back of St Dymphna's. Get someone to call the police but get here first – please.'

'I'm on my way,' said Hubert.

Hearing his voice so calm, calmed me a little. Even so, I couldn't stay in the house. I knew I should, but courage had deserted me. I rushed out into the road and stood on the edge of the pavement.

Outside the world seemed to have changed. It was bright and

crisp and clean. I began to tremble as I stood there waiting as if in a trance, without my coat and without my car keys.

Hubert arrived within minutes. He said nothing but wrapped me in a blanket and once I was in the car handed me a pocket flask of brandy. I managed one swig but it made me heave.

'Try not to puke on the seats,' said Hubert.

Back at Humberstones, Hubert helped me up the stairs to my office. That was where I wanted to be when the police arrived. In place of the old floral armchair and my hard office chair were two softly upholstered swivel chairs in dove grey.

'Very classy, Hubert, thank you,' I said, trying hard to force a smile. 'Can I try them out?'

He took my arm and I sank gratefully down on to the nearest, and he swivelled me round, just the once.

'I've had a terrible experience, Hubert,' I said, trying to choke back the tears.

'Did you crack the case?'

'I think you could say that. I thought perhaps you might have turned up in the nick of time to save me.'

'Saved yourself, didn't you?' said Hubert. 'Apart from that cut on your arm. I would have come, only the chairs turned up and I had to unpack them.'

'Never mind,' I said wearily, pushing up the sleeve of my jumper to reveal a long, but not deep cut on my upper arm. And for the first time I was aware of just how much it hurt. Hubert busied himself with water and antiseptic liquid that smelt like something you clean drains with, and began to dab timidly at my wound.

Later the police rang to request the pleasure of my company.

'How's Margaret?' I asked guiltily, aware that perhaps I should have stayed, tried to help her.

She was in hospital, the police told me. It had been close: she'd lost a lot of blood and would be transferred to a mental hospital. She'd probably never be fit to plead. I hoped they would be kind to her.

'Cheer up, Kate,' Hubert said, as he admired his bandaging. 'I don't think it will need stitches and you've solved your first case, and I've just heard about a nursing home that's losing a patient a week. It's quite a dodgy set-up and I'm sure it's right up your street.'

If I hadn't still been trembling so much, I would have laughed.